In a country divided,
Eden and Logan found only one
passion stronger than loyalty... love.

PARADISE

Eden heard Logan's quiet call and looked up. Her eyes widened at the riveting vision he made as he came toward her in the night, so tall and broad-shouldered, moving with an easy grace, his expression darkly intense. Her heartbeat quickened, and a surge of sensual awareness shot through her as he drew near.

Logan stopped beside her.

"This really is the Garden of Eden, you know," he said, his voice deep and husky.

She smiled up at him. "I try to make it as heavenly as I can. I want it to be a place where I can come and pretend the real world doesn't exist—at least for a little while."

Time seemed to stand still as their gazes met. They were alone under a canopy of stars.

Eden was breathless as Logan closed the distance between them. He stood over her, staring down at her, the flame of desire burning in his eyes.

As if in slow motion, Logan lifted one hand to cup her cheek, then bent to claim her lips, whispering, "Ah, but there was temptation in the garden—" His mouth took hers in a tender-soft exchange.

Eden went still at the touch of his hand, and when his lips moved over hers, she gave a small blissful sigh.

This truly was paradise—

BOBBI SMITH

EDEN

LEISURE BOOKS NEW YORK CITY

*To John Backe, with thanks and appreciation, and
to everybody at Dorchester Publishing. We did it!
We made* The New York Times! *Wow!*

A LEISURE BOOK®

December 2001

Published by

Dorchester Publishing Co., Inc.
276 Fifth Avenue
New York, NY 10001

ISBN 0-8439-4942-2

The name "Leisure Books" and the stylized "L" with design are trademarks of Dorchester Publishing Co., Inc.

Printed in the United States of America.

Visit us on the web at www.dorchesterpub.com.

ACKNOWLEDGMENTS

I'd like to thank all my friends at Standard Drug on Hwy. 94 for their support and for keeping me supplied with bubble gum when I'm on deadline. Pat O'Connor, Theresa Gage, Steve Fine, Jim Brown, Cathie Day and Jenny O'Day.

Thanks, too, to Diana Tucker, Ruth Fell and Lucy Lockley of St. Charles County Library who always come to my rescue when I need help with research and to Jeanette Grider at KTRS Radio, the Big SSO, in St. Louis.

A special thanks, too, to Kathy Baker and her terrific husband/emergency chauffeur, Bobby. I appreciate your kindness and hospitality.

EDEN

Chapter One

New Orleans, 1863

"Miss Eden! Wait!"

The sound of the young boy's call stopped Eden LeGrand as she prepared to leave the Homeless Haven Orphans' Asylum. She turned to see ten-year-old Paul Kalsbeek running toward her down the main hall, ignoring the calls of Miss Jenny, his teacher, to get back in line.

"Miss Eden—don't leave!" Paul pleaded desperately as he stopped before her. She was the one person at the home he'd allowed himself to become attached to, and he'd heard from the others this morning that she was leaving them today.

"I'm just going on a short trip, Paul. I'll be

back soon. I promise." Eden opened her arms, wanting to hug and reassure him.

The boy stood back, refusing her offer of comfort, his expression almost angry. "That's what my pa said before he left."

His words were accusing. His father had been killed in the early months of the war and his mother had died shortly thereafter of the fever, leaving him alone in the world. During his months at the orphanage, he'd come to trust Miss Eden because she was so much like his mother—kind and beautiful with her dark hair and dark eyes. But now she was going away, and sheer terror ate at him. He would have cried, but he told himself he was too old to cry now. He was almost a man. As soon as he could, he was going to get a gun and go fight the damned Yankees and avenge his father's death!

"I know, Paul." Eden felt the sting of his words and reached out to touch his cheek. She could see the torment in the depths of his blue eyes. "But I have to travel upriver with my mother to visit a sick relative." The lie ate at her, but there was no way she could tell the boy—or anyone else—what she was really about to do. "You be good and help Miss Jenny all you can with the younger boys, and I'll be back before you know it."

Paul wanted to throw himself into her arms. He wanted to cling to her and beg her not to go, but he couldn't show any weakness. Instead, without another word, he turned and ran back to join the other children.

Eden understood Paul's unspoken rejection. She understood his fear and his need. He was young, and life had been hard on him—too hard.

Her gaze was warm and loving upon the orphans. Paul and the others were the reason she was going on this trip. She was going to try to make things better for them. No innocent child should have to live through what these children were living through. She would do everything she could to help the Cause and see this war ended as quickly as possible. She wanted all the hatred and carnage to stop.

Eden was saddened that she'd hurt Paul, but she had to be on her way. She turned to go and caught sight of Adrian Forrester, the director of the orphanage, standing in the door of his office watching her. Adrian had been grievously wounded early in the war and had lost his right leg. He'd been fitted with a wooden replacement but was unable to fight anymore. Adrian had returned to New Orleans, wanting to help in some way. He worked to successfully establish the Haven for the orphaned children of Confederate soldiers in a large, three-story home that had been donated to him for that purpose.

"Trouble with young Kalsbeek there?" Adrian asked as he made his way to stand with her.

"No. No trouble. Paul just wanted to tell me good-bye before I left."

"So you're leaving now?" Adrian asked, his expression carefully guarded.

"Yes. I'm scheduled to meet my mother on the riverfront in half an hour."

"Be careful."

Their gazes met and locked in complete understanding.

"I will," she promised.

As she left the building, Eden didn't see Paul watching her from the upstairs window.

Steamboats were lined up endlessly along the riverfront, and the levee was bustling with activity as Eden's carriage made its way to the place where the *Bayou Belle* was tied up. For a moment, seeing how busy everything was, Eden allowed herself to believe things were as they used to be, but then the sight of Yankee soldiers jarred her from her fantasy.

Vicksburg had fallen.

Nothing would ever be the same again.

Eden saw her mother, Francene, waiting for her, and she directed the driver to stop there and unload.

"You made it." Her mother greeted her with a warm hug. "How did everything go at the Haven?"

"Just fine. I'm going to miss the children, but we should be back soon—I hope."

Eden's driver got a steward to carry their trunk for them and then left them to board. Eden and Francene followed the steward onto the *Bayou Belle*, each woman carrying her own hat box. Eden was nervous, but she didn't let it show as they climbed the steps to the upper deck and entered their stateroom. The steward placed the trunk in the space provided and then excused himself, closing the cabin door behind him as he left.

"We did it." The relief in Eden's voice was obvious, and she managed a tight smile as she placed the hat box she'd been carrying on one of the beds.

"Your father would be proud of you," her mother said as she gingerly set her hat box down beside Eden's.

"He'd be proud of *us*," Eden said, appreciating her mother's support, "but it's not over yet." She lowered her voice for fear that someone might overhear them. They couldn't be too careful. There was too much at stake.

True, their boarding of the *Bayou Belle* had proven uneventful. To all outward appearances they were simply a mother and daughter traveling upriver to visit relatives. No one had any idea that they had guns and ammunition hidden in their trunk and hat boxes.

"What are we supposed to do now?" her mother asked.

"We just act like normal passengers. We can even take a walk around the deck, if you want."

"I'd like that. I'm afraid if I stay here in the cabin, I'll get too nervous worrying."

Eden had an ulterior motive in suggesting they stroll the deck. They would play the role of genteel Southern ladies, and while they were walking about, she would take careful note of the number of Union soldiers posted to guard the arms shipment that was being transported on this steamer. She planned to do everything she could to make sure their mission was successful.

"How long do we have?" her mother asked.

"I don't know for sure, but nothing is going to happen until we're well away from New Orleans."

They left their room and walked casually about the deck as the steamboat backed into mid-stream and then started north against the current.

Eden was glad the *Bayou Belle* was one of the smaller vessels plying the river. When the time finally came for their plan to be put into action, things were going to get dangerous. The fewer crew members they had to worry about, the better.

After making a round of the ship, Eden and her mother found two chairs in the shade on deck and settled there to pass some time. It was late afternoon when they finally returned to their cabin to get ready for dinner. They had only been back a few moments when a knock sounded at the door. Eden opened it to find a workman standing there, a toolbox in his hand.

"I'm here to make the needed repairs, ma'am," he said.

Eden recognized Steve Rednauer immediately. She'd met the tall, fair-haired man in Adrian's office some weeks before. Standing aside, she let him in and quickly closed the door behind him.

"Is everything going all right, Steve?"

"Yes. Everyone made it safely on board. We'll make our move after midnight when we're sure it's going to be quiet. Do you have the guns?"

"Right here." Eden opened the trunk and hat boxes for him.

Steve opened his toolbox and quickly stowed the guns and ammunition there.

"Mother and I took a walk around deck, and from what I could see, there were only two Union soldiers on board."

"We've been checking, too. If everything goes as we hope, there will be little chance for resistance and no one will get hurt."

"It'll work. It has to," she told him firmly.

"Thank you." Steve glanced down at the guns one last time before he closed the toolbox. His expression was determined.

"Be careful, and Godspeed," Francene bade, looking at the young man and seeing in him her son, Robert, who was off fighting with her husband, James, somewhere back East.

"Yes, ma'am." He left the stateroom, looking once again the workman.

Eden and her mother shared a knowing look, then continued to get ready to go to dinner.

The meal that was served was delicious, but Eden didn't notice as she ate. She was only going through the motions, making small talk with the others seated at their table and wishing that the night to come was already over. When at last they retired for the evening, the tension within Eden grew almost unbearable. She had helped Adrian and his men before with their schemes, but only in small ways. This was the first time she'd been so deeply involved in one of their plans to aid the Confederacy. She was proud to do it, but it was also very nerve-wracking. She silently prayed that everything would go off as they'd planned.

"Good night, dear," her mother told her as they lay in the darkness.

"I hope it is a good night," Eden said.

"It will be. Steve and the others will be careful. Everything is going to be fine."

"I hope you're right."

It was in the wee hours of the morning that the sound of shots being fired jarred Eden and Francene from their uneasy slumber.

"It's happening!" Eden breathed as she all but threw herself from the bed.

"What should we do?"

"Act like frightened passengers," she answered, grabbing a blanket to wrap around herself.

"I don't have to act," Francene told her, trembling at the sound of the chaos that was rocking the boat. She was excited by the prospect that they had helped the South, but still fearful that something might go wrong. If their plan failed and any of their men were hurt or taken captive, their role in the plot might be revealed and they might be sent off to prison. The possibility terrified her.

Eden opened their stateroom door to see a steward racing by. Pretending ignorance of the situation, she called out, "What's happening? I heard shots! Are we under attack?"

"Stay inside your cabin, ma'am!" he shouted without stopping, and he disappeared on down the deck.

"We'd better get dressed so we can be ready for whatever happens," Eden said as she shut the door and turned back to her mother.

Though it was the middle of the night, both women hurried to don their daygowns.

It seemed an eternity, but it was really only a short time later when a deep-voiced man came pounding on all the stateroom doors. He was demanding that all passengers leave their cabins and take only the barest of necessities with them. Eden and Francene hurried to comply. Once they'd emerged from the safety of their room, they saw one of the Rebel agents, gun in hand, hustling the unarmed and defenseless passengers down the steps to the lower deck.

The passengers were truly frightened by what was transpiring. Some women and children were crying as they rushed to obey the man's harshly issued orders. Some of the male passengers were daring to question the man, demanding to know what was wrong, but he refused to answer, only waving his weapon at them in a threatening manner and telling them to keep moving down to the deck below. It wasn't until Eden and Francene had been herded together with all the other passengers on the main deck that they saw some of the crew members and the two Yankee soldiers who'd been guarding the shipment sitting on the deck together, their wrists bound behind them. Armed men stood over them, watching and waiting for any kind of trouble.

At the sight, several of the women started screaming, fearing for their lives. They were quickly silenced by orders from the guards.

Eden and Francene cowered convincingly as they watched all that transpired, but inwardly they were satisfied that all had gone well. No blood had been shed, and the Yankees would not be getting any of the guns on this ship to use against Southern soldiers.

The *Bayou Belle* slowed as she neared the western riverbank, and the men who'd commandeered her made short order of tying her up. A gangplank was quickly lowered.

"Listen up! Everybody off the boat!" Steve shouted, taking charge.

The plan was simple, yet devastating. They would unload all the passengers and some of the nonessential crew here, where eventually another steamer would find them sometime the following day and transport them to safety. Once the passengers had left the *Bayou Belle*, they would push off again and steam farther upstream to the prearranged meeting place to unload the arms shipment and ultimately burn the steamer.

In response to Steve's command, cries of protest came from the passengers, but their cries were ignored as they were hustled down the gangplank, off the *Bayou Belle* and onto the shore.

Lieutenant Braden Matthews was furious as he sat on the deck, his hands bound, nursing a vicious headache. He realized now that he should never have allowed himself to relax once the ship had set sail. He should never have let down his guard. He'd been in charge of the arms shipment, and he'd failed miserably. Disguised as workmen, the Rebs had outsmarted him. They had sneaked up on him from behind and knocked him unconscious before he'd realized what they were about. It was a terrible lesson to learn, and one he would never forget.

"Lieutenant—" Corporal Danner whispered to him as the Reb who was guarding them momentarily moved off to help with the passengers. "What are we going to do?"

"Nothing—right now," Braden answered, carefully working at the ropes that bound him without drawing attention to himself.

Braden watched the armed Rebs herding the people from the ship and noticed that there were a number of able-bodied men among the passengers. If he could get free, he could attack one of the guards, and hopefully then some of the male passengers who were Northern sympathizers would help him overpower their captors. As far as he'd been able to tell, there weren't that many raiders—maybe twenty at the most. Braden didn't know what the Rebs planned to do next. The way things were going, he might end up dead anyway, so he silently vowed to do everything in his power to stop them from getting away with the guns.

Braden's wrists were raw and starting to bleed, but that didn't matter to him. Time was running out. He had to act soon or lose his only chance to save the shipment. When at last he managed to free one hand, he was careful not to betray his elation.

He waited, watching for the right opportunity. When the Reb guard turned his back, Braden made his move. He charged to his feet and threw himself bodily at the armed man, catching him unawares and knocking his gun from his grip. Braden had always been a determined man, but never more so than now. His fury driving him, he pummeled the man. They were locked in a desperate struggle.

The other Rebs who'd been helping the passengers disembark ran to help their comrade.

Eden had been just about to leave the steamship when she saw the Yankee soldier attack the guard. She froze and looked on in horror as the fight raged.

Braden managed to overpower the Reb and then made a dive for the gun. He grabbed the weapon and turned toward the men who were coming after him.

But the others were ready. One of the Rebels fired.

"No!" Eden screamed as she saw the Yankee fall.

Chaos erupted around her.

Francene cried out in horror, as did the others who'd been filing from the boat. Several of the Rebels hurried to quiet the panicked passengers, while others turned their guns back on the remaining Yankee and the crew members still tied up on deck. Eden dropped the few personal things she'd been carrying and started to run to help the fallen man.

"Stop right there! Get back!" the Rebel who'd shot the Yankee ordered. He glared at Eden, his gun ready in case there was more trouble.

"Let me help him!" Eden said.

Steve Rednauer had heard the shot and now hurried down to the main deck.

"What happened?" Steve demanded, pushing through the crush of people to get to where the Union soldier lay wounded on the deck.

The Rebel quickly explained.

"Sir, please, I have to help him!" Eden spoke up, her gaze imploring upon Steve as he turned to face her. "You can't just let him die!"

Steve did not acknowledge that he knew her, but he nodded tersely. "Go ahead."

Eden wasted no time. Unmindful of the blood, she dropped to her knees beside the injured

Union soldier and quickly examined him. The bullet had hit him in the shoulder, and the wound was bleeding profusely. She tore strips from her petticoat and pressed them against the torn flesh. She wished there had been a doctor on board to take care of him, but she was alone. Even her mother had been restrained from helping her. As Eden attempted to stanch the flow of blood, the Yankee soldier stirred and groaned.

"Easy," Eden said in what she hoped was a calming voice. She couldn't decide if he had been brave in his desperate attempt to try to stop what was happening despite such overwhelming odds or if he'd been crazy.

Braden's consciousness returned with a vengeance, and he tried to sit up in a sudden move. Pain rocked through him, jarring him to the depths. He collapsed back, only distantly aware of gentle hands pressing him down and a soft voice trying to calm him.

"Don't move."

Braden fought against the physical agony that threatened to sweep him back into unconsciousness. He looked up to see a beautiful, dark-haired woman hovering over him, and he wondered if she was some kind of angel. He struggled to focus his thoughts on all that had happened. It came back to him then—how he'd fought the Reb and tried to grab the gun in his desperate bid to save the arms shipment.

"You're going to be all right. Just stay still," Eden said soothingly.

"Is he going to live?" Steve asked, coming to stand over them.

Eden looked up at him. "He needs to see a doctor. The bullet's still in him."

"Bind him up as best you can, and then get off the boat." It was an order.

"But this man needs help—" she protested.

"Do what you have to do to stop the bleeding and then go."

Eden struggled against the emotions that raged within her. She knew he was right. This soldier was the enemy. He was a Yankee. Yet the thought of his suffering horrified her. "He needs to come with me. Let me take him with us. He needs—"

"He's a Yankee. He's lucky I let you tend to him at all," Steve said coldly.

"But he might die—" she protested again.

Steve shrugged and turned away. He planned to take the two Union soldiers with him as prisoners.

Eden was upset but realized there was nothing more she could do except try to ease the man's suffering. She tore more strips from her petticoats and worked feverishly to bind the wound as tightly as she could to stop the bleeding. She was amazed at the inner strength the Yankee displayed. The lieutenant never made a sound as she treated his wound. His eyes were shut, but she knew he wasn't unconscious by the muscle that worked in his jaw as he battled to control the pain.

25

When at last she had finished treating him, Eden started to get up and move away, but the soldier reached out and snared her wrist in an iron hold. Eden was surprised by the strength in the Yankee's grip, and she looked down at him to find his dark-eyed gaze upon her. The fierce intensity of his expression startled her.

"Thank you, angel lady," Braden said in a hoarse voice.

"Take care—" Eden whispered.

His grip weakened then, and his hand fell away. The effort he'd exerted to speak to her had sapped what little strength he had left.

Eden stood and made her way toward the gangplank to follow the others on shore. She glanced back once to see how the wounded soldier was faring and then hurried on into the darkness of the night.

Her mother rushed up to meet her. "Are you all right?"

"I'm fine, but that soldier—"

"Is he dead?"

"No, but I fear he might be soon if he doesn't get help."

Both women watched as the Rebels forced the last of the unneeded crew off the boat and then drew back the plank. Slowly the *Bayou Belle* backed into the river and churned away, leaving them stranded on the riverbank, abandoned in the night.

Chapter Two

St. Louis

"How did it happen?" Logan Matthews demanded, fury and fear gripping him as he stared across the desk at Larry Cotlar, his superior in the Union's Secret Service.

"Your brother was assigned to guard a shipment of arms coming upriver from New Orleans. Evidently, some Rebels in disguise boarded the steamer and took it over. They stole the shipment. From what I've been able to learn, your brother tried to stop them, but he was shot during the fight."

Logan went still at the news. "Is he—?"

"No. He was only wounded, but they took him and the other guard along with them as prisoners." Larry quickly explained how the passengers and most of the crew had been abandoned on the riverbank, and how the thieves had sailed the *Bayou Belle* farther upriver before making off with the shipment and setting the boat afire.

"I'm going to New Orleans."

"I thought you'd be interested in this assignment." Larry gave him a tight smile. Logan was one of their best operatives. If anybody could find out who was running the spy ring, he would—especially since his brother was involved.

"What do we know about them?" Logan turned coldly logical as a fierce determination gripped him.

"Very little. The records of who sailed on the *Bayou Belle* that day burned with the ship. We've been able to gather a few names of those who were on board from newspaper accounts of the story. You might be able to learn something there." He handed Logan a file. "According to our sources in the city, there are several suspects in and around New Orleans who might have been involved in the planning of the theft."

"The Army wasn't able to learn anything?"

"No. By the time the steamer was located, there was nothing left of her but a burned-out hull. The Rebs either escaped through the bayou or transferred to another steamer. There was no trail to follow."

Logan grew grim as Larry described the possible suspects who might have masterminded the raid.

"Adrian Forrester served in the Confederate Army but lost a leg early on in the fighting. He returned to New Orleans and established an orphan asylum for children of dead Confederate soldiers. It's called the Homeless Haven Orphans' Asylum. Nathaniel Talbott is a banker who is well connected on both sides and could possibly be relaying information to spies. There have been other disruptive incidents in and around the city that might be related to this same group, but we've been unable to catch any of those responsible. And neither one of these men is known for being an ardent Unionist. That's where you come in. How soon can you be ready to leave for New Orleans?"

"Today." Logan had no ties to keep him in St. Louis. His brother had been wounded and taken captive in Louisiana. The sooner he reached New Orleans and began his investigation, the better.

"Good."

"And I know exactly what disguise I'll use." At Larry's questioning look, he went on. "The Reverend Matthews will be traveling south to save souls."

"Perfect."

Larry had always known Logan was a brilliant operative, and he'd just proven it again. Traveling as a minister, he would be accepted and trusted by both sides in the war. In that disguise, he would have no difficulty if he had to cross into enemy territory. Larry quickly filled him in on the two informants he already had in place in the city and told him how to make contact with them.

"I'll get word to them about you. When you meet with them for the first time, just mention that you're searching for lost souls."

"All right," Logan agreed, knowing it wasn't a lie. The real lost soul he was looking for was Braden.

Larry stood and extended his hand to him. "Good luck, Logan. Send word and let me know how to get in touch with you in case there's any news of your brother."

"I will."

The two men shook hands, their intent serious.

Logan left the office anxious to get to New Orleans. Since the war had begun, he'd had several important assignments, but none as vital as this one. His brother's life depended on him. He had to work quickly. He would not fail.

The trip to New Orleans seemed endless to Logan. Once he'd arrived in the city, he took a room at a hotel and got ready to begin his mission. He pushed all personal worries aside, for he couldn't afford to be distracted by emotions. He had a job to do, and he would do it. He was going to track down those responsible for stealing the arms shipment and try to break up whatever spy group was operating out of the city.

Logan donned a simply tailored dark coat and pants with a white shirt and tie. There was nothing unusual about his clothing, nothing that would draw attention to him. Ready to venture out, he picked up the leather-bound Bible he'd been carrying with him on the trip down. His disguise was complete. The Reverend Matthews was ready to go out in search of lost souls.

Logan planned to head to the riverfront first to meet with Larry's contact there—a free man of color named Sam Hall. Logan hoped the man might have some information about who knew of the arms shipment and the arrangements to send them upriver. Sam Hall would be his starting point.

After meeting with Sam, Logan planned to pay a visit to the orphanage. He'd brought extra cash to ensure his acceptance at the home. His story was simple. There were Southern sympathizers in St. Louis who'd heard of Forrester's efforts on behalf of the Confederate children, and they wanted to help Homeless Haven. They had entrusted him with their donations. As difficult as life was now due to the shortages created by the war, Logan doubted that anyone would question his story when he showed up with cash in hand. He was simply a man of the cloth, trying to do God's work on Earth.

Logan got his horse and made the trip to the riverfront. It was still a crowded, busy place, but he could imagine how much busier it had been before the fighting had disrupted regular trade. Tying up his horse near a warehouse where

Larry had told him Sam Hall worked, he made his way along the levee, Bible in hand.

Sam was hard at work loading goods on a steamer when he saw the minister walking along the waterfront. He remembered the message he'd received from his contact and finished his task at hand before heading his way.

"You lost, preacherman?" Sam asked gruffly as he confronted him.

"No. I'm doing God's work, searching for lost souls," Logan answered, looking up at the big, burly man who stood before him. Intelligence shone in the man's dark eyes.

"You'll find them here in this town, that's for sure," Sam told him. Their gazes met in understanding and acknowledgment of each other's identity.

"I'm Reverend Matthews."

"My name's Sam—Sam Hall. Good luck with your work, Reverend."

"Thank you, but I'm going to need more than luck if I'm to be successful." Logan needed any and all information Sam could give him.

"That you will," Sam agreed, then lowered his voice. "I can meet you tonight—here, around midnight. Can you make it, preacherman?"

"I'll be here," Logan promised. He started to say more when he heard shouts coming from the area where he'd left his horse tied up.

"Stop! Thief!"

He turned to see a boy racing along the riverfront with a man in hot pursuit.

The youth spotted Logan's horse and raced straight for it.

"Tonight," Logan confirmed to Sam quickly. Then he started back up the levee to see what the problem was.

The boy had already snatched up Logan's horse's reins and was just about to vault into the saddle when the man who'd been giving chase caught up with him. Grabbing the boy bodily, he held on tight as the youth twisted and turned in a violent effort to free himself.

"Let me go!"

Logan reached the scene as the man was struggling to subdue him.

"What's the problem?" Logan asked, looking from the red-faced man who was obviously a merchant to the fighting boy he held in an iron grip.

"This little bastard stole some food from my shop," the merchant snarled, tightening his grip even more.

"Did not! Let me go!" the boy yelled, still fighting for his freedom. "Let me go!"

"If you didn't steal anything, then you'll have no objection to this gentleman searching your pockets, will you?" Logan asked him in a calming tone. "Surely you've nothing to fear if you're innocent and have been falsely accused."

The boy glared at Logan, and then he saw the Bible Logan carried. He paled a little and stopped his struggles. The merchant eased his grip and started to check the boy's pockets. Realizing he was about to be found out, the boy bolted, but he wasn't quick enough.

Logan had anticipated his move and was ready for him. He snared the youth by the collar.

"Look!" The merchant held up the bread roll and piece of fruit the boy had jammed in his pockets. "I told you he was a thief! I'm going to beat him within an inch of his—"

Logan gave the youth a censoring look, then said to the man, "Let me pay you for what he's taken."

"But he ain't nothing to you. Why would you—?" The merchant was shocked by Logan's offer.

Logan didn't respond to the merchant. He looked down at the boy and asked, "Can I trust you not to run?"

The boy's expression was as defiant as it was angry. "I ain't gonna run."

"Give me your word," Logan said.

"I told ya, I won't run!"

Logan let go of his shirt and turned to the merchant. "How much will satisfy his debt to you?"

The man quoted a price and Logan paid him.

"You know him?" the man asked, wondering why he would help the boy out.

"I know him. He's a child of God," Logan answered, looking down at the dark-haired youth as he rested a hand on his shoulder. That single touch told him that under the baggy, ill-fitting clothing he wore the boy wasn't much more than skin and bones.

"You paid for this. It's yours." The merchant handed him the fruit and bread. "Good luck with your 'child of God' there, preacher. I think God needs to have a little talk with him about stealing and lying," he sneered, giving the boy a dirty look as he moved away, pocketing the money.

"Everything all right, preacherman?" Sam asked. He'd followed along with some of the other workers to see what the ruckus was about.

"Everything is fine," Logan told him. They exchanged a knowing look, confirming their rendezvous for later that night.

Sam moved off with the others to return to their work, leaving Logan alone with the boy.

"What's your name, son?"

"I ain't your son." He was sullen.

"I asked you your name," Logan repeated in a tone that this time brooked no defiance.

"It's Mark. Mark Williams."

"Well, Mark Williams, my name is Reverend Matthews."

The boy only looked up at him. He did not speak.

"Do you have something to say for yourself?" Logan guessed the boy to be about nine or ten years old.

"I ain't got nothing to say."

"Where are your parents?"

"They're dead."

"Where do you live?"

Mark glowered at him in silence. It was bad enough that he'd been caught, but he wasn't going to be telling this man his business. He wasn't nothing to him. He didn't owe him anything.

"Mark, when was the last time you had a decent meal?"

He still didn't answer, refusing to admit that he needed help. No one had ever helped him before, and he didn't expect anyone to start helping him now.

"Here." Logan held the food the boy had stolen out to him. "Eat this."

Mark eyed him for a minute, then grabbed the food. He took a big bite of the bread.

"Now get on the horse," Logan ordered.

The boy was tempted to run, but the look in the minister's eyes stopped him. He saw no threat there, only understanding and kindness. It had been a long time since he'd known either. Still, he hesitated, unsure.

Logan understood his indecision. "No harm will come to you. I give you my word as you gave me yours."

Mark nodded and mounted the horse. "Where are you taking me?"

"I have business at an orphanage here in town—The Homeless Haven Orphans' Asylum."

"I ain't going to no orphans' home!" He was ready to bolt.

Logan fixed him with a steady regard. "You don't want to be someplace safe and have a clean bed every night and three good meals a day?"

"Have you ever lived in a home?" Mark countered.

36

"I plan to be working in this one."

Mark eyed him skeptically, still not ready to trust him. "Why are you helping me? What's in it for you?"

"It's my calling," Logan answered as he looked up at the boy whose innocence and youth had been stolen from him.

Logan understood Mark's cynicism. He realized, too, that if Mark knew the truth about his own motives—that taking the money to the orphanage might win Forrester's thanks, but rescuing a child off the streets would provide him with real credibility—it would only have deepened his distrust of others. Logan recognized that Mark was a survivor, and though he was using him for his own purposes right now, ultimately the boy would be better off for it.

Logan realized his reasoning was cold and harshly logical, but he told himself this was war, and Mark was his means to an end. He wanted to learn everything he could about Adrian Forrester, and working from inside the orphanage would provide him with that opportunity. He took up the reins and, leading the youth on horseback, began the trek to the home.

Chapter Three

Paul was upstairs in the boys' quarters on the third floor doing his cleaning chores with several of the other boys when he heard angry voices outside. He hurried to the window. Below on the sidewalk in front of the house, he could see several Union soldiers who looked like they were drunk arguing with two ladies. He recognized the women immediately as Miss Gabrielle and Miss Veronica, two friends of Miss Eden's who volunteered at the Haven and were just on their way home.

"You damn Southern women think you're better than us!" Yankee Corporal Tom Layton snarled, looming threateningly over them.

Gabrielle could smell the rank odor of liquor on his breath, and it disgusted her. She straightened her shoulders and, lifting her head high, looked him straight in the eye.

"We don't think it, Corporal," she replied with dignity. "We know it."

"You stupid bitch!" Layton growled. "This city is ours. We conquered you!"

"You filthy Yankees may have conquered New Orleans, but you will never conquer our spirit." Veronica bravely defied him. "Gabrielle, let's go."

"Yes, Veronica. If you *gentlemen* will please excuse us?" Gabrielle gave them both a cold, dismissive look.

The women stepped into the street to walk around them, but the soldiers were enraged by their arrogance.

"I'll show you what conquered is!"

Layton reached out and grabbed Gabrielle. She cried out and struggled to break away, but his grip was bruising. Veronica tried to help her escape. She swung out at the hated Yankee, using her purse as a weapon, but the other soldier was there, snaring her wrist, stopping her attack with brutal force of his own.

"Let me go!" Veronica shouted.

"Help!" Gabrielle cried.

Paul had been watching from the window, and his anger had grown by the minute as the Yankees were disrespectful to the ladies who he knew were kind and gentle. When the drunken soldiers dared to lay their hands upon them, he was desperate to help them in any way he could.

He turned from the window to look for something he could throw at the Yankee attackers to drive them away.

"I hate them filthy damn Yankees!" Paul swore, his eyes wild as the furious need to save the women possessed him.

"What is it?" one of the other boys asked, seeing his rage. "What's the matter?"

Paul didn't take the time to answer, he just grabbed up the only thing handy he could use as a weapon to defend the ladies—the slop jar.

"Paul—what are you doing?" another boy asked.

Paul didn't hesitate, but leaned as far out the window as he could and heaved the heavy china pot, contents and all, at the soldiers who were manhandling the defenseless women.

"Leave them alone!" Paul shouted at the two, determined to do everything he could to stop the savage Yankees from hurting Miss Gabrielle and Miss Veronica.

Paul was thrilled when he saw that his aim was true. The heavy pot bounced off the porch roof and struck one of the soldiers, knocking him away from the woman he'd held, freeing her. The contents drenched both soldiers and partially soaked the women as well before the pot crashed to the ground and shattered.

Freed by their unseen savior's attack, Veronica and Gabrielle fled the scene, unmindful of the way their rescue had been accomplished. They were just thankful to be escaping their abusers.

"What the hell?" Layton raged as he struggled to right himself, still a bit dizzy from the glancing blow of the chamber pot.

"Where did that come from?" Private Rich Moran was furious and disgustingly wet as he looked up at the building, trying to catch sight of their attacker.

He could see a group of boys looking down from a window on the third floor and knew the culprit had to be among them. Leading the way, Moran rushed toward the front door of the building. He was intent on catching the one who'd done this and when he did, he was going to beat him within an inch of his life.

"What the hell is this place?" Layton raged, the vile odor that clung to him feeding his mindless fury.

Moran saw the sign out front and swore loudly. "It's the damned home for the Reb orphans."

That knowledge only made them angrier and even more determined. The two didn't bother to knock. Their fury had taken them past any trace of civility. They tried to open the door and found it locked, so undeterred and in a drunken rage, they kicked at it full-force, breaking it open, and rushed inside.

Eden had been in the kitchen talking to the cook about the children's evening meal when she heard the sound of a crash in the front hall. Thinking one of the children had been hurt, she ran to the front of the house to help, only to find two Union soldiers barging into the Haven.

"What are you doing here? What do you want?" Eden demanded, confronting them. She was shocked by the damage they'd done to the front door and knew sudden fear. She'd heard the stories of Yankees raiding private homes, but she never thought they would invade an orphanage. There were no riches or valuables here to steal. The only priceless treasures at the Haven were the children.

"Get the hell outta my way, woman!" Layton ordered as he and Moran advanced on her.

Eden stood her ground in the middle of the hall, refusing to be cowed by their threatening looks. She was in charge of the Haven while Adrian was away, and she would protect the children at any and all cost. "You must leave at once! You have no right to be here!"

The evil-looking men kept coming, ignoring her demands.

As they got closer, Eden saw that their clothing was wet, and she smelled the horrible stench about them. She wondered what had happened to them. There was no time for Eden to ask, though, for they pushed right past her. They headed straight for the staircase where some of the children were standing, having come down from the second and third floors to see what the shouting was about.

"You can't go up there!" Eden told them, giving chase and grabbing one of the Yankees by the arm to try to stop him.

Layton turned on her and shoved her roughly from him. "Stay out of my way, you stupid bitch!"

Eden was thrown back against the wall as they moved closer to the orphans. The children shrieked at seeing Miss Eden so mistreated, and they started to panic.

Eden wasn't about to give up. She couldn't let these two harm the children! Chasing after the two invaders, she grabbed at them again, desperate to stop them.

"Stop! They're only children! You can't harm them! Get out of the Haven right now!"

Layton didn't even think. He was too drunk and too furious—and too wet. First the two women on the street had defied him, and then the boy upstairs had dared to throw the chamber pot at him. He turned on the female who was trying to stop him from exacting his revenge and backhanded her full-force. He had had enough.

The power of his blow knocked Eden down. She fell to the floor, stunned, her lip bloodied and her cheek bruised by the Yankee's violent assault.

"Miss Eden! *No!*" A cry of absolute terror went up from the children.

They all wanted to go to her and help, but the mean Yankees were coming after them now. Frantic to escape, they ran shrieking up the steps and out of sight. They had to hide from the dreaded, hated soldiers who caused nothing but pain and terror in their lives. Even the cook who'd come to see what the noise was about, fled back to the safety of the kitchen.

Eden struggled to fight back. Outrage pounded through her as she tasted blood. How dare these animals invade the Haven and threaten the children this way! Miss Jenny was upstairs teaching, but the middle-aged widow would be no deterrent to these animals anyway.

Eden realized she was the only one who could keep the children safe from these madmen, and she sorely regretted that she didn't have a gun close at hand for she certainly wouldn't have hesitated to use it right then. Adrian had suggested keeping one in the office, but she'd worried that one of the children might find it. After today, that was going to change, but for right now, it was up to her to find a way to save them and she was unarmed.

Eden started to get up, unmindful of the blood that seeped from her injured lip. Her only concern was to stop the drunken soldiers before any child was hurt.

It was then, at her darkest moment as she was struggling to summon the strength she needed to fight them, that the deep, authoritative voice rang out in command from the doorway behind her.

"What is going on here?"

Layton and Moran had just started up the steps when they heard the man's call. They stopped to look back, fearful that it might be their commanding officer. They saw only a tall, dark-haired stranger in a black suit standing just inside the door.

"It ain't none of your God-damned business what's going on here! Come on, Moran!" Layton swore at the man who dared to interrupt them. He didn't know who the man was, and he didn't care. He had only one thing on his mind, and that was to find the boy who'd thrown the chamber pot down on him.

"My name is Reverend Matthews, and God's business *is* my business." Logan glared up at the two drunks as he spoke with bold authority.

The two saw the Bible the man was carrying and realized he really was a preacher and might be able to cause trouble for them.

"Some little Reb bastard up on the third floor threw a piss pot down on Layton and me when we were out in the street," Moran snarled. "I'm going to find him and beat the living hell out of him!"

"Watch your language, Private, there are children and a lady present," Logan reprimanded him.

Layton snorted in derision and sneered at Eden, "That ain't no lady. She's a whore just like the rest of the Southern bitches around here, and there ain't no children in this place worth anything. This is a Reb orphanage, ain't it?"

"Why, you—!" In a blind fury, Eden got to her feet and started toward them. She felt a little dizzy, but she was determined to do her best to keep them away from the boys and girls.

"Stay here, Mark," Logan ground out in low tones to the youth who was standing outside on the porch just behind him.

Logan went after the woman. He could tell she was filled with righteous anger, but she was defenseless against these two. He knew their kind—they were mean, ugly drunks, and he wanted her out of harm's way.

His gaze never left the soldiers as he moved quickly down the hall to the woman's side, taking her arm to stop her advance on the two. He took one quick glance down at her to make sure she hadn't been seriously injured. Her lip was bloodied and there was a mark on her cheek, but otherwise she appeared to be all right. Their gazes met for a moment, and he could see the outrage in her dark-eyed gaze. Satisfied that her injuries weren't serious, he looked back at the soldiers who were watching him cautiously.

"You men are to leave this place. Now." Logan's order was firm and brooked no argument.

Eden stared up at the stranger, amazed by the power of his presence. He had declared himself to be a minister, and to her that meant he was a man of peace and love. Yet here he was, confronting these drunken soldiers without any fear at all, acting almost as if he were their commanding officer.

"Like hell we will! Some boy up on the third floor deserves—" Layton started to argue.

"He deserves to be punished," Logan interrupted his tirade, "and I will find the youth and reprimand him myself, but I wonder what you did to provoke such an attack from a mere child? The children who make their home here are little more than babies. You, sir, are a soldier of the United States, and yet you have come into this haven and beaten an innocent woman who was only trying to defend the young ones in her charge."

"She shouldn't have tried to stop me from finding the little bastard who did this!" the corporal said hotly, turning back toward Logan in a threatening move. "It's her own damned fault she got beat! She's just lucky I didn't hit her harder!"

At his words, rage tore through Logan. There were few things lower in the world than a man who would hit a woman, and right then he couldn't think of a one.

Logan tightened his grip on his Bible. He had hidden a small derringer within the Holy Book in case he was ever trapped in a desperate situation, and he was beginning to think he might have to use it now.

He didn't want to use the gun.

He had come here to establish himself at the Haven as the generous, peace-loving Reverend Matthews.

If he resorted to violence at this moment, his cover would be destroyed before he even had the chance to begin his investigation, and he couldn't let that happen.

Determined to try to intimidate the drunks one last time before he gave up and overpowered them, Logan strode confidently forward, never looking away from the two troublemakers.

"You have already wreaked enough havoc here. Get out now." It was a command, and the look in his eyes was cold and deadly enough to back it up. "Leave this place and never come back."

"Who the hell are you to tell us what to do? You ain't got no right to order us around!" Moran was defiant of the minister. "We don't have to listen to you! You ain't nobody!"

"Perhaps I should send for the authorities and notify them of the damage you've caused here— to the building and to the children. I'm sure the young ones who witnessed your savagery now have an even lower opinion of Yankees than they did before. You've done your country no service or honor by your degenerate behavior, *gentlemen*. Now get out and don't ever come back!"

Layton and Moran exchanged glances. They considered fighting the man. After all, he was only a preacher. They stood their ground for a moment longer, then seeing the fierceness of the look in the man's eyes, they backed down. Their captain wouldn't understand them beating up on a minister. Stalking down the hall past the minister and the woman, they went out through the broken front door, cursing out loud as they went.

They gave the young boy on the porch a dirty look as they passed him.

Logan followed the two all the way to the door to watch them leave. He didn't trust them, and he wanted to make certain they were really gone from the property.

Mark was more than a little impressed with the way the minister had handled everything. He had always thought preachers were just smooth talkers, always spouting off about the Lord but never really doing much of anything to help anybody. But this man —this Reverend Matthews really was different. He had helped him, and now he had come to the defense of the lady inside, not to mention the children. While he'd been living on the streets, Mark had witnessed a lot of confrontations, and they'd all ended in violence. Reverend Matthews had just faced down two very dangerous men, and he hadn't lifted a hand in anger to do it.

"Reverend Matthews? Is everything all right?" Mark asked, staring up at him in awe.

"Now it is," Logan said confidently, although secretly he was relieved that the two had gone on their own. He held out an arm to Mark, realizing the boy needed some reassurance right then.

Mark immediately went to his side. He looked up at him, respect shining in his eyes.

"Let's go see to the lady. She needs our help," Logan told him, drawing him inside the Haven with him.

This wasn't quite the way Logan had meant to make himself known at the Homeless Haven Orphans' Asylum, but there was no way to change what had just happened. He wondered where Adrian Forrester was and found he was a bit angry that the man had not been there to help the young woman protect the children. He wondered, too, if the woman had ever considered keeping a weapon on hand for just such incidents as what had happened today. He realized, though, that as a "minister" he could hardly recommend she arm herself. It didn't seem quite the godly thing to do.

Eden was certain the children were frightened, and she wanted to comfort them. She was just starting toward the steps when the man who'd called himself Reverend Matthews came toward her accompanied by a young boy.

Logan said. "Are you all right?"

"I'm fine—I think." She stopped as Logan joined her.

Mark stood quietly by, looking on.

Eden was still torn between fury and shock over the soldiers' invasion and attack on her. She was even more stunned by the actions of this complete stranger who'd appeared out of nowhere to save her and the children. She had no idea who he was, but she would forever be grateful.

Logan set his Bible aside, then took out his handkerchief and pressed it gently to her bloodied lip.

His kind gesture touched Eden even more. She lifted her hand to hold the handkerchief in place. When she did, he stepped slightly away from her.

"Are you my guardian angel?" Eden asked, gazing up into the face of the darkly handsome, powerful man.

"I can be if you'd like me to be," Logan said, a slight smile quirking his lips at her question.

In that moment, Eden thought she'd never seen anyone more attractive. From his raven-dark hair to the hard, lean line of his jaw, he looked every bit like what she'd always imagined the fierce warrior St. Michael the Archangel would look like. All that was missing were his wings, and she was almost tempted to look at his back just to make sure. This man was strong and powerful, a glorious warrior, a defender of justice and of the innocent. And he had just chased the evil men from the orphanage without even using a weapon.

"Is your first name Michael by any chance?" She tried to smile back at him, but the effort left her grimacing in pain.

"No. My name's Logan."

He was relieved that she hadn't been traumatized by what had happened, but as his gaze went over her features and he saw the bruise forming on her cheek from the soldier's vicious blow, rage pounded through him. No woman should ever be abused, and certainly not this one. She was too fragile, too beautiful. She seemed the portrait of innocence, and he felt a sudden unexpected need to protect her and shield her from harm. In that moment, if the two men had stood before him again, he would have forgotten all about posing as the peace-loving reverend and exacted some savage revenge for what they'd done to her.

"Well, thank you, Reverend Logan Matthews. I don't know what the children and I would have done if you hadn't gotten here when you did." She kept his handkerchief pressed to her lip as she started to turn and go for the children. As she moved, a wave of lightheadedness threatened, and she swayed a bit on her feet.

Logan saw her distress and was quick to help, moving closer to put a helping hand at her elbow. He thought again how fragile she seemed to his touch, and yet she had bravely defended the children at the risk of her own life without thought.

At his simple touch on her arm, a shiver of awareness went through Eden, surprising her. Suddenly, she found herself confronted with the hard manly strength of him up close, and it was a solid, comforting feeling. When he stepped back and moved away from her, she felt strangely bereft. Only Miss Jenny's call as she came rushing down the steps distracted Eden from her unexpected desire to be back in the safety of the stranger's arms.

Chapter Four

"Eden! Is everything all right? The children told me some terrible Yankees were down here and that you'd been hurt!" Jenny Jones appeared at the top of the steps surrounded by frightened children, some of whom were clinging to her skirts and making it difficult for her to descend. She had been teaching in a classroom at the rear of the second floor and hadn't heard the commotion in the main hallway until the children had come to get her. "Oh, my dear! Do you need the doctor?" she cried when she saw Eden's injury.

"No, I don't need the doctor. My cheek's only bruised. I'll be all right."

"But you're bleeding. Are you sure?" Jenny reached the hall and hurried to Eden's side. She wondered who the gentleman and the boy were, standing with her.

"Yes—yes, I'm sure."

Reassured by her words, the children ran forward to surround Eden in a loving crush. "Miss Eden—"

She hugged them back as best she could.

Jenny looked down the hallway and noticed the damage to the front door. "What happened?"

"Two Yankees broke in, but everything is fine now, thanks to Reverend Matthews here," Eden said simply. "Reverend, this is Jenny Jones. She's a teacher here at the Haven."

Logan turned to the attractive, middle-aged, blond-haired woman. "It's a pleasure to meet you, Mrs. Jones."

"Just call me Jenny," she invited. "And you're a minister? Well, thank heaven you showed up when you did, Reverend. You saved Eden and all of us at the Haven today."

"I was glad I could help," he answered sincerely.

"Why would the Yankees do something like this?" Jenny still couldn't believe what had happened. "They've never bothered us before."

"They were drunk," Logan explained. "And they said somebody threw a chamber pot at them from an upstairs window. They wanted to find the one who did it."

"Someone threw a chamber pot out a window?" Jenny repeated incredulously, aghast. She was a lady through and through, and could not fathom such behavior from one of their charges. She turned a questioning look on the older boys who had been up on the third floor unsupervised.

Paul and the boys who'd been with him stood a little back from the other younger children, their expressions guarded, their eyes downcast.

"Do you boys know anything about this?" Eden asked them pointedly.

Guilt ate at Paul. He realized with chagrin that it was all his fault. He was responsible for the attack on Miss Eden. His hands tightened into fists at his sides. He had thought he was helping to rescue the ladies outside. He had thought he was saving them from the filthy Yankees, and yet his actions had had terrible consequences. He swallowed tightly. He knew the other boys wouldn't tell on him, but he also knew he couldn't lie to Miss Eden. He had to tell her the truth.

"Miss Eden," Paul said in a flat voice as he stepped forward, lifting his gaze to look her in the eye. "I'm the one who threw the pot at them."

A murmur of surprise ran through the children. Everyone turned to stare at Paul.

"Paul? You did it?" The shock was evident in Eden's expression. Paul was such a quiet boy. She would never have suspected him, for he had never been in any trouble before.

"Yes, ma'am. I did it, but I never thought this would happen! I'm sorry!"

"But why?" she asked, trying to control the

anger she was feeling over his actions. This wasn't like Paul at all. She knew there had to be more to it than a stupid prank.

"I was trying to help—"

"Help who?" Eden asked.

"It was Miss Gabrielle and Miss Veronica. They'd just left to go home when the Yankees—"

"Gabrielle and Veronica?" Eden gasped, horrified. They were two lovely ladies who volunteered to help out at the Haven one day a week, and they had left a short time before. "What happened to them? Why didn't they come back inside?"

"I don't know. I guess because those *Yankees*"—he said the word with pure loathing—"were hurting them and they couldn't get away. That's why I threw the chamber pot. I had to try to make them stop—to make them let the ladies go! I never thought they'd come in here or hurt you." Tears threatened, but Paul fought against them. He did not want to appear weak before the other children.

Eden saw his distress and went to put her arm around his shoulders.

"What you did was a brave thing, Paul," she told him. "Not everyone would have tried to come to their aid." She added quietly, "We'll talk more in the office." Looking to the others, she said, "Everything's fine now, Miss Jenny"

"Good, good," the older woman answered, then turned to the minister. "Thank you so much for your help, Reverend Matthews. I hate to think what might of have happened to us if you hadn't come to our aid." She shuddered visibly, for she had heard just how vile the Yankees could be.

"It was fortunate Mark and I arrived when we did."

"Yes, it certainly was. What do you say to Reverend Matthews, children?"

"Thank you, Reverend Matthews," they told him in unison.

"All right, children. Let's go back up to the classroom," Jenny announced.

Jenny herded them up the stairs, leaving Eden, Reverend Matthews, and the two boys alone in the main hall.

Eden turned to Logan and the boy standing at his side.

"So your name is Mark?" Eden smiled at the youth, assuming he was the reverend's son.

"Yes, ma'am."

"And you're Eden?" Logan countered with a slight smile.

"Oh—I'm sorry. I never did introduce myself," she said quickly, embarrassed that in all the confusion she'd never told him her name. "Yes, I'm Eden. Eden LeGrand."

"It's a pleasure to meet you, Eden LeGrand," he said.

"Some other way, I think, might have been better for a first introduction," she said.

"Yes, it would have been, but I'm just glad everything turned out all right."

"Why don't we talk in the office?" She and Paul led the way into Adrian's office.

Logan and Mark followed. Eden went to sit behind the desk and Paul took the chair to its side, leaving the two visitors the seats in front of the desk.

"As Miss LeGrand said, that was a very brave thing you did, Paul," Logan began, studying the boy who was sitting beside Eden, his expression sullen. "I don't doubt for a minute that those two soldiers were accosting ladies on the street, just as you said they were. It was good of you to try to help them."

At his words, Paul's expression subtly changed. He'd been feeling bad enough that Miss Eden had been hurt, and he was expecting to be punished for his actions. This stranger's unexpected praise startled him.

"Paul's a very special young man, Reverend," Eden put in, smiling at the boy.

"I can see that, and I can tell that you're smart." He looked Paul in the eye. "That's why I want you to learn from what happened here today. In the future, if you ever witness anything like that again, go get an adult to help you. If I hadn't arrived at the Haven right as the two soldiers were breaking into the building, things would have turned out very differently for everyone this afternoon."

"Yes, sir."

Eden was pleased that the minister cared enough to take the time to talk to Paul. "Reverend Matthews is right. Those were two very big, very mean men, and they were coming after you."

Paul nodded in understanding. "I'm sorry for the trouble I caused, Miss Eden. And I'll fix the door for you, I promise."

"Do you think you can?" She was worried that it might be too badly damaged.

"I'll go look at it." Paul got up and started from the room.

"If you need any help, Paul, let me know," Logan volunteered.

"Yes, sir."

"You are being so good to us," Eden told the reverend.

"I'm just glad I can help in some way."

"Did you say you had been coming here to see us today?"

"Yes, I wanted to meet with your director, Adrian Forrester, but I take it he's not here." Logan's plans had changed drastically since he'd started out that morning to make his first contact with the Haven, from his encounter with Mark to the drunken Yankees, but it didn't matter. He was prepared to do whatever was necessary to win the trust of those who worked here at the orphanage. He had to get close to Forrester in some way, and fate had handed him another opportunity to ingratiate himself by confronting the drunks at the home. He was going to take full advantage of it.

"Adrian is away. He won't be back until sometime next week. Was your visit personal, or is there something I can help you with? I'm in charge while he's gone," Eden offered, surprised by the news that the minister had really been coming to see them. They didn't get many visitors at the Haven. She'd thought he'd just been passing by and had heard the commotion the soldiers had made breaking through the door, and had come to their aid.

Logan was immediately suspicious of Forrester's absence, and he wondered what had called him away from the orphanage. He would let Sam know that Forrester was gone when he met with him later that night. If the director of the home proved to be the mastermind behind the Rebel group that had raided the *Bayou Belle*, he might be off planning another attack. Logan would have to keep a careful eye on the man when he returned.

"I would like to speak with you, but it can wait until another time, considering what you've just been through."

"I'm fine, really," Eden insisted. Her lip had finally stopped bleeding, and though her cheek still ached, the pain wasn't too severe. "There's no need for you to go. What can we do for you? We owe you so much already—"

"You don't owe me anything. I'm just glad things worked out the way they did."

"Why were you coming to the Haven?"

"I'm from St. Louis. A month or so ago, news reached us there about the Homeless Haven Orphans' Asylum and the wonderful job you're doing here. There are quite a few Southern sympathizers in St. Louis, and they were touched by your undertaking with the children. They wanted to help you in some way, so I took up a collection from several congregations to support your work. I've brought it with me." He reached inside his coat and took out the envelope that was thick with the funds he'd been carrying for just this moment. He presented it to Eden.

Eden's eyes widened in disbelief as she opened the sealed envelope and counted the donations. She was shocked by the generosity of the gift.

Mark was looking on, too, and he had never seen so much money all at one time before—and the minister was giving it all away!

"Reverend Matthews—this is so . . ." She paused and looked up at him, her eyes misting with heartfelt tears. "Wonderful. How can we ever repay you?"

"It's a present. Don't even think of any repayment. The pleasure is all mine, believe me."

And Logan meant it.

The pleasure was his, for things were definitely going his way. Eden LeGrand, the acting director of the Haven, was accepting him without question. He was right where he wanted and needed to be.

"Thank you."

"I'm just glad to be able to offer some aid. These children need all the help and moral support we can give them."

"You're right about that. Times are very hard right now. Some days, we have trouble getting enough food for everyone."

"I am planning to stay in New Orleans for a while. If you're in need of help, I'd be more than happy to work with you here."

"We'd be honored to have you with us, Reverend. We have prayers every day, but it would be wonderful if the children could have regular contact with a minister." Eden couldn't believe their good fortune. She'd been praying for a miracle, and it looked as if her prayers had been answered. Reverend Matthews had come to them in their desperate hour of need, and now he was going to stay on and help. "Do you know how long you'll be in town?"

"Until God's calling sends me elsewhere," he answered.

"Is there anything we can do for you? You've been so generous and caring—"

"No. My needs are few, but young Mark here—"

"Mark is your son?"

Mark had remained quiet as he'd sat at Logan's side listening to all that transpired, but he tensed at her words.

"I ain't his son," he spoke up quickly, a sharpness in his tone as he denied the reverend before the reverend could deny him.

"You're not?" Eden was honestly surprised by the news. With their dark coloring, she had thought them father and son.

"No, we're not related," Logan affirmed. "Young Mark here is in need of a place to call home. He's fallen upon hard times with the death of his parents, and I was hoping he could find shelter with you at the Haven."

"Of course, Mark is welcome here," Eden said as she looked over at the boy, then back at Logan. "Did Mark travel down from St. Louis with you?"

Mark cast a sidelong, nervous glance at the preacher, unsure of how Reverend Matthews was going to answer her. If the reverend told this lady the truth—that he'd tried to steal his horse and that he'd stolen food from the store—she might not want him there at the orphanage. He remained silent, waiting to hear the reverend's response. Defensively, he told himself he didn't want to live there at the orphanage anyway, so it really didn't matter what Reverend Matthews told her. If she didn't want him to stay there, that would be just fine with him.

"Mark and I met down by the riverfront just today," Logan began, carefully choosing his words. "He was admiring my horse, and we struck up a conversation."

Mark had been prepared for the worst. The preacher's answer shocked him. As he listened to this man of God, he realized that Reverend Matthews had not only avoided all the ugliness of their first encounter, but nothing he'd revealed to the woman was a lie. He'd told Miss Eden the truth, he just hadn't added all of the details.

Deep within him, Mark felt the ache of a long-absent, more tender emotion begin to grow, but he fought to ignore it. Any gentle feelings were a weakness, and he couldn't afford to be weak. The preacher meant nothing to him, and Mark didn't really care if he ended up in this asylum or not. Eventually Reverend Matthews was going to leave, and they'd never see each other again, so it didn't matter.

Eden looked over at the boy and said gently, "It seems like the Lord made sure the both of you were in the right place at the right time today so you could meet."

"Yes, ma'am," Mark answered respectfully, but all the while he was thinking that he seriously doubted that God had wanted him to try to steal the minister's horse to make his getaway after stealing the food.

She was about to say more when Paul returned to stand in the doorway.

"I think I can fix the door, Miss Eden," he told her.

"Good. Why don't you let Mark here help you with it, while I show the Reverend around the Haven?"

"Yes, ma'am." Paul looked at Mark.

The other boy got up to follow him.

"Mark, do you have any personal belongings

with you?" Eden asked as he was about to leave the office.

"No, ma'am."

It never failed to touch Eden when she learned of the children who suffered so much at the hands of this merciless war. To be destitute and alone in the world at such a young age could be heartbreaking. That was why she volunteered to work here. That was why she did all she could to make Homeless Haven more than just a building to house orphans. She wanted this place to truly be a haven. She wanted the children who lived here to know that they were loved. She wanted it to be their home. She would make sure that Mark had a change of clothing before the day was out.

"Reverend, would you like to take a look around? I can give you a guided tour right now." She locked the envelope with the money in the top desk drawer and stood up.

"I'd like that," Logan told her. His smile was genuine as he, too, got to his feet. He picked up his Bible to carry it with him.

At his smile, Eden found herself once again thinking what an attractive man he was. She'd been around many handsome men before, but there was something about Reverend Matthews that really appealed to her.

The old adage "drawn like a moth to a flame" echoed in Eden's thoughts, and she was momentarily puzzled by it. There was nothing dangerous about this man. If anything, he truly was like a guardian angel. He was a minister doing God's work. She had only to look at the donation he'd just given to the home to know that. He was the answer to her prayers—a godsend.

"This is Adrian's office, and his personal living quarters are there." Eden pointed to a door leading off to the side of the room.

It was then that she noticed he was still carrying his Bible.

"You can leave your Bible here in the office, if you'd like. We'll come back here before you leave," she offered.

"Thanks, but I always carry it with me." Logan didn't want to risk leaving it behind just in case one of the children might pick it up. There would be no explaining the gun secreted inside. He added with a smile, "It makes me feel as if I'm 'armed.' "

Eden led the way from the office, thinking him a most dedicated clergyman.

Logan was impressed with the Haven. It was clean and spacious. It housed seventeen children now with the addition of Mark—nine boys and eight girls. The youngest was four, and at ten, Paul was the oldest. From what he'd seen so far, the children seemed quite well behaved.

Eden showed him the main-floor dining room first. It was large and filled with tables and benches for the children. A single round table with chairs was at the front of the room for the adults. They made their way to the third floor next to see the boys' quarters.

Logan walked to the open front window to look out at the street below.

"It's amazing that Paul's aim was as good as it was. It's a long way down there," he remarked.

Eden came to stand beside him. "That must have been very traumatic for him to witness."

"He's a brave young man."

"Yes, he is. Especially coming forth and admitting he'd done it. I'm proud of him."

"There is one problem, though," Logan added, seeing the shattered remains of the chamber pot on the ground below.

"What?"

"The boys are going to need a new chamber pot up here."

As terrible as the day had been, his response evoked a laugh from Eden. "They certainly will."

The sound touched Logan, and he realized it had been a long time since he'd heard anyone laugh. He gazed down at her.

Eden looked up at him and found herself staring into his dark eyes. Though his expression was unreadable, she was suddenly, intensely aware of him as a man. A shiver of sensual recognition went through her. Confused by her reaction to Logan, she stepped back to distance herself from him.

"Let's go downstairs and I'll show you the girls' rooms."

Nervous, she moved off a bit quickly, leaving him to follow. They continued on.

"What's a typical day like for the children?" Logan asked as they made their way downstairs.

"We get up early, usually by seven A.M. We have breakfast and then prayer. Miss Jenny teaches from around nine until noon. Then we have lunch and play for a while. In the afternoons, we're flexible. Sometimes we do chores, sometimes we study, and sometimes we just play some more. Dinner is usually around six o'clock, and bedtime is at nine."

"Sounds like you're very busy."

"Yes, but it's rewarding work. The children are special, and we love them like our own."

Eden showed Logan around the second floor and took him to the classroom.

Eden interrupted Jenny as she was teaching her class.

"Miss Jenny, I have some news for everyone. Mark, the boy who came in with Reverend Matthews today, is going to be staying on with us."

"That's wonderful." Jenny was sincere, but she was a bit surprised, for she'd thought the child was the reverend's son. "Where is he now?"

"He's helping Paul repair the front door."

"We'll have to make sure we give Mark a proper welcome later at dinner."

"Good. And I have even more wonderful news. While Reverend Matthews is in New Orleans, he's going to help us out here at the Haven."

"When will you be starting, Reverend?" Jenny asked, delighted with the news.

Logan looked at Eden. "Tomorrow, if that's all right with Miss Eden?"

"Fine," she agreed, truly pleased, for she knew what a good influence he would be on the children, and on the boys in particular after the way he'd counseled Paul.

They started back down to the main floor.

"You've done a fine job here. The children seem happy."

"Thank you. I'm just glad we're able to keep them safe. So many of the children have suffered devastating losses. It's a harsh, ugly world out there right now."

"Indeed it is," Logan agreed, thinking of his brother and hoping he was still alive.

Paul and Mark were still hard at work repairing the lock on the door when Eden and Logan made their way back to the office. Eden glanced out the window as she went to the desk, and she saw several Union soldiers passing by on the street. The sight of them left her trembling, and she fought hard for control.

Logan saw her reaction to the men. "I'm sorry about what happened to you today. Are you sure you're feeling all right?"

Eden turned back to him and managed a half-smile, even though her cheek still ached. "Yes, I'm fine. Thanks to you."

"I'm going to be on my way now, but I'll be back first thing in the morning."

"We'll be looking forward to it," she told him as she saw him to the door.

"I'll see you tomorrow, Mark," Logan promised as he stopped to talk with the boy.

"You're coming back?" Mark asked, not really believing he would.

"I'll be here."

Mark nodded and returned to his work.

"Do a good job," Logan told the two.

"We will," Paul assured him.

Logan left the building.

Eden returned to the office. She found herself drawn to the window, wanting to see Logan one more time just to make sure he really existed. She glanced out just as Logan swung up onto his horse's back, and her gaze lingered on him. He was tall and confident in the saddle, and he commanded his mount with practiced ease. She lingered there, watching as he rode away, not wanting to lose sight of him.

Only when the reverend had disappeared from sight did Eden turn back to the desk. She sat down and wrote notes to both Gabrielle and Veronica, letting them know that she'd heard about the Yankees accosting them and that she hoped they were all right.

That done, she wrote another note, but this one was short and terse. It contained only the names of the Yankee private and corporal who'd attacked the women and invaded the Haven, and requested information about them. She sealed it in an envelope and slipped it into the pocket of her gown. She would see it personally delivered to her contact that very day. Once she got an answer to her request, she would decide what action to take. Men like Layton and Moran needed to be taught a lesson, and she planned to do the teaching.

There was one other thing Eden needed to do to ease her fears, but she knew it would have to wait until she went home for dinner that night. Never again would she be caught defenseless before the hated Yankees. She was going to get one of her father's guns and bring it with her to the Haven. From this day forward, she would always be ready to protect and defend the children with whatever force was necessary. She couldn't always count on someone as wonderful as Reverend Matthews showing up to defend them.

As she went out to see to the children, Eden thought of the minister again and smiled. She found she was looking forward to seeing him the next day.

Chapter Five

Fever ate at him. Burning him. Searing him. Braden struggled against the agony that tore at him with razor-sharp claws. Thrashing about on the pallet, he sought peace from the torment, but there was no peace—no release.

Union Corporal Jim Danner felt helpless as he tried to ease his lieutenant's suffering. They were trapped in a prison camp where no one cared if they lived or died.

"Is the lieutenant getting worse?"

Danner looked up at young Private Taylor who had only been brought into the camp a few days before. Taylor didn't look much older than fifteen or sixteen.

"Yes, and there's not a damned thing I can do to help him."

"Let me see if I can help," Taylor offered, dropping down beside the wounded man. "My pa was a doctor."

Danner was glad for his aid and moved back to let Taylor tend to the lieutenant. "The bullet's out, and he seemed like he was getting better for a while, but now a fever's got him."

Taylor nodded and set to work. The private took the blanket off the injured officer, then removed his shirt and the bandage to examine the wound. "Can you get me some water?"

Danner hurried off, anxious to do whatever he could to help.

"Easy, Lieutenant," Taylor said as the officer tossed about restlessly in his delirious state.

Taylor made sure the wound was clean and then rewrapped it, all the while talking in low, calming tones.

Danner returned quickly with a bucket of fresh water and a dipper.

"Good. Thanks. What's your lieutenant's name?" Taylor asked.

"Braden Matthews."

Taylor nodded and, lifting the officer's head, pressed the dipper to his lips to try to force him to drink. "Lieutenant Matthews —you need to drink this."

As if from a distance, Braden could hear someone talking to him, calling to him, but he wasn't sure who it was. He knew it wasn't Corporal Danner. This voice was different, higher than the corporal's. He thought maybe it was the woman from the *Bayou Belle* who'd helped him when he'd first been shot. He tried to concentrate on the voice, to use it to pull himself back to reality. He fought for a grip on his sanity and awareness, and for a moment Braden managed to focus on the face above him. He didn't recognize the soldier speaking to him and couldn't reason well enough to understand what was happening.

"Drink," Taylor ordered, recognizing the momentary look of clarity in the officer's eyes.

Braden swallowed thirstily of the proffered water.

"That's good. That's the way."

The pain threatened to overwhelm Braden again. He closed his eyes against it, welcoming the relief from his agony in the darkness of unconsciousness.

Taylor put the dipper aside, tore a strip of cloth from the lieutenant's shirt, and began to bathe his brow with what was left of the water. His fever was dangerously high and had to be broken soon or he might die.

Together, Taylor and Danner worked through the night to try to ease Braden's suffering.

"Eden! What happened to you?" Camille Le-Grand gasped, coming face-to-face with her sister when Eden returned home for dinner that evening.

At the sound of her youngest daughter's remark, Francene hurried from the dining room where she'd been setting the table to see what was wrong. She was stunned by her first look at Eden. The bruise on her daughter's cheek was vivid and her lip was slightly swollen. Francene rushed to her side, horrified as she tried to imagine what had happened to cause the injury.

"My darling! You're hurt. Look at your face! Who did this to you?"

Eden had known her mother and sister would be upset, and she hurried to calm their fears. "I'm fine. There was a problem at the Haven today."

"What kind of problem? What happened?" Francene exclaimed, worried.

Eden quickly related everything that had happened and how the reverend had arrived just in time to save them.

"Oh, my God," Francene said weakly, her color turning ashen at the news of her daughter's peril. "You could have been killed."

"But I wasn't, thanks to Reverend Matthews." She noticed how pale her mother had become. "Let's go sit down in the dining room while I tell you the rest of my news."

"There's more?" Francene asked weakly, not sure she could handle anything else right then. It was traumatic enough worrying about her husband and son away at war, but the realization that something terrible could happen to one of her daughters right here at home was unnerving.

"The rest is all good, Mama. I promise," Eden reassured her as they entered the dining room.

"Who is this Reverend Matthews? Where did

he come from?" Camille asked. In her mind, all ministers were white-haired old men. She was having trouble understanding how an old, decrepit minister could have driven two angry, drunken Yankee soldiers from the orphanage all by himself.

"Reverend Matthews is from St. Louis, and not only did he help with the Yankees, he brought the Haven a sizable donation." Eden told them about the money he'd collected for them. "Logan Matthews is one very special man."

"He sounds like it," her mother agreed. "I'm going to have to meet him and thank him for what he did for you and the children."

"He said he was going to come to the Haven regularly, so he'll be there working with the children. Why, he even brought a homeless boy he found on the streets with him today in hopes that we could take him in."

"Did you?"

"Oh, yes. We never turn away anyone in need. There's always room for one more. The boy's name is Mark. When I first met him, I thought he was the reverend's son."

"How old is this reverend?" Camille asked, instantly alert at the suggestion that the reverend could have had a young son. That meant he wasn't quite in his dotage yet. Her hopes elevated as she awaited her sister's answer.

"Oh, I don't know—maybe thirty or so," Eden told her as their maid began serving dinner.

"Tell me more about him, Eden," Camille urged. She tried to sound casual, but in truth, there was nothing casual about the way she was suddenly feeling. Because of the war, available, able-bodied men were few and far between. At eighteen, she was of marriageable age, and she had no intention of becoming an old maid. She was after a husband, and she was going to get one. Just the fact that this reverend was a man and was physically fit made him wonderful in her eyes. "What does he look like? He's not married, is he?"

"Camille!" Eden gave her sister a censorious look as she realized where her thoughts were going. "Logan's a minister!"

"So? He's a minister, right? He's not a priest. Besides, you still haven't answered my question. Is he married?"

"We really didn't discuss his personal affairs," Eden replied with dignity.

"Too bad. Is he handsome?" Camille pressed, sensing that Eden was acting strangely reticent where this man was concerned.

The image of the way Reverend Matthews had looked as he'd ridden away from the Haven played in Eden's mind.

She finally answered her sister, "Yes, as a matter of fact, I think he is quite good-looking, but he is a man of God, and he's very serious about his calling."

"Ooh," Camille cooed. "I just love serious men."

"Camille!" Francene scolded. She understood her daughter's interest in eligible young men, but she had raised Camille to be a lady and she should act like one.

"Sorry, Mama," Camille apologized, but she didn't mean it. She was suddenly seriously considering volunteering to help out at the home. It had never appealed to her before, for she wasn't all that fond of children, but if this handsome young reverend was going to be there, well, she might be able to find a few hours a day to dedicate to the less fortunate little brats.

"Eden, what's going to happen to the soldiers who hurt you?" her mother demanded.

"Nothing."

"But they should be punished!"

"I'm afraid if I did report them, they might make more trouble for Paul or for the Haven. It's better to just let it go. The children weren't harmed, and that's all that matters." She did not reveal any of her own plan to wreak revenge, knowing it would only upset her family.

As they finished eating, Eden looked over at her mother.

"I want to take one of Papa's guns with me tonight when I go back to the Haven," she told her. Eden had expected her mother to be terribly upset by the suggestion; instead she nodded her head in approval.

"I have two of them in the study. Let's see which one is easiest for you to use," Francene said.

"You aren't angry?"

"Heavens, no," she reassured Eden. "I think you're smart to do it. In fact, if you hadn't brought it up, I was going to. I don't want you to be alone and at anyone's mercy ever again. We don't have your father or brother here to protect us, and while you were fortunate that the minister showed up today, there's no way of knowing when this might happen again, with the way the war is going and the way the city is these days. You've got to be able to defend yourself."

Eden hugged her spontaneously, glad to have her mother's support. "I was hoping you'd understand."

Camille was about to suggest that Eden stop going to the orphanage, but then held her tongue. If this handsome young minister was going to be there, she had to have a way to get introduced to him, and her sister was it. Not that Eden would listened to any advice she'd give her any way. Camille knew Eden well enough to know that she would never stop working with the children. "Well, you'll have Reverend Matthews there with you for the next few days until Mr. Forrester gets back, so maybe it will be safe."

"It will be safe once I have the gun with me," Eden declared as she and her mother went into the study.

A short time later, carrying the gun in her reticule, Eden made the trip back to the Haven. She spent her nights at the home when Adrian was gone because she didn't want to leave Jenny alone with all the children in case there was any emergency.

As she reached the front door, Eden was pleased to note that the boys had finished repairing the lock. The wood around the door was still damaged, but the portal itself was secure. She was glad, for she didn't trust the two soldiers not to return. With the door locked, if they ever did try to break in again, she would have enough time to get her gun.

Eden used her key to let herself in. She left her things in the small room off the main hall that she slept in when she spent the night, carefully storing the gun in the bedside table. That done, she went to seek out Jenny, who was in the kitchen talking with the cook about the meals for the following day.

"Paul and Mark did a good job on the door," Eden told Jenny.

"Yes, they did. I was quite pleased with their work, and I think they were, too," Jenny said.

"How is Mark doing?"

"He and Paul seem to be getting along very nicely."

"That's good for both of them." Eden was glad. She had hoped that they would become friends, for she knew Paul was very much a solitary child. "I'm going to go upstairs and take a look in on them before I retire."

"Is the reverend really coming back tomorrow?"

"He said he'd be here in the morning.

"The children are looking forward to it. They saw how he helped you, and they think he's wonderful."

"Reverend Matthews is wonderful," Eden agreed on her way to speak with Paul and Mark.

It was almost lights-out time, but all the boys were still awake. Some were reading, others were talking among themselves in small groups.

"Miss Eden's back!" The cry went up as she entered the room.

"Good evening," she told them as she greeted each boy individually, working her way around the bedroom.

Some of the younger boys came to hug her, and she returned their embraces warmly, cherishing the sweetness of the moment. The bigger boys remained sitting on their beds, and she made her way back to where Paul and Mark were, to tell them what a good job they'd done fixing the lock.

"Do you have everything you need, Mark?" she asked.

"Miss Jenny gave me some new clothes, but she made me take a bath and wash my hair," he answered gruffly.

"That's good. Cleanliness is next to godliness, you know," she teased with a smile. "I'm glad she took care of you tonight. You get a good night's sleep, and I'll see you in the morning."

"Miss Eden," Mark spoke up as she turned to leave.

She stopped and looked back.

"Is Reverend Matthews really coming back?"

She saw a fleeting look of pain in his eyes as he asked her. She understood that it was hard for him to allow himself to care about anyone. A lot of the children had that problem when they first arrived at the Haven.

"Yes, he is. He told me he'd be here in the morning, and I don't doubt for a moment that Reverend Matthews is a man of his word. He will be here."

Mark nodded. He knew she was right. Reverend Matthews was a man of his word. He stretched out on his bed, but sleep did not come quickly as his thoughts went over all that had happened to him that day. So much had changed and so quickly. He had gone from sleeping in an alley to the safety and comfort of this bed in the Haven. He thought of Reverend Matthews, and silently said a short prayer of thanks for the man. When he finally fell asleep, Mark slept deeply for the first time in weeks.

Downstairs, Eden locked the door to the small bedroom she was using before changing into her nightgown and lying down. She missed the comfort and privacy of her own room at home, but she knew it was important to be there.

Closing her eyes, Eden sought rest, but memories of the horror of the day returned. Visions of the drunken soldiers crashing through the door and invading the Haven haunted her. She tossed and turned as she recalled in vivid detail how the

Yankee had hit her. The image of Logan Matthews came to her then, appearing so tall and powerful and invincible in the doorway ready to vanquish the invaders. He had been a guardian angel. He'd defeated the enemy and driven them away, leaving the home safe for the children once again.

In the darkness, a soft smile curved her lips as she thought of Logan. She remembered how safe she'd felt when he'd come to her after the attack and how strong he'd been when he'd helped to steady her as she'd stood before him. As sleep finally claimed her, Eden was thinking about the day to come and how she was looking forward to seeing the reverend again.

Time passed slowly for Logan as he sat alone in his hotel room, waiting for the hour when he was to meet Sam on the riverfront. He had tried to rest, but his thoughts were too troubled. Concern about his brother ate at him endlessly. He'd made some headway at the Haven that day, but with Forrester gone, he would not be getting any quick answers to his questions. He was going to have to bide his time, but time was the one thing he didn't want to waste, for Braden's very life depended on him.

Logan thought of Eden then and how lucky it had been that he'd arrived at the Haven when he had. She was a beautiful, spirited young woman. The fierce courage she'd shown in the face of the soldiers' brutality had been amazing, considering how fragile she'd seemed when he'd helped to steady her. He thought of her laughter again, and found that he was almost looking forward to going to the orphanage in the morning.

Logan frowned, for he realized he could not allow himself to think about anything but his mission. He was there to learn the identity of the ones responsible for the raid on the *Bayou Belle* and in the process save Braden. Nothing else mattered.

As the midnight hour finally drew near, Logan quit his room and made his way to the designated place to meet Sam. The riverfront was dark and deserted, and he was glad for the anonymity the night gave him. Logan walked quietly along the levee, Bible in hand.

"That you, preacherman?" The hushed voice came to him out of the enveloping darkness.

"I'm here looking for lost souls," Logan answered.

"You found one," Sam returned with a grin, appearing out of nowhere. He came to Logan's side and then led him off to a secluded spot where they wouldn't be seen or overheard. "What happened with that boy who tried to steal your horse?"

"I took him with me to the Homeless Haven. He's staying there now."

Sam nodded in the darkness, seeing the brilliance of Logan's actions. "That was smart, real smart."

"I've been accepted at the Haven, but Forrester isn't there. He left a woman in charge while he's away, and according to her, he won't be back until next week. Have you heard anything about where he might have gone?"

"Nothing," he answered. "But I'll see what I can find out."

Logan quickly told him where he was staying in case he had any messages to relay to him.

"We have another helper here in town, you know. Be watching. They'll be contacting you when they get some information you might need."

"Who is it?"

Sam refused to give him a name. "Someone whose soul could use a little saving just like me, preacherman."

With that, Sam disappeared into the darkness.

Logan returned to his hotel room and bedded down for the night, satisfied that things were going as well as could be expected.

Chapter Six

Eden awoke early, excited about the new day. Her thoughts were of the minister and his coming visit as she got up and started to get ready. She realized there were very few men like Logan Matthews—men who were generous and self-sacrificing. He had put himself at risk to save her and the children. Eden wished she could repay him, but she didn't know how.

Eden studied her reflection in the mirror as she worked at pinning back her hair in the practical bun she always wore at the nape of her neck. The bruise on her cheek was darker this morning. She didn't like the thought that every time the children looked at her today, they would be vividly reminded of yesterday's terror. Eden wished she had some face paint like actors used on stage to cover the mark, but her mother would never have approved, no matter what the circumstances. She covered it as best she could with a little powder.

As Eden reached for her daygown, she wondered why she hadn't brought something from home that was a little more attractive than this drab, serviceable dress. Oddly, before this morning, she'd never noticed how faded the gown was. She studied it now, realizing it was in very poor condition. The thought surprised her. Camille was the one who always worried about her clothes and her appearance; she seldom did.

Eden frowned as she slipped into the dress, trying to understand her own reasoning. It took her only a moment to realize why she was acting this way: Reverend Matthews would be spending the day at the orphanage. She wanted to look her best for him.

Eden emerged from her room and hurried down the hall to join the children as they were filing down the steps in an orderly fashion to the dining room for breakfast.

"Good morning, everyone," she greeted them cheerfully.

"Good morning, Miss Eden."

"Is Reverend Matthews here yet?" six-year-old Connie Curtis asked, her blue eyes shining with excitement. She had been among those hiding on the steps yesterday who'd watched first in fear, then in awe as the minister had singlehandedly driven the Yankees from the home. She thought him most wonderful and was eager to see him again.

"No, not yet. But he will be," Eden assured her, following her into the dining room.

The children lined up behind their chairs and waited for Miss Eden and Miss Jenny to reach their seats. With Eden leading them, they said grace.

"—from thy bounty through Christ, our Lord—"

"Amen," came the deep sound of the reverend's voice from the doorway.

Everyone looked up to see Logan standing there, smiling approvingly at the scene before him.

A unexpected thrill surged through Eden at the sight of him. She told herself she was excited about seeing him only because she was glad he'd kept his word to the children. In truth, she suspected that her own feelings had a bit to do with it, but she ignored that possibility. Eden did admit to herself, though, that seeing him this morning proved what she'd been thinking about all night: Logan Matthews was every bit as good-looking as she'd remembered him to be, and possibly even more so. His tall, commanding presence dominated the room filled with children, and they were all watching him a bit in awe.

"Good morning, Reverend Matthews," the children greeted him happily.

"Good morning," he responded as he strode

into the room. He was looking for Mark but hadn't spotted him yet when a little blond-haired girl jumped up and grabbed him by the hand. She tugged him toward her table.

"You can sit here with me!" little Connie declared, holding tightly to him. "There's lots of room."

Logan had been intent on speaking with Mark first and then breakfasting with Eden, but he could hardly refuse the child. "I'd like that," he accepted. "Thank you."

There was plenty of room on the bench for him, so he moved to stand next to Connie. Everyone sat down then as breakfast was served.

Eden watched from the head table as Logan engaged in conversation with the girl.

"He's so good with the children," Jenny remarked, noticing how the children sitting around Logan were all laughing at something he'd said. "They love him already."

"He's a godsend, that's for sure."

When the meal ended, Eden stood up to speak.

"As you know, our good friend Reverend Matthews is going to be visiting the Haven regularly now. Reverend? Would you like to say a few words to the children?"

Logan had been anticipating this moment since he'd gotten up that morning. He knew Eden was expecting him to minister to the children, and he was as prepared as he was ever going to be. Smiling easily, he rose and moved to stand at the front of the room.

"It's my pleasure to be with you today," he began. "As Miss Eden told you, I hope to be spending a lot of time here at the Haven while I'm in New Orleans, and I'm really looking forward to it. Thank you for the warm welcome you've given me. Since this is our first day together, let's get to know one another. I want you to call me Reverend Logan, and I want to learn all your names, too."

He looked to the children sitting at the table closest to him, and they quickly introduced themselves. It went around the entire room, ending with Mark where he was sitting with Paul and the other older boys toward the back. Logan was glad to see that the boy looked as if he was doing fine.

"It's going to take me a while to remember everyone's name, but I'll do my best," he promised when they'd finished. "Miss Eden said that you always start your day with a prayer, so this morning I'd like to lead you in one. Everyone stand, please."

They all rose and stood in attentive silence, their heads bowed as he began to pray.

"Dear Lord, bless us this day and teach us to love each other as You have loved us. Amen."

"Amen," they repeated dutifully.

Eden came to stand with him.

"Thank you, Reverend Logan, for sharing

your time with us. Children, you can go to class now."

As the children left the room, Logan turned his attention to Eden.

"How are you feeling this morning?" He had an urge to reach out and touch her bruised cheek, to soothe her somehow, but he held himself back.

"I'm fine. My cheek looks much worse than it feels," she admitted a bit self-consciously.

"Is there anything in particular you'd like me to do today? Anything you need? I know a little about carpentry and was thinking I could finish up the work the boys started on the front door frame, if you want me to."

"Why, yes, thanks." She was surprised by his offer. "But I never thought you were coming here to do manual labor or carpentry work." She appreciated his thoughtfulness and his willingness to help in any way he could.

"Jesus was a carpenter," he answered simply, glad that he'd thought of the response.

Eden showed him where the tools were, and Logan began straightaway. He had specifically suggested working on the front door, knowing it would keep him near the office. He wanted to keep watch in case someone of interest came or went.

Camille was excited as she got dressed that morning. She made sure her hair was perfect, and she made certain to wear her finest daygown. Confident she looked her best, she was ready. She had planned everything perfectly.

Today was the day.

Granted, she wasn't thrilled to have to be around all the orphans, but if that was the price she had to pay, so be it. Her mother had gone off to visit friends, so the time was right. She left the house and eagerly made the trip to the Haven.

The children were outside playing on the grounds as she made her way up the walk toward the front door, but she ignored them. She truly didn't care about the children. She had bigger prey on her mind. She just hoped the reverend was there.

Camille reached the steps to the porch and stopped. There before her, working on the door with his back to her, was a man who looked to be a common day laborer. He was wearing dark pants and a white shirt that was sweat-stained and dirty. She paused for a moment, pondering what to do. To get inside, she had to walk right past him, and she didn't want to get dirty if she accidentally brushed against him. She planned to look her absolute best when she met the minister for the first time.

As if sensing there was someone behind him, the man turned to look, and then smiled at her.

His good looks surprised Camille. He was tall and darkly handsome, but she quickly told herself that that didn't matter. He was obviously only a manual laborer. She was looking for the reverend. He had to be around here somewhere.

"Good morning," Logan said, seeing the young woman and immediately noticing her resemblance to Eden. "Let me hold the door for you."

"Thank you," Camille said, sweeping inside as quickly as she could, and holding her skirts so they didn't brush against him.

Camille hurried down the hallway toward the office. The door was open, and she swept into the room without hesitation.

"Camille?" Eden had been working at the desk, and she looked up in astonishment at the sight of her sister. Camille rarely, if ever, came to the Haven. This was truly a shock, and she was immediately worried. "What are you doing here? Is something wrong at home? Is Mother all right?"

"There's nothing wrong, dear sister. I just decided that it was time for me to help. I want to volunteer to work here with you," she said sweetly.

It took Eden only an instant to realize her sister's true motive, and she frowned. "Are you sure?"

"I am positive. Mother and I had a long talk about it last night, and we agreed I should help you."

Eden's eyes narrowed suspiciously, for she knew her sister far too well.

"That's wonderful of you," Eden said, then added to call her bluff, "The cook could use some help fixing the noon meal."

Camille's expression soured a bit. "Isn't there something in the way of book work I could do? I'd be much better at that than I am at working in the kitchen."

"That's a wonderful idea. You can read to the little ones after they eat, right before they take their naps," she answered, deliberately making sure she would be with the children.

"Eden!" Camille glared at her sister, her hands on her hips in defiance. "I meant paper work."

"I know what you meant. I was just seeing if you were really serious about helping the children or if you only came here to meet the reverend."

"Well? Where is he?" Camille demanded, her temper flaring at her sister's ploy. She should have realized that Eden would know what she was up to. She had never been able to fool her.

"You didn't meet him already?" Eden wondered if Reverend Logan had finished his work on the door. "He was just out front—"

"No, the only one in front was your workman."

Eden hid her smile as she got up and led the way back into the hall. Camille followed, puzzled. She wondered how she'd missed seeing the minister.

"Reverend Logan," Eden called out to him where he was repairing the door frame.

Logan put aside the tools and came inside to see what she wanted. He wiped his hands on his pants as he went to join the two women.

"Reverend Logan, I want you to meet my sister, Camille. Camille, this is Logan Matthews."

Camille's eyes widened as she realized the truth. Then her gaze went over him again, this time with even more appreciation. She was seeing him in a whole new light, and she liked what she saw. After a bath, wearing clean clothes, this man would be strikingly handsome. He was healthy. He was handsome. He was perfect.

"It's nice to meet you. Eden told me all about you."

"It's a pleasure to meet you, too," he responded.

"I see you're in disguise today," Camille said, smiling coyly at him. "I'd expected you to be wearing a dark, serious-looking suit and carrying your Bible."

"My coat's hanging up and my Bible is always close by." Logan returned her smile, knowing just how close to the truth she really was when talking about his disguise. "A minister's calling can come in many ways, Miss LeGrand. True, our main goal is saving souls, but there are times when we have to do work in the physical world to help those we're trying to save." Thoughts of his brother were with him as he spoke.

"Well, I know Eden is just delighted to have you here, and so am I. What you've done for the Haven is wonderful."

"I'm glad to help. Speaking of which, I'd better get back to work now. Miss LeGrand—"

"Please, call me Camille, Reverend," she said quickly.

"And I'm Logan," he responded. "If you'll excuse me—Camille, Miss Eden."

Logan nodded to them and had just started down the hall when Camille's call stopped him.

"Oh, Reverend Logan?"

He looked back.

"We were wondering if you'd care to join us at our home for dinner tomorrow night?" Camille brazenly asked. "We'd be honored to have you." She hadn't discussed it with either her mother or Eden, but that didn't matter. What mattered was getting this man to the house, so she could spend time with him.

"That's very kind of you to offer. Thank you. I'll be there," he accepted.

Eden went back in the office, and Camille was practically floating on air as she followed her.

"Oh, you were so right, dear sister!" Camille told her in a hushed, excited voice. "The reverend is handsome! You didn't do him justice in your description of him last night. He's even better than I'd hoped. I can't wait to tell Mama that he's coming to dinner. In fact, I'm going home right now to let her know."

"I thought you wanted to do some work here with the children. I thought you were going to volunteer to help out?"

"Later." Camille dismissed her sister's suggestion without a thought. "Right now, I have to get things ready for tomorrow. Reverend Logan is coming to dinner! I'll see you at home tonight."

Eden walked with her sister to the office door, then watched as she passed by Logan. As Eden had expected, Camille stopped to speak with him. The sound of her flirtatious laughter drifted down the hall to her, and Eden turned back into the room, her mood slightly annoyed as she returned to her work. As she did, she glanced down at her own plain gown and sighed.

The day passed quickly. Eden received notes from both Veronica and Gabrielle letting her know that they were fine, but they would not be returning to volunteer at the Haven for a while for they didn't feel safe there anymore. The two women had been a great help to her and Jenny while Adrian was away, and Eden was disappointed by their decision. Her anger at the two Yankees grew and so did her desire for revenge.

After the noon meal, Eden took some of the older children outside to work in the garden they kept in the backyard. Because of the shortages caused by the war and low funds, they had to raise as much of their own food as they could right there on the grounds. Eden also spent time working in the flower garden that bordered the rear of their property. Several seasons of neglect had transformed it into almost a wilderness, so she dedicated as much time as she could to taming the lush, overgrown plants and shrubs. Eden loved flowers, and the time she spent there was her favorite time of the day.

Eden set the children to weeding while she cut some of the more fragrant blooms to take inside.

Logan had finished his repairs to the door and was ready to leave for the day. He wasn't sure where Eden had gone. She wasn't in the office, and he didn't want to just disappear without telling her good-bye.

The sound of children's voices outside drew him from the house. He went out the front door and made his way around through the side yard.

"Is Miss Eden here?" he asked one of the boys.

The boy pointed him in the right direction.

Logan headed toward the back of the property to find her. The flowering bushes were tall, lush, and full. The heavenly scent of the blossoms filled the air. A narrow path wove its way among the shrubs and trees, and as he followed it, Logan almost felt as if he were in a maze. He came upon Eden as she was cutting a bouquet of flowers, and he paused. She hadn't heard his approach, so he took advantage of the moment to observe her.

Logan had thought Eden was lovely from the first moment he'd seen her. Now, standing there among the blossoms she looked even more beautiful. Framed by nature's glory, she was radiant, the epitome of innocence and beauty.

The fleeting thought that this was the Garden of Eden came to Logan, and he smiled.

But the smile quickly faded. He grew irritated

with himself for allowing his thoughts to stray that way. He knew little or nothing about Eden. True, she was dedicating her life to helping the children, and there certainly seemed to be no guile in her, but even so, the only thing he should concern himself with was finding those responsible for stealing the arms shipment. He was a man on a mission. He could afford no distractions. The stakes were too great.

"Eden?" Logan said her name softly, not sure why he felt the need to lower his voice, except that the place seemed so serene he hated to disrupt it by talking.

"Oh, Reverend Logan." She looked up in surprise.

"I think when we're by ourselves you can just call me Logan," he told her with a conspiratorial smile.

She grinned back. "Are you leaving now?"

"Yes. My work on the door is finished, and I think it turned out rather well."

"Thank you. Will we see you in the morning?"

"I'll be here."

"We'll be looking forward to it."

Eden stood before him, holding the bouquet of fragrant blossoms in her arms, her eyes aglow as she gazed up at him.

This time, Logan didn't try to stop himself from touching her injured cheek. "Are you sure it doesn't hurt?"

"Not so very much," she answered, her voice soft. She was mesmerized by the concern she saw in his expression and the gentleness of his touch.

He nodded and let his hand drop away, then said quietly, "Until tomorrow."

With that, he was gone.

Eden stood there, staring after Logan, feeling suddenly lost and alone without him and wishing she could think of a reason to call him back. The sounds of the children's voices forced her back to reality, but she knew she was already looking forward to his return in the morning. She smiled in anticipation.

Chapter Seven

"What shall we do for fun today?" Eden asked the children the following afternoon when they'd finished their chores and were gathered in the dining room. "Whose turn is it to choose?"

"The girls!" all the girls called out.

As usual, the boys were less than enthused to be at the mercy of the opposite sex, and they let their displeasure be known by their grumbling.

"I don't want to hear any more complaining, gentlemen. It is the ladies' turn to decide. So what would you like to do? Just raise your hands, and I'll call on you to hear your suggestions," Eden told the girls as Jenny and Logan looked on in amusement.

"Miss Eden!"

"Yes, Amanda?"

"I think we should do needlepoint."

The boys all groaned aloud.

Eden tried not to smile.

"That's a good suggestion. Anyone else have another idea?" She looked around and saw little Connie with her hand up. "Yes, Connie?"

The young girl smiled shyly as she answered, "I think we should practice dancing, Miss Eden."

The rest of the girls seemed to like that idea, while the boys looked suitably tortured at the prospect.

"I think dancing sounds wonderful," Jenny put in, knowing it would be just the thing to quiet the boys down.

"Very well," Eden agreed. "Boys, why don't you push the tables back so we have some room for a dance floor."

The boys went to work clearing the area. The girls were so excited, they decided to help. Jenny made her way to the back corner of the room where the old piano that had been donated to the Haven was kept. The piano was in poor condition and had a few keys missing, but the children never noticed. When Jenny played, they generally just enjoyed the music—except for the boys when they were forced to dance.

"Since this is ladies' day—girls, you may pick your own partner," Eden instructed, again trying not to grin when she saw the looks of pure misery on the boys' faces.

The girls quickly scattered to grab their favorite available male.

"Reverend Logan." Little Connie went straight to him and took his hand. She looked up at him adoringly. "I want you to dance with me first."

"I'd be honored," he answered.

Eden watched over the children as they paired up and went out onto the makeshift dance floor. The boys outnumbered the girls so, being the new boy, Mark ended up not being picked. He was looking delighted at the prospect of sitting this one out, so Eden decided to take him for herself.

"Mark? Will you dance with me?" she invited.

The boy was a bit stunned by Miss Eden's invitation. His expression became guarded as he tried to refuse her. "You don't want to dance with me, Miss Eden. Ask one of the others."

"Oh, no. You're not getting out of it that easily," she challenged him. "Come on." She took his arm.

"No, ma'am." Mark hesitated again, drawing back from her, scowling a bit and wanting to escape.

"When a lady asks you to dance, Mark, you're not supposed to refuse her."

He looked almost pained as he finally admitted to her, "But I can't dance, Miss Eden. I don't know how."

He was shocked when Miss Eden laughed. It wasn't a mocking laugh, but a laugh of pure delight.

"None of us can dance, Mark. That's why

we're doing this. It's all for fun and for practice so we can learn how. Come on. Don't be afraid. I'll show you what to do." She took his arm again and led him out among the others.

Mark looked tense and self-conscious, but Eden kept talking to him, and he relaxed a bit.

Logan had watched the exchange between the two of them with interest. He was amazed that a youth who had suffered through what Mark had, being orphaned and living hand-to-mouth on the streets, would be afraid of dancing with Eden. Logan had no more time to think about it, though, as the music began and little Connie demanded his full attention.

They practiced the quadrille and then the schottische, changing partners after each dance. Sometimes things went smoothly, and sometimes everyone ended up laughing at their own missteps and the missteps of others. Eventually the boys began to have fun, too, though they were less than wont to admit it.

Eden always enjoyed herself when they danced. She especially liked watching the bigger boys dancing with the youngest girls. It brought out the gentleness in them that they tried so hard to hide. She was pleased that Mark had not fought her too strongly in her effort to get him on the floor. He'd proven rather adept once he'd learned the basic steps, and he was now quite sought after by the girls.

"All right," Jenny announced. "It's time for a waltz."

Eden was wondering who she should choose to dance with next, but before she could decide, Logan appeared at her side.

"I was hoping you'd do me the honor of choosing me to be your partner for this waltz, Miss Eden," he said, giving her a courtly bow.

She was surprised and delighted by his request. She smiled up at him as she curtsied before him. "Reverend Logan, I would love to share this dance with you."

Around them, the children mimicked their behavior, bowing and curtsying.

As the slower melody began, Logan swept Eden into his arms. A shock of awareness shot through him at the touch of her body against his, and it startled him. He'd known she was beautiful. He'd known he was attracted to her, but he'd had no idea that holding her this way would prove so disconcerting. He began the waltz, guiding her expertly around the room. With every step he took, Logan was reminded of just how perfectly she fit against him. Gliding about the dance floor, they moved as if they were one.

Eden was surprised to discover that Logan was such an accomplished dancer. She'd thought that since he was a minister he probably didn't have too much dancing experience, but she realized now that she'd been wrong. Following his lead, she allowed him to swirl her gracefully about the floor, and she found she was loving every minute of being in his arms. It had been one thing when he'd helped her to stand the other day; it was another thing altogether to be held close to him as they moved in perfect unison. She lifted her gaze to look up at him.

Logan happened to glance down just then to find Eden staring up at him. It was a timeless moment for them both as their gazes met and locked, and it seemed as if the rest of the world had faded away. There were only the two of them—alone, caught up in the sensuous rhythm of their dance.

As Eden looked up at Logan, a revelation came to her. In that moment, for the first time, she saw him not as a minister, but simply as a man. She had always thought him attractive, but now as they danced together, every fiber of her being was aware of him—of the warm touch of his hand at her waist, the strength of him as he guided her flawlessly to the music. There was power and grace in his every move, and she instinctively followed him, reveling in the sensual awakening he was stirring within her.

And then Eden heard the laughter of the children around her.

Jarred from her reverie, Eden reminded herself who Logan was and why they were dancing together.

She tore her gaze away from him and looked down to hide the slight blush that stained her cheeks. She scolded herself for her reaction to him. She told herself that this was Logan—Reverend Logan. He was here to help the children and the Haven. Yet she had to admit that there was something about this man who had come into her life so unexpectedly that touched her in ways she'd never been touched before.

When at last Jenny stopped playing, Eden and Logan stood facing each other, marveling at the intimacy they'd just shared.

"Thank you for the dance," Logan said, and he meant it. He found he was sorry he had to let her go. If they'd been anywhere else, he would have paid the musicians to continue playing waltzes for the rest of the day and night. He wanted to keep her in his arms.

Eden smiled up at him, trying to make light of what had passed between them, wondering if she'd imagined it, but realizing that she hadn't. She felt almost bereft at no longer being held in his arms. "No—thank *you*, sir. You were a most worthy partner. I'm sure the children learned a lot just watching us."

"It was my pleasure," he answered.

"I'm just glad your religion doesn't prohibit you from dancing," she said, her eyes shining.

"So am I," he replied, giving her a wicked grin, and then he was gone, drawn away by another of the little girls.

A short time later, the time for dancing came to an end, and the children went off to see to their chores before dinner.

"I'm leaving now, but I'll see you later tonight," Logan told Eden when he sought her out in the office.

"We're looking forward to having you join us,"

Eden said. She had given him directions to her home earlier in the day.

As he left the Haven, Logan realized he truly was looking forward to the evening to come. Thoughts of their waltz and the way Eden had felt in his arms stayed with him until he finally forced himself to put the remembrances aside. He cautioned himself yet again not to even think about getting involved with Eden in any way. There was a very good possibility that the men he was after were somehow connected with Forrester, and he couldn't let any personal concern for Eden interfere with his mission. Beautiful woman that she was, he had no time for any kind of romantic dalliance. He had to find a way to save Braden.

Eden remained at the Haven with the children until they had all come down and settled in for the evening meal. Once she was certain all would be quiet, she left them with Jenny and went home for dinner.

The day before, Eden had been upset by her sister's brazenness in asking Logan to dinner, but now Eden found she was glad that he had accepted the invitation. She was looking forward to spending the evening with him. Logan truly was a gentleman and, she added in her thoughts, a very fine dancer.

As Eden made the trip home, she found herself wondering when she would get a response to the letter she'd sent to Adrian's contact. She had hoped she would hear something quickly, but she knew that wasn't always possible. Still, Eden held on to her anger and her need to make sure those Yankees never tried to harm another Southern lady.

He wasn't dead.

Braden knew that because the pain was there, taunting him at the edges of his consciousness.

He didn't want to come fully awake. He wanted to lose himself in the pain-free darkness again, for he knew what true awareness would bring.

But the outside world would not be denied.

Braden's inner world lightened, and with the light came the agony. He struggled to avoid it. He stirred, trying to escape, but it enveloped him. Even that simple movement evoked agony, so he lay still. His jaw locked against the excruciating torment that radiated through him as he opened his eyes to see his surroundings clearly for the first time in days.

Sunlight.

He could see that it was day, and he was lying in a tent. There was a Union soldier sitting nearby, but the man was turned so he couldn't see his face. He knew it wasn't Danner, though, for Danner was a big man and this one was much smaller.

"What happened?" Braden asked, his voice hoarse and barely above a whisper.

"You're awake!" Taylor was startled by the

invalid's words and rushed to kneel beside him. The private touched his patient's forehead to discover with great relief that the lieutenant's fever had actually broken and the look in his dark eyes was clear and sane.

Taylor couldn't believe his patient was better. The hours of nursing him had seemed endless, and there had been a few times when Taylor had worried that he truly might not make it, but there had been no giving up in trying to save him. That wasn't in Taylor's nature.

"Who are you?" Braden stared up at his caregiver, realizing he wasn't much more than a boy. He was certain he'd never seen him before.

"I'm Private Taylor. You've had a high fever, but it's finally broken."

"How long—?"

"It's been a few days, but it looks like you're going to make it now."

Braden gave a weak nod as his eyes drifted shut.

Once Taylor was sure that the lieutenant was just resting and had not lost consciousness again, Taylor stood and hurried from the shelter to find Danner and give him the good news.

Danner was sitting around a small campfire with a few of the other prisoners when he looked up and saw Taylor heading his way. He couldn't read the private's expression, and he worried that the lieutenant had taken a turn for the worse.

"Something wrong?" Danner asked as he got quickly to his feet to go meet him.

Only when Taylor smiled did he realize the news wasn't bad.

"He's awake. The fever's broken."

The two hurried back to Braden's side.

"Lieutenant?" Danner said quietly as he knelt down next to the makeshift bed.

Braden recognized his friend's voice and opened his eyes.

"You are better," Danner said with relief.

"Better than what?" Braden managed. "Dead might feel better than this." He tried to shift positions, seeking some bit of comfort, but there was none to be found on the hard pallet.

"Rest easy, Lieutenant," Taylor cautioned. "Don't move around too much. You don't want to go opening up that wound again."

Danner spoke up. "Taylor here's been taking care of you. His pa was a doc, so he seems to know what he's doing."

Braden glanced at the young soldier. "Thanks."

Taylor nodded, glad that his patient was improving.

"Any news?" Braden asked.

"We haven't heard anything, sir. It looks like we're going to be trapped here awhile."

In spite of his pain, his expression grew determined. "Not if I can help it. Once I get my strength back, we're going to find a way to get out of here."

Danner didn't want to tell his lieutenant that their guards were mean and very well armed. He knew that if there was any way they could escape and save themselves, his lieutenant would find it. "Yes, sir."

The effort to talk had cost Braden dearly. He closed his eyes and drew a ragged breath. As soon as he was able, he would start planning. They would escape. It wouldn't be easy, but they would do it.

Chapter Eight

Camille sat before her dressing table mirror primping and putting the finishing touches on her hair. She'd been in her room working on her appearance since early that afternoon, for she wanted to look her absolute best tonight for the reverend. She couldn't remember the last time she'd been this excited. Certainly it had been before the war began.

Her sister had already returned home from the orphanage, so Camille knew Reverend Logan would be arriving soon. She'd left her bedroom door open, and she saw Eden walk past on her way downstairs.

"How soon will he be here?" Camille called out.

"Any time now," Eden answered, pausing for

a moment in Camille's bedroom doorway.

"Good. I can't wait!" Camille smoothed one last errant curl into place, then stood up and turned to her sister. "Well, how do I look?"

"You look beautiful, of course," Eden answered sincerely.

Eden knew Camille was very conscious of her appearance and always took great pains to look her best—not that she had to work very hard at it. With her raven hair and green eyes, Camille was strikingly lovely. Tonight was no exception. She wore an emerald gown that set off her coloring, and she had pinned her hair up in an attractive style. Eden suddenly felt quite plain in her sedate, dark blue gown, wearing her hair down around her shoulders and held back only by a simple ribbon.

"Good." Camille swept across the room to join her. "I'm all ready."

They made their way down the hall and descended the staircase together.

Francene heard her daughters' voices and came out of the dining room to speak to them. The sight of Eden and Camille coming down the staircase looking so pretty lightened Francene's heart. Life had been terribly harsh these past few years. Sometimes she almost forgot all the beauty, elegance, and joy that had once been theirs before the Yankees had come.

"Is he here yet, Mama?" Camille asked eagerly, but in a quiet voice just in case Reverend Logan was already there, seated in the parlor.

"No, dear, not yet." Francene smiled, understanding her younger daughter's excitement. Camille had already described the minister to her in glowing terms. Francene looked at Eden. She knew how busy she was at the Haven with Mr. Forrester off on one of his trips, and she was glad Eden had made the time to come home for dinner. "Let's sit in the parlor while we wait for him."

They had just settled in when a knock came at the front door. Sarah, their servant and cook who'd stayed with the family through all the hard times, hurried to answer it.

"Good evening, miss. I'm Logan Matthews, and I'm here to see Miss LeGrand," Logan told the servant.

"Yes, sir. Please come in." She held the door wide for him to enter.

Logan stepped into the front hall as Eden and her mother came out of the parlor with Camille close behind.

"Logan, I am so glad you could join us," Eden said, moving forward to welcome him into their house.

"Hello, Eden," he said in a low voice.

He had meant to concentrate on his real reason for being there—finding out all he could about the activities of Adrian Forrester—but the sight of Eden wearing the simple yet flattering blue gown with her hair hanging loosely around her shoulders reminded him all too vividly of what it had felt like to hold her in his arms as they'd waltzed earlier that day. He smiled warmly in greeting as his gaze went over her.

She smiled up at him. "I want you to meet my mother, Francene. And of course, you've already met Camille. Mother, this is Reverend Logan Matthews."

"Reverend Matthews—" Francene began.

"Please call me Logan," he insisted as he greeted them both in a courtly manner. "Camille, it's good to see you again."

"I'm so glad you were able to join us tonight," Camille cooed as they moved into the parlor to visit for a few minutes until dinner was served. "Eden told us about all the wonderful things you've been doing for the orphans."

"That's right, Logan. I have to thank you. What you did for Eden that day with the Yankees—why, you are a true hero," Francene said with heartfelt sincerity, her expression earnest as she took a seat beside him on the sofa.

"I'm just glad I arrived in time to stop them." He looked up at Eden as she took a chair nearby. The thought of what might have happened to her and the children if he hadn't gotten there when he did still troubled him.

"What you're doing for the children is wonderful, too." Francene added. "Not only the money you gave them, but volunteering to work with them. You're a very special man."

"Thank you, but Eden and those at the Haven deserve all the credit. I'm just lending a helping hand."

"Well, you are most appreciated," Eden told him. "I know you've won the children over. They adore you."

"I just wish they'd never been orphaned. It's sad that any young child has to suffer as these children have."

"That is so true," Francene agreed.

"Mark seems to be doing fine, don't you think?" Logan asked.

"He's quiet, but that's not unusual for someone who's just joined us. At least we did get him to laugh today with the dancing." Eden felt quite proud of that accomplishment.

Logan smiled as he remembered the boy's reluctance to dance. "I think most boys that age react the same way at the thought of dancing."

"Who's Mark?" Camille interrupted. Not that she really cared who Mark was, she just wanted the preacher's undivided attention on her as she sat down directly across from him.

"Mark is the boy Reverend Logan brought to the home," Eden explained.

"He was homeless, wasn't he?" Camille asked, looking at Logan.

"Yes, I met him on the streets and brought him with me when I visited the Haven for the first time. Your sister was kind enough to find room for him there."

Camille did not understand why Eden wasted time working at the orphanage. Their own lives were difficult enough without getting involved with anyone else's troubles, too. She realized she couldn't complain too much about it right now, though, for Eden's work at the Haven had brought the minister into her life, and she was definitely grateful for that.

"It was kind of you to take care of a child of the streets that way." Francene was impressed.

"This war is a terrible thing, and I want to help whenever I can. I want to try to make a difference in people's lives." Logan knew it wasn't a lie. He was definitely trying to make a difference in a life right now—his brother's.

"Your work with the children makes a difference," Eden praised him.

"You haven't met Adrian Forrester yet, have you?" Francene asked.

"No, I haven't, but I hope he will approve of my work at the Haven when he returns."

"Adrian will," Eden assured him. "He is always glad for any help we can get. You've been so generous already with your monetary donation, he'll be thrilled that you're sharing your time and talent with us as well."

"He said he would be back sometime next week, didn't he, Eden?" her mother asked.

"Yes. Logan will get to meet him then."

And Logan couldn't wait. Forrester's absence had slowed his investigation, but it wouldn't be long now. What troubled Logan the most was the knowledge that Braden had been wounded before being taken prisoner. Every day his brother passed in the prison camp had to be a pure horror for him. Logan had heard how terrible the conditions were in the Southern prisons.

"Was there any news of the war today?" Francene asked.

"I didn't hear anything," Eden responded.

"Sometimes no news is good news when it comes to the fighting," Logan said.

"I wish we'd heard that our men had sent the Yankees back to Washington at a dead run," Camille spoke up with very real venom. "I hate the Yankees for all they've done to us! Things have been so terrible. Why, the only good news we've had lately was what happened on the *Bayou Belle*."

"What happened on the *Bayou Belle*?" Logan was instantly alert at her mention of the steamer, but he played innocent.

"I guess the news didn't reach St. Louis," Eden remarked.

"Some of our men stole a shipment of Union guns right out from under the Yankee guards," Camille boasted, interrupting her sister. "Then they burned the ship."

At her unknowing reference to his brother, Logan tensed, but he managed to conceal his reaction. "I hadn't heard about it."

"Well, it was quite the talk around New Orleans," Camille went on, glad that she finally had his attention. "I still can't believe Eden and Mother were on board and saw it all."

Eden and her mother had been on the Bayou Belle*!*

The revelation caught Logan by surprise. Their names hadn't been on the list that Larry had given him, and neither woman had been mentioned by those he had managed to locate and speak with before coming to the Haven. He looked at Eden. "You were actually on the steamer during the attack?"

Camille was irritated that he was paying attention to her sister again. She didn't give Eden time to answer as she told him, "Yes, they were, and I am so glad I didn't make the trip with them. Why, it must have been just terrifying."

Francene spoke up, telling Logan how she and Eden had been on their way to visit a sick relative upriver when the Rebels took control of the *Bayou Belle* and seized the shipment. "I was most afraid."

Logan's mind was racing as he considered the possibility that they had had a connection to the raid. If Forrester was one of the key men in the group behind it, had Eden—and her mother—been on the steamer working for him? The suspicion ate at him.

"It was frightening," Eden agreed, "but I have to admit I was glad the guns weren't going to end up in Union hands. We thought the raiders were just going to take the guns and go, but then there was the shooting." Eden paused, paling a little as she remembered what had happened. "I always thought I hated the Yankees, too, but when that guard was shot—"

"You saw someone shot and killed?" He was

shocked that she'd witnessed his brother being wounded.

"A Yankee guard was shot, but he wasn't killed, thank heaven," Eden went on. "He was wounded when he tried to stop them. I still can't believe he thought he could do it all by himself. The other men were bound, but somehow he managed to get loose. It was crazy for him to even try. He was only one man against so many."

To Logan, that sounded just like Braden. His brother took his responsibilities seriously, and he would never have given up the arms without a fight.

"Well, I still can't believe what you did." Camille said to her sister disparagingly.

Logan looked over at Eden, wondering what Camille was talking about.

"Eden was so brave," Francene told him. "She tried to help the wounded Yankee."

"Weren't you putting yourself in danger?" Logan asked.

"It didn't matter. I had to do something. I couldn't just let him bleed to death."

His suspicions about Eden's involvement suddenly faded. *She had helped Braden.*

"What happened to him?" he asked, trying not to sound too intense.

"I don't know. All of us passengers and most of the crew were forced to go ashore on the west bank. The raiders took the guards and some of the crew with them when they left. We weren't rescued until the following morning, and we didn't find out what had happened to the *Bayou Belle* itself until several days later when we heard that they'd found what was left of it abandoned upriver. It had been burned."

"It's a miracle no one was killed and that you got away safely," he said.

"We're very thankful everything turned out the way it did," Eden said. "I still worry about what happened to the guard, though. There were no bodies found anywhere near where the steamer was located, so I guess he lived through it."

"Don't be ridiculous, Eden." Camille countered. "Who cares what happened to him? He was a Yankee. Do you think for one minute any Northern woman would waste her time worrying about a wounded Rebel soldier?"

Eden looked over at her. "I would hope so."

"We are all God's children," Logan put in, fighting to keep the anger he was feeling over Camille's words from reflecting in his tone.

"Well, you're wrong, Eden, and I am tired of talking about the war," Camille pouted. "Let's talk about something else—something pleasant." She turned her gaze to the reverend and smiled sweetly. "Reverend Logan, is your family here in town with you? Did your wife and children come along on the trip, or did you travel alone?"

"I'm not married. I made the trip alone."

Camille's spirits soared to even greater

heights. Logan was a bachelor! She was delighted.

"Will you be staying with us here in New Orleans for very long?" Francene asked.

"As I told Eden, I'll be staying until the Lord calls me to move on."

"That's wonderful."

Sarah interrupted them to announce that dinner was ready, and they made their way into the dining room.

"Logan, would you do the honor of leading us in saying grace?" Francene invited.

Logan did, and as he prayed over the meal, he truly was thankful. He had learned valuable information tonight.

Chapter Nine

"Thank you so much for dinner. It was wonderful to meet you," Logan told Francene as they stood in the entry hall.

"It was wonderful to meet you, too. Please come visit us again, Logan."

"I will."

"Oh, good," Camille said sweetly, priding herself on her acting abilities. She was more than a little irritated by the way the evening had gone, but she wasn't going to show it in front of him. "I hope to see you at the Haven."

"I'll be there."

"Good night, Mother." Eden gave her a kiss on the cheek as she prepared to return to the orphanage.

"You be careful, now," Francene cautioned.

"I'll see her safely there, ma'am," Logan promised.

As soon as the door closed behind them, Camille's expression turned ugly.

"Camille, dear, what is it?" her mother asked. She'd thought the evening had been a pleasant diversion, and she couldn't imagine why her daughter would be so angry.

"Oh, Mother—Logan is so handsome and intelligent, and tonight he all but ignored me!"

Francene realized Camille had been flirting with the minister, but she hadn't thought the man had been anything but a gentleman. "Nonsense, child. Logan is different from other men. You must remember he's a minister—a man of God."

"But he's still a man!" she pouted. "Didn't I look pretty enough tonight?"

"You look absolutely lovely, but Logan isn't in New Orleans because he wants a social life or, for that matter, because he's looking for a wife. He came here to work with the orphaned children."

"I suppose." Camille's expression turned from angry to pouty as she began to try to figure out a way to win his attention—and ultimately his heart.

"I feel quite blessed to know him," Francene went on, thinking again of how he'd rescued Eden. "And I'm certainly thankful that he saved your sister."

At the thought of Eden, jealousy stung Camille. Logan had paid more attention to Eden that evening. "He is a wonderful man," she agreed.

Camille went upstairs to her room for the night, her thoughts on the handsome minister.

The night was dark and warm and sultry. A canopy of stars twinkled high above them as Logan and Eden made their way back to the Haven. Logan had offered to accompany her once he'd learned that she would be spending the night there. He had tied his horse to the back of her small buggy for the trip.

"Do you have to stay overnight at the Haven very often?" Logan asked casually, wondering how often Forrester went out of town and trying to see if there was any pattern to his absences.

"No. Adrian doesn't go away very often—maybe a few days every other month, so I don't mind. I know my mother worries when I'm there, but I can't leave Miss Jenny alone with all the children. If anything happened to them, I'd never forgive myself. Besides, after the other day, I've made up my mind that I won't ever be caught defenseless again."

He cast her a sidelong glance. "What do you mean?"

"Mother and I both agreed I should take one of my father's pistols and keep it at the Haven, just in case anything like that happens again."

"Do you know how to use one?"

"Papa taught me before he left for the war. He didn't like the idea of Mother, Camille, and me being here unprotected, so he made sure I learned how to load and fire."

"Your father's a wise man."

His words surprised her. As a minister, she would have thought that he abhorred violence of any kind. "You approve?"

"There is no sin or dishonor in protecting yourself."

Eden had worried that he would disapprove of her arming herself. She felt better now, knowing that he didn't condemn her for having the gun, and she relaxed a little more as they made the ride together.

They fell silent as they drew near the Haven. When they reached the building, Logan stopped the buggy and jumped down to tether his own horse there.

"Is there a carriage house around back?" Logan asked as he climbed back up beside Eden.

"Yes."

At her direction, Logan guided her horse and buggy around to the rear of the building. He reined in, climbed down, and tied up the horse, then returned to the side of the conveyance to help Eden descend.

Eden was grateful for Logan's aid. She leaned forward and rested her hands on his broad shoulders for support as he took her by the waist and lifted her easily to the ground. Eden brushed against him as he set her on her feet. The contact was electric, startling them both. They stood motionless for a moment, staring at each other in the quiet of the night.

Eden studied Logan in the dark shadows, seeing the strength in his chiseled features. He was arrestingly good-looking, and she was drawn to him in a way she'd never been drawn to any man before. Her gaze dropped to his mouth, and she wondered suddenly what it would be like to press her lips to his—to kiss him fully on the mouth. Eden shocked herself with the boldness of her fantasy. Forbidden excitement shivered through her as she pictured the exchange in her mind. She told herself this was Reverend Logan, believing that admonishment would discourage her runaway imaginings, but the answering thought came: *I know*.

Logan was gazing down at Eden, his hands still resting on her waist. He had always thought she was pretty, but standing there before him now on this warm, starry night, she was exquisitely lovely. He knew Eden was a strong woman, and yet at this moment she seemed so incredibly fragile. His gaze traced her delicate features, settling on her lips. He knew a sudden driving need to taste of her sweetness, but he held himself back. He struggled for logic, fighting against the need that urged him to draw her to him and kiss her.

It was only when the horse stirred that reality returned, and Logan let his hands drop away from Eden. He turned quickly from her to see to the horse, relieved for the interruption. Eden was proving too tempting to him—too irresistible. He couldn't afford a weakness, and Eden could easily become his if he wasn't careful.

"I'll take care of the horse and then walk you in," he said, keeping his back to her and concentrating on unharnessing the animal. He wanted to keep Eden at a physical distance from him. He had always prided himself on being a man in control, but she was testing his limits.

"I can take care of the horse," she told him, coming to his side. She was used to tending to it by herself. "It's all right if you want to go ahead and leave."

"No," he said, stopping to look at her. "I want to make sure you're safely inside before I go. I don't trust those Yankees not to come back. I'd like to think they wouldn't dare, but I want to be sure."

"Thank you."

The thought that Logan was concerned about her and wanted to protect her touched Eden. Leaving him to his task, she moved away to walk the path in her flower garden. Eden cast one last glance back at him as she went, and she was surprised by the longing that filled her. She had really wanted to kiss him.

Sternly, Eden reminded herself that she shouldn't be having those kinds of thoughts about Logan—no matter how handsome he was. She made her way down the narrow path, enjoying the heavenly scent of the blossoms that surrounded her. The flower garden truly was an idyllic place, and she needed the peace and serenity of it right then to help her forget her attraction to Logan.

Logan finished tending to the horse and buggy, and then went in search of Eden. He found himself worrying about her being alone on the grounds in the dark. True, he was nearby. All she would have to do was call out if she needed him and he would be there in an instant, but the realization didn't calm his concern. He knew what evils could be lurking in the night, and he didn't want her at risk. He would make sure she was safely inside the Haven with the door locked behind her before he left.

Logan followed the narrow path Eden had taken and caught sight of her a short distance ahead of him. She was standing in profile to him, and he was once again struck by her sheer beauty. He paused, his gaze raking over her in a visual caress. Eden was slender, but every bit a woman. Her dark hair was loose about her shoulders in a cascade of untamed, silken curls that he longed to caress. He moved forward.

"Eden." He said her name softly.

She heard Logan's quiet call and looked up. Her eyes widened at the riveting vision he made as he came toward her in the night, so tall and broad-shouldered, moving with an easy grace, his expression darkly intense. Her heartbeat quickened, and a surge of sensual awareness shot through her as he drew near.

Logan stopped beside her.

"This really is the Garden of Eden, you know," he told her with a half-smile, his voice deep and husky.

She smiled up at him. "I try to make it as heavenly as I can. I want it to be a place where I can come and pretend the real world doesn't exist—at least for a little while."

"Your own paradise."

"Yes."

The night was dark, and time seemed to stand still as their gazes met. They were alone under the canopy of stars.

Eden was breathless as Logan closed the distance between them. He stood over her, staring down at her, the flame of desire burning in his eyes.

As if in slow motion, Logan lifted one hand to cup her cheek, then bent to claim her lips, whispering, "Ah, but there was temptation in the garden."

His mouth took hers in a tender-soft exchange.

Eden went still at the touch of his hand, and when his lips moved over hers, she gave a small blissful sigh.

This truly was paradise.

She had longed for Logan's kiss, had wanted Logan's kiss.

It was heavenly.

Logan heard her sigh, and it emboldened him. He gathered Eden to him, deepening the exchange.

A whirlwind of emotion swept through Eden.

Dancing with Logan had been delightful, but kissing him was pure ecstasy. She'd been kissed by several suitors before, but no other man's embrace had ever affected her this way. Logan's lips were a searing, demanding brand upon hers. She responded fully to him, looping her arms around his neck to draw him even closer.

Logan wanted her. There was no denying it. Passion flared within him at the feel of her crushed so intimately against him, and it was the power of that passion that jarred him to the depths and forced him back to reality. With painful clarity, he realized that this was wrong—very wrong. He stifled a groan as he ended the embrace and, taking her gently by the upper arms, put her from him.

"Logan?" His name was an endearment upon her lips as she looked up at him questioningly. She couldn't imagine why he'd broken off the kiss when it had been so wonderful and she had been enjoying it so.

"I'm sorry, Eden."

Sorry? Eden was surprised and a little hurt by his apology. She didn't know why he was apologizing.

"Let me see you inside." Logan had not meant for this to happen. He had not meant to touch her, let alone kiss her, but she had proven too much of a temptation for him.

Like Adam in paradise, he had fallen.

But he wasn't Adam.

And this wasn't Paradise.

It would not happen again.

"Oh—all right." Eden struggled to hide her disappointment as they continued on the path toward the front of the building.

Logan was very conscious of her beside him, and he deliberately did not walk her all the way to the door. He stopped at the top step and watched as she crossed the porch to unlock the portal and let herself in.

"Good night, Eden."

She looked back at him as he started to turn away from her. "Good night."

Eden did not wait to watch him mount up and ride away, but went quietly inside, closing and locking the door behind her. She made her way to the bedroom and paused to light the lamp on the small bedside table. The glow filled the room, and it was then that she spotted an envelope lying on the bed along with a note from Jenny. She snatched both up and, not recognizing the handwriting on the envelope, quickly scanned Jenny's note.

This was dropped off tonight for you. Thought it might be important.

Tearing the envelope open, Eden pulled out the single-page missive and read it.

I have the information you requested. Meet me outside at midnight.

The note was unsigned, but she knew it was from one of Adrian's men. She glanced at the mantel clock; it was only a little after nine. Midnight seemed an eternity away, but she could wait. She wasn't sure yet what she was going to do with the information. She guessed it would depend on what she found out. But she would be ready at the appointed hour no matter what.

The time passed slowly. When finally it was midnight, Eden silently left the house.

"Over here," came the whisper from the side yard in some trees.

Eden made her way to join the man. He was not a total stranger to her, for she had seen him before with Adrian, but she had never learned his name. "You sent the note?"

"Yes."

"What did you find out?"

"There's a tavern near the riverfront that they frequent called the Palace."

"How often do they go there?" Somehow she was going to find a way to pay the Yankees back for what they'd done at the Haven.

"I talked with George Sosson, the bartender, and he said they're in there pretty regularly."

"What about tonight? Would there be a chance that they might be at the tavern, or is it too late?"

"There's no way of knowing until we check and see. Can you get away?"

"Just give me a minute."

"What about a horse?"

"We can ride double on yours." Eden was not about to be deterred. She had no saddle for her own horse, and she didn't want to risk taking the carriage, for she was certain someone would notice that it was missing.

The contact was surprised by her daring declaration, but said nothing. He knew she worked with Forrester, so she was capable and could be trusted. He faded back into the night as she returned inside the house.

Earlier after reading the contact's letter, Eden had hoped there would be a chance to go after the soldiers tonight, so she had gone through the laundry during her hours of waiting and gotten a pair of boys' black pants and a dark shirt to wear. She donned them quickly now, then tied up her hair and put on a boy's hat, tucking her hair under it. After getting a dark scarf to use as a mask when the time came to confront them, her disguise was complete. As ready as she would ever be, she got her father's gun, checked to see that it was loaded, then stuck it in the waistband of her pants.

Eden unlocked and opened the window in the bedroom and slipped out through it, closing it behind her. She would reenter that way, too. She didn't want to risk being discovered. Certain that no one had seen her and that all was quiet in the Haven, she was ready to go. No one would miss her, and she would be back before dawn.

"Do you have a name?" Eden asked the contact as she went to him where he was waiting in the yard.

"I'm Darrell. Darrell Ankarlo," he replied, staring at her in amazement. Moments before, she had been the image of the perfect lady, and now she could pass for a youth. He again admired Forrester's choices of operatives. The man had surrounded himself with a very capable group. Then Darrell saw the gun tucked in her waistband. "Do you think you're going to need that?"

"You never know," was all she answered.

Darrell had tied his horse in back behind the carriage house, and they made their way there, walking down the path she had traversed with Logan. Eden was grateful that Darrell hadn't arrived earlier when she'd been in the garden with Logan.

Eden blushed at the memory of Logan's kiss, and she was glad for the cover of the night to hide her emotions. The thought of Logan filled her with longing, but she put it from her. Right then, she had only one thing she wanted to think about, and that was finding the Yankees Moran and Layton. She wanted to make sure that they never thought about bothering a Southern lady or any children ever again.

They reached the place where Darrell had tied his horse. He mounted first, then reached down to help her up behind him. They headed off to the tavern at a slow pace, not wanting to draw attention to themselves.

When Darrell had been to the Palace earlier that day to speak with the bartender about the two soldiers, he'd noticed that the alley across the street from the place offered an unrestricted view of the tavern's main doors. He knew they could safely keep watch from there.

"I thought this would be a good place to hide out and watch for them."

"It is, thanks," Eden told him as she slid to the ground and went to take a position near the alley's opening.

"Will you be able to recognize them from here?"

"Oh, yes. I'll never forget those two." She rested her hand on the gun and felt confident.

Darrell tethered his horse farther down the alley, out of sight, and then came to stand with her. For all that she was armed, she was still a lady and deserving of protection.

"Why are you after these two? What did they do?"

Eden told him about the attacks.

"So that's what happened to your cheek," he said, having noticed the bruise even in the darkness.

"Yes," she answered.

"Once we find them, what are you planning to do to them?" He didn't think cold-blooded murder was her style.

"I don't know yet, but once I see them, I'm sure I'll think of something."

They remained there in the darkness, watching and waiting. It wasn't until the early hours of the morning that Eden finally gave up her vigil.

"Can you meet me again tomorrow night?" Eden asked.

He was surprised by her request. He'd expected her to give up after the long hours they'd spent there.

"Are you sure you want to do this?"

"I'm sure." She looked up at him in the darkness. "If you don't want to, it's all right. I'm going to find them either with you or without you. It doesn't matter."

Darrell stared down at her, seeing the very real determination in her expression. He knew he couldn't let her seek the Yankee soldiers alone. "I'll be back for you at midnight tomorrow night."

He returned her to the Haven, and she crept silently back in through the window.

Chapter Ten

Eden got no sleep. Lying in bed, she tossed and turned, too tense and too excited by all that had happened that day to get any rest. Thoughts of the Yankees and the revenge she wanted to exact from them played in her mind, but were quickly forgotten as the memory of Logan's kiss returned. Her thoughts of Logan's embrace were most satisfying, and she smiled.

Eden wondered how Logan could have come to mean so much to her in such a short period of time. It had only been a few days since he'd arrived at the Haven, and yet it seemed as if she had known him forever. Her heartbeat quickened as she relived the touch of his lips on hers. She remembered his clean, manly scent, and the warm strength of him as she'd been held in his arms. His embrace had been heavenly, and she still wondered why he had apologized for it. It left Eden fearing that he hadn't enjoyed the kiss as much as she had. The only regret she'd had was that he had ended it too soon.

Eden sighed as she turned to stare out the window at the eastern sky. Weariness threatened now, but she could not give into it. Logan would be arriving soon, and then, later tonight, she would meet Darrell again and continue her quest to find the Yankees. She would find no rest today.

As the sky grew ever brighter, Eden arose to wash and dress. She found she was a bit nervous in anticipation of Logan's arrival. She feared she'd been far too bold with him the night before. Certainly she'd responded fully to his kiss, but he was a minister. Had she been too brazen? Too forward? Doubts began to assail her.

As Eden started from the bedroom, she glanced out the window and caught a glimpse of the flower garden. A soft smile curved her lips.

Logan was frustrated and angry as he arose that morning. He had gotten little sleep, and what sleep he had managed had been restless and filled with troubled dreams of Braden.

Logan always considered himself a man of action, but the situation he found himself in now left him feeling useless and thwarted. There had been no word from Sam, and no contact from Larry's other operative. It would be days before

Forrester returned—days during which his brother was suffering God-only-knew what torment in the Rebel prison camp. The reality of Braden's plight tortured Logan.

And then there was the memory of Eden's kiss that would not be dismissed.

Damn, but the woman was wreaking havoc on his sensibilities. He'd known many women in his life, yet none of them had affected him the way Eden did. He didn't understand what it was about her that attracted him so. True, Eden was beautiful, but he'd been around many beauties in his day. There was something else—something deeper and more elemental that drew him to her, and he had to fight against it.

Their kiss should never have happened, and yet Logan could not deny that he had enjoyed it. Eden was a very desirable woman, but he had no time for any involvement with her. He told himself that she wasn't important to him. She was simply a means to an end—just as Mark had been. He was using her, biding his time at the orphanage until he could discover whether Forrester was involved with the raiders.

Thinking of the raid brought his thoughts back to Eden—and her unusual presence on the *Bayou Belle*. He remembered, too, how she had gone to his brother's aid, and he was grateful to her for that.

Logan admitted to himself that he had never known another woman like Eden. She was self-sacrificing. She thought nothing of putting herself at risk to save others—first Braden, and then the children.

As tempting a distraction as Eden was proving to be, Logan wondered how he was going to keep his distance from her. Even as he thought about it, he knew the answer: the children. He would make sure he never allowed himself to be alone with her again. That would be the safest way.

He was Reverend Logan Matthews, and he was in New Orleans to work with the orphans. In the back of his mind, though, Logan added, he was also a Yankee. Eden's enemy.

Logan got dressed and picked up his Bible. It was time to head to the Haven and see the children—and Eden—again.

Logan reached the orphanage and went to join everyone in the dining room. Little Connie commandeered him as soon as he stepped into the room. After leading everyone in saying grace, he found himself seated with the youngest girls to have his breakfast. He was caught up in their conversation, but found himself glancing Eden's way. She looked even lovelier this morning, and he tried to ignore the feelings just the sight of her aroused in him. When the meal ended and the children were filing from the room, Logan made his way toward her.

"Good morning." Logan grinned at her.

Eden had been pleased that he'd arrived in time for breakfast, and watching him with the girls had warmed her heart. She wanted to talk with him, and just as she would have replied to his greeting, her sister's call interrupted them.

"Eden." Camille appeared unexpectedly in the doorway of the dining room. "Why, hello, Logan." She spotted the two of them and didn't waste any time heading their way.

"Camille—I didn't know you were coming to the Haven today." Eden was surprised to see her, but after last night she knew she shouldn't have been.

"I wanted to help you in any way I could," Camille said coyly, her gaze upon the handsome minister. "So I thought I would get down here bright and early this morning."

Eden actually felt a sting of jealousy over the way her sister was ogling Logan. She tried not to let it show. She had no claim on the minister. He was there for the children.

"That's very generous of you," Logan said, smiling at Camille. "I'm sure the children will be delighted to see you."

Camille didn't care one bit what the children thought. She wanted to know if *he* was delighted to see her.

"What would you like me to help you with?" she asked, only barely paying any attention to Eden. She looked straight at Logan. "Is there anything you're doing that could use my help?" On the way there, she had envisioned herself working by his side for the whole day, making herself indispensable to him.

"I was planning to work outside cleaning out the carriage house," Logan answered, having noticed its run-down condition the night before. "That's hardly work for a lady."

Camille's expression faltered. "Oh."

"Would you like to spend some time in the classroom with the children?" Eden offered. She knew her sister hated working out of doors, and she doubted Camille had any desire whatsoever to spend any time with the children, but she didn't want to see her humiliated in front of Logan.

"That will be fine, Eden." Camille turned to her sister, the only sign of her irritation the spark of annoyance in her eyes.

"Logan, would you like some of the boys to help you with the carriage house? I'm sure Jenny could spare them from class." Eden knew it would be good for the boys to spend some time with him. At their age, they needed a strong male influence.

"I'd love to have Mark and Paul work with me. Send them out," he answered. "May I leave my Bible and coat in the office?"

"Of course."

Camille stood with Eden watching Logan as he left the dining room.

"Clean the stables!" Camille muttered in almost a curse. "Why is a man of Logan's stature cleaning the stables?"

"Because he saw that it needed it. He truly does want to serve us here. I've never met anyone quite like him," Eden said, and she meant it.

"Neither have I," her sister agreed, her eyes narrowing as she already began to calculate a legitimate excuse to go outside and talk to Logan, one that didn't include doing any kind of physical labor on her part.

They went upstairs to the classroom.

"Miss Jenny, children, this is Miss Camille. She's my sister, and she's here to spend time with you today."

The children all welcomed Camille, and she went to sit by Jenny at her desk.

"And I need Mark and Paul to come with me, please."

Both boys looked a little shocked at being singled out. For a moment, the fear that they were in trouble of some kind shone in their eyes.

"No, you're not in trouble," Eden quickly told them. "Reverend Logan needs your help today."

At this news, both boys brightened. They quickly rose from their desks to follow her from the room.

Camille watched them go and fought not to let her irritation show. She was trapped for now, but she promised herself she would find a way to see more of the reverend a little later. Surely it wouldn't take him all day to work in the carriage house, especially not with the two boys helping him.

"What are we going to be doing?" Paul asked Eden as they went downstairs. He was more than pleased at having gotten out of class.

"Reverend Logan's working outside this morning, and he requested you both specifically."

"He did?" Mark was delighted.

"That's right."

Together they went outside and around to the rear of the grounds. They had to pass through the flower garden, and Eden couldn't help remembering what had happened the last time she'd been there—last night—in the dark—with Logan. She forced herself to think of other things. As they neared the carriage house, they could see Logan already hard at work inside.

"Here are the boys for you," Eden announced, coming to stand in the doorway.

Logan looked up from straightening a pile of equipment and smiled in welcome. "I can use all the help I can get."

"Yes, sir."

Paul and Mark were glad to have escaped lessons for one day. They quickly grabbed up a shovel and rake and pitched in.

Logan took a break to visit with Eden.

"I never imagined you'd be doing anything like this for us when you volunteered your time," she said ruefully. "I thought you'd be doing a lot of praying and saving souls."

"But I am," he said with a grin.

"You are?" Eden's heartbeat quickened at his rakish smile, and she remembered far too vividly the feel of his mouth upon hers. She gave herself a mental shake. He'd apologized. The kiss had meant nothing to him. It had been a mistake. He'd been sorry that it had ever happened.

"If I can teach these boys by example that honest work is hard work and has its own rewards, they'll be ready to make their way in the world."

"I hope so. I just wonder what kind of world it's going to be when they're old enough to leave the Haven."

"None of us have the answer to that right now. It won't be easy for them, but they're smart. They'll survive." Thoughts of surviving reminded him of Braden. "We just have to do everything we can to prepare them for real life." *And he had to do everything he could to help his brother.*

"You are. Just by being here today, you're teaching them the importance of sharing your gifts and aiding those who are less fortunate."

Logan ignored the twinge of conscience he felt at Eden's praise. His cover was working. That was all that was important. "I'd better get back inside before Mark and Paul start thinking that I'm not helping the less fortunate very much when it comes to the real dirty work."

Eden lingered for a minute longer, watching the three together, then returned to her own duties inside.

Camille was bored as she sat in the classroom listening to Jenny lecture the children on first geography, then spelling. This was definitely not what she'd had in mind when she'd planned to spend her morning at the Haven. There was absolutely nothing for her to do except pass out paper and pencils to the students as they worked on various assignments.

Casting a glance toward the window that overlooked the rear grounds, Camille grew frustrated. Logan was out there somewhere, and she had to find a way to spend some time with him. As she sat there in complete and utter irritation, she finally thought of a believable excuse to go to him. She quietly excused herself from the classroom.

It took Camille only a few minutes in the kitchen to get the pitcher of water and cups she needed to take out to the carriage house. Surely, after all this time working outside in the heat, Logan and the boys would be ready for a cool drink. The cook said nothing as Camille swept outside to seek Logan out.

"You boys want to take a break?" Logan asked.

They had been hard at work since Eden had left them and were making good progress in repairing the building.

"Sure," Paul said, more than ready to rest for a while.

Mark didn't say anything, but he put aside his rake and went to sit with them in the shade nearby.

"So, Mark, how are you doing here at the Haven? Is everything going all right?"

The youth cast a sidelong glance at him. In the few days that he'd been there, his life had changed completely. He was no longer hungry or homeless. And he had friends now, too. He knew

Reverend Logan had been right to bring him to the Haven. "It's fine."

"Good. I was hoping it would work out for you. Is there anything you need?"

Deep in his heart, Mark wished he could have his parents back, but he knew that wasn't going to happen. "No. Miss Eden takes good care of us."

"Miss Eden is special," Paul added, then turned more serious as he looked at the minister. It was rare that he allowed himself to open up to anyone, but he felt he had to thank Reverend Logan for what he'd done. "I sure am glad you got here when you did that first day. I love Miss Eden, and those men were real mean. They might have hurt her even worse if you hadn't been here to stop them. So—thanks, Reverend."

"You're welcome," Logan said, knowing how much it took for the boy to talk to him that way.

"Yeah, I'm glad she's all right, too. She sure is a nice lady," Mark put in. "And real pretty, too."

"Reverend Logan?" Camille called out, wanting to interrupt their conversation. The last thing she was interested in hearing about was how pretty Eden was.

Logan and the boys looked up to find Camille approaching with the water.

"I thought you might like a cool drink since you've been out here working so hard."

"Why, thank you. That's most thoughtful of you, Miss Camille," Logan said.

She handed each one of them a cup, then poured water for them.

"It looks like you're making good progress," Camille remarked, casting a glance inside the carriage house.

"That we are," Logan said with a smile. "The boys have been a big help to me."

Camille was wishing that the two boys would just disappear, but she knew that wasn't going to happen. She managed a benign smile in return.

"I'm sure they are. You know, Reverend, since you're new to the city, if you ever want anyone to show you around, I'd be more than happy to do it. There are several theaters, too, that would be worth attending if you're in the mood for some entertainment."

"That's very kind of you to offer, Miss Camille. Right now, though, I don't have much time to do anything but my work here at the Haven."

His answer hurt, but she didn't let on. She was certain that where there was a will, there was a way. She wouldn't give up. "Well, you just let me know when you have the time."

"I'll do that." Logan was polite, but deliberately kept his interest cool. The last thing he wanted to do was encourage Camille.

Before she could say more, Paul spoke up.

"Reverend Logan, we better get back to work. We still got a lot to do if we're going to be done before lunch."

"You're right, Paul. Mark, are you about ready?"

"Yes, sir."

"Miss Camille, thank you for bringing us the water. We appreciate it." Both boys thanked her.

"We'll be in as soon as we're finished," Logan told her.

He followed the boys back inside, leaving Camille standing there fuming at being so easily dismissed. She found it infuriating that he would rather be cleaning out the carriage house than visiting with her. Her head held high, she returned to the Haven. As she went, Camille was already trying to figure out how she could get to sit with him during the noon meal.

Chapter Eleven

The day passed quickly for Eden. She wasn't surprised when Camille made her excuses and left shortly after lunch. She'd known her sister had wanted to sit with Logan during the meal, but she had been thwarted in that plan when he'd been surrounded by the children the moment he'd entered the dining room and dragged off to sit with them. Camille had tried to hide her irritation when she'd announced that she was leaving, but Eden knew her too well. Eden didn't doubt for a moment that her sister would be back, though. For, as long as Logan was going to be at the Haven every day, Camille would continue to show up, too.

Logan left the orphanage in mid-afternoon with the promise to return the following morning and accompany the children to the Sunday church service at nine A.M. Eden found herself wondering what he was going to do that night, but she didn't ask, for she didn't want to be too forward with him.

As the day aged, Eden's thoughts turned to her own plans for that evening. Darrell would be back to meet her at the agreed-upon hour, and they would once again lay in wait near the bar for the two Yankees. She hoped tonight was the night they found them. She wanted to make sure Layton and Moran never mistreated anyone again.

Eden was tired, but the tension within her grew as evening came and midnight approached. After making sure the children were all asleep and Jenny was abed, Eden pretended to retire herself. She locked herself in her bedroom, but sleep was not on her mind. Eden donned the trousers, shirt, and hat from the previous night, and she made sure she had the scarf to complete her disguise. She was ready. Now all she had to do was wait for Darrell; she hoped nothing delayed him.

Right on time Darrell appeared in the side yard, and Eden silently escaped the house through the bedroom window to meet him. He had brought a mount for her, and they rode off together as quietly as possible. She realized the two soldiers might not still be in town, but she didn't want to miss the opportunity to seek her revenge. She planned to continue her search for them until she'd accomplished what she'd set out to do.

Eden and Darrell reached the alley and took up their vigil once again. They tied their mounts out of sight, and then, with the blackness of the night and the stench of the alley surrounding them, they waited.

"Are you always this determined?" Darrell asked in a low voice after about an hour.

"When something's this important to me, yes," she answered without hesitation.

Eden realized she could have forgotten the attack—put it from her mind and gone on with her life. If she'd been the only one involved, she probably would have, but these two soldiers had invaded the Haven and threatened the children. She'd considered reporting them to the authorities, but any action of that kind might have caused trouble for Paul. So she'd decided that she would handle it herself. She would seek her own justice.

Darrell looked at her in the shadows. Eden wasn't a physically big woman, but there was something about her courage that made her a force to be reckoned with. It was no wonder Forrester trusted her. Darrell only hoped that these two Yankees would be as easy to control as she thought they would be.

"Cornering these two could prove tricky." Darrell warned her.

"That's why I'm glad you're with me," she told him, appreciating his company. "Once we finally do find them, we have to surprise them. As mean as they are, they might try to give us a fight, so we have to have the upper hand from the start."

"So you're ready."

She nodded. "Yes."

"And you know what you want to do."

"Yes." Eden quickly explained her idea to him.

Darrell nodded his head in appreciation. "I think that might just work."

Eden grinned. "Now, if they would only show up."

They fell silent again as they waited to see if fate would deliver the Yankees into their hands.

Another hour passed.

And then Eden saw them.

Layton and Moran came staggering down the street in front of the bar together.

Eden tensed as she rested her hand on her gun.

"There!" she whispered excitedly to Darrell, pointing the two men out. "That's them!"

"Do you want to do it now or later after they come out of the bar?"

"Later. They'll be even drunker then. It'll be easier to confuse them."

"You're sure about this?" Darrell asked, wanting to give her one last chance to reconsider.

"Yes. The big thing is, when the time comes, we have to act quickly and quietly."

They turned their attention back to the bar's

entrance and kept careful watch. Eden knew it might be hours before they reappeared, but she didn't care.

Logan had met with Sam after leaving the Haven late that afternoon, but the operative had nothing new to report. After he ate dinner alone in a restaurant, the night stretched before Logan long and empty. He made his way back to his hotel and crossed the lobby to the stairs leading up to his room. He longed to be doing something, but there was nothing to be done—yet. Unlocking his door, he stepped inside.

It took Logan only an instant to react once he realized someone else was in the darkened room. He opened the Bible and grabbed for his gun, unsure of who the intruder was.

"There's no need to start shooting, Reverend," the deep voice said, amusement evident in his tone. "I've come here to save my soul."

Logan froze, peering into the heavy shadows, trying to make out the face of the stranger. "Who are you?"

"A friend," the man replied obliquely. "My name's Holder, Jim Holder. Larry sent word that I should pass on all the information I have about the raid to you."

Logan relaxed and put his gun away. He closed the door and walked to the small dresser to light the lamp and put his Bible aside. That done, he turned to face the informant. "Have you heard anything new?"

Jim smiled grimly at him. "Yes. I have news I think might prove important. I work for Nathaniel Talbott at the bank, and I see and hear a lot that goes on around town. You're right to suspect Forrester, and I wanted to let you know that Talbott has been gone for almost a week, too. Word at the bank is that he's away on family business. Once he returns, I'll be able to find out exactly where he's been; then we can try to figure out what they're planning next."

"So there is a definite connection." Logan was glad to have this confirmed.

"Yes. Forrester and Talbott meet on a regular basis at the bank. If I could find out exactly what goes on in those meetings, I could take action, but so far I haven't had any success. If I tried to go in and have them arrested, without definite proof, they could always claim that they were talking about raising funds for the orphanage."

"I don't want them arrested—not yet. This organization could be a lot bigger than we suspect. If we were to bring in Forrester and Talbott now, whoever they're working with would disappear before we ever had the chance to find them."

Logan knew, too, that if the group disbanded that way, he would never find the lead he needed to locate his brother. Unbidden thoughts of Eden came to him then. He had no conclusive proof that she had been involved with the theft in any way, yet just the fact that she worked with Forrester at the Haven and had been on the *Bayou Belle* on the day that the guns had been seized, seemed far too much of a coincidence to him. His suspicions troubled him.

"Stealing that arms shipment was no simple operation. We know that. I don't doubt for a minute that there are more than just the two of them involved," Jim agreed. "As soon as I find out anything else, I'll get word to you."

"It will be interesting to see if Talbott and Forrester get back to New Orleans at the same time."

"If you need to contact me before then, just come to the bank and ask for an appointment with me to set up an account." Jim grinned as he rose from his chair next to the bed. "And in the meantime, Reverend, say a prayer or two for my soul. I need all the prayers I can get."

The two men shook hands. Jim left the room and disappeared down the hallway.

Alone and troubled, Logan locked the door and lay down on the bed. Thoughts of Eden stayed with him. The memory of the pleasure of her kiss, coupled with the possibility that she might be part of the conspiracy, haunted him.

Eden was nervous, but her determination kept her from dwelling on her fear. Each minute seemed an hour as she hid out with Darrell, keeping watch from their vantage point. She was not going to give up—not now, not when she was so close.

And then the doors to the bar swung open and Layton and Moran staggered out.

Eden and Darrell were ready. Eden slipped on her mask and ran to mount her horse. Gun in hand, she waited. Darrell came out of the alley, but stayed in the shadows so the Yankees couldn't see him clearly. The less they remembered about him, the better.

"Layton! Moran!" Darrell called out, wanting to lure them across the street. He was relieved that no one else had followed them out of the bar.

The two soldiers stopped and looked his way. They were so drunk they were unsteady on their feet, and Darrell was glad. That meant they'd be easier to handle when the time came.

"Who is it? What d'ya want?" Moran called out in a slurred voice.

"Come here. I got something to show you, something you'll want to see."

Intrigued, the two changed course and crossed the street. Drunk as they were, they were eager for even more excitement that night.

Darrell backed into the alley, staying away from any light, encouraging them to follow him.

"What d'ya got?" Moran asked in a slurred voice as he followed him.

Darrell hid in a darkened doorway.

Layton and Moran had ventured about five feet into the alley, but then stopped. They looked around in confusion to see where the man who'd called them over had gone, but there was no sign of him anywhere. Puzzled by his disappearance, they started to turn to leave when a gruff voice rang out.

Bobbi Smith

"Hold it right there!" Eden shouted, deliberately deepening her voice.

Peering farther down the alley, Layton and Moran saw a figure on horseback. They tensed as the horse moved slowly toward them. It was then that Moran noticed the rider was masked. He started to go for his gun.

"Don't even try," Eden said tersely.

Moran froze as he saw the gun in the rider's hand pointed directly at him. "What the—"

Darrell had put on his own mask, and he stepped out then, revealing himself, his gun drawn and ready. "Drop your guns right now."

Darrell and Eden were pleased and relieved when the two soldiers obeyed without question.

"Kick them over here," Eden ordered.

They did as directed while Layton protested, "We ain't got much money, but what we got you can have—"

"I don't want your money. There's something else I'm after," Eden said.

"What?" Neither drunk could imagine what these two strangers wanted of them if not their cash.

"Your pants."

Both men went still in shock as they looked between their two captors.

"Take your pants off. Both of you."

"Hell, no! I ain't taking off my pants!" Moran protested.

Eden and Darrell both cocked their guns.

"I'd hate to have to shoot you just to get them," she said easily, "but I will."

The steely edge to the voice, along with the gun barrels pointing directly at them, convinced the two to act. They pulled off their boots, hopping around awkwardly as they did, then stripped off their pants. The two stood unarmed, in little more than their shirts and stocking feet before Eden.

Darrell grabbed up the rope they'd brought with them and quickly moved behind the Yankees to tie their hands.

"We'll get you two bastards for this!" Moran swore as his wrists were bound.

"I don't think we're the bastards here," Eden chuckled, enjoying his outrage.

"Why don't you quit laughing and get down off that horse and fight me like a man?" Layton challenged.

Eden's gaze raked insolently over him as he stood there in his underwear. She deliberately paused in her appraisal to let her regard linger on his groin. She turned her attention to Moran as well, then sneered, "I don't see any men here at all, except for me and my friend. Mother Nature wasn't too kind to either one of you two, was she? Looks like she forgot a vital part or two when she was putting you together."

"Why, you—" Layton started to charge forward in his state of drunken outrage.

"I wouldn't if I were you," Darrell said in a harsh voice, pressing the barrel of his gun fiercely into the man's back. "Just put your hands behind you real slow."

Suddenly terrified at the feel of the cold metal against him, Layton went still and obeyed.

Darrell quickly bound his wrists and gave him a shove. "Both of you, get over by the wall."

"What are you going to do to us?" Moran was finally growing afraid, now that they were completely helpless to stop their unknown assailants.

"Sit down on the ground," Eden ordered.

The two men sat. Darrell bound their ankles and then tied the two men to a post. He made certain that they couldn't reach each other's hands, so they couldn't free themselves. They would be trapped, without their pants, in the alley until someone stumbled upon them.

"Here." Eden rode slowly forward. She handed the note she'd written and had been carrying with her to Darrell along with a pin.

He attached the note to Moran's chest.

"What are you doing?" Moran demanded, scared. "What's that for?"

"It's just a note that tells everybody what fine, upstanding citizens you are," Eden told them.

Moran strained to read it, but he couldn't.

"What's it say?" Layton asked.

"You'll find out soon enough," Eden said with satisfaction. She hoped someone paid attention to her message. The note read:

These drunken men are abusers of women and children.

Darrell gagged both men. He did not want

them to be discovered too quickly, and they would be if they started shouting once he and Eden had gone. That done, Darrell grabbed up their pants and handed both pairs to Eden. He got his horse, and together they rode quietly away from the scene. They took off their masks before they entered the street and disappeared into the night. Eden discarded the pants on the riverfront. The drunks were left alone in the darkness, shuddering in terror and humiliation.

Eden turned to Darrell as they made their way through the deserted streets on the way back to the Haven.

"Thank you. I couldn't have done it without you," she told him, her tone serious. She was feeling great satisfaction in having taught the two Yankees a lesson. Maybe when they finally sobered up, they would realize the error of their ways and never drink or hurt anyone again.

"I won't say it was a pleasure, but I'd sure like to be around when someone finds them. It'll probably be after daylight, and whoever shows up first is going to be in for quite a show."

Eden found herself grinning at the thought. "I know."

When they reached the carriage house behind the Haven, Eden dismounted and handed her reins to Darrell. They shared one last look of understanding before he rode away.

Eden made sure she moved silently as she passed through the garden and reached the side of the house. She didn't want to draw any atten-

tion to herself, dressed as she was and sneaking
back into the Haven in the middle of the night.
She heard a horse out in the street in front of
the house, so she was extra careful not to make
any noise. She quietly pushed the unlocked window up far enough to allow her to climb inside.

The night before, Eden had been very nervous
when she'd returned, but tonight, having accomplished her goal, she was almost calm. She pulled
herself in through the open window, glad to be
back in the orphanage, glad to be safe in the Haven once again.

Logan had sought rest, but sleep didn't come. He
tried to keep his thoughts off Eden, but he failed.
Over and over, he'd found himself questioning
her connection to the arms theft. He wondered
if he could trust her or if she really was a part of
Forrester's organization.

The sense of unease that filled Logan drove
him from his bed, and he left the hotel. He decided to go for a ride, and after saddling his
horse, he headed out. His path took him past the
Haven. He hadn't consciously gone there, but for
some reason he felt drawn to the place that night.

Logan was frowning as he rode slowly by the
orphanage. He studied the darkened building,
asking the silent structure for a clue, for some
hint of what really was going on there.

And then he caught a glimpse of an elusive,
darkly clad figure slipping into the house through
the side window.

Logan was immediately worried. He feared it was one of the Union soldiers returning to harm Eden and the children. He gave no thought to anything except going to Eden's aid. Reining in, Logan jumped down from his horse and raced toward the window where he'd seen the intruder enter the building.

Chapter Twelve

Eden started to unbutton her shirt as she walked to the dresser to put away the gun and light the lamp. She was more than ready to change clothes. She had to get some rest, for it would be dawn soon.

Logan was determined to get inside the Haven as quickly as possible. Eden was in danger! He regretted that he was unarmed, but he hoped to take the invader by surprise. Relief filled him when he saw that the window was still open. Without pause, he climbed in.

Eden put the chimney back on the lamp and turned it up to a soft glow. She was reaching for her nightgown when she heard a noise behind her. Startled, and realizing she'd forgotten to close the window, she turned to find that a man had climbed in and was advancing on her. Eden made a grab for her gun.

Logan was ready for trouble as he came into the room, but the moment he eyed the stranger standing with his back to him lighting the lamp, he realized he wasn't one of the soldiers. This man was physically too small to be Layton or Moran. Even so, Logan felt no relief. He took a threatening step toward the man just as he turned on him.

"Eden?" Logan went still, and his gaze raked over her as she stood before him, the gun in her hand aimed at the center of his chest.

"Logan!" She'd been shaking with fear from the thought of an intruder in her room, but now that terror turned to confusion. There was no intruder. It was Logan. Relief flooded through her.

"What are you doing here?" Eden asked, lowering her gun and placing it back on the dresser.

"What am I doing here?" Logan repeated in disbelief, frowning as his suspicions about her involvement with the spies returned full force. "The real question is: What are you doing dressed like that, running around in the middle of the night carrying a gun? I was riding by, and I saw you climb in the window. I thought you were a thief or one of the Yankees breaking into the orphanage. I was afraid that someone was going to hurt you."

For all that his doubts about Eden's loyalties were plaguing him, he had to admit to himself, with some surprise, that he had really been worried about her safety. He was vastly relieved to discover that she was all right.

As Eden stared up at Logan, she could see the concern in his expression, and she was touched by it. Since he was a minister, though, she didn't think he'd appreciate what she'd done to the Yankees that night, and she didn't want to tell him. She thought it would be better if he left, now that he knew everything was fine at the Haven. "As you can see, there's nothing wrong. So you can go."

"But, Eden—why are you disguised this way?" Logan took a step closer to her. He wanted to find out what she'd been up to, but on an instinctive level, he was also very aware of the way her pants accented the curve of her hips and the way the unbuttoned shirt revealed the lace camisole she wore under it. He grew irritated with himself and struggled to keep his focus on her possible spying. "If you're in any kind of trouble, I can help you. All you have to do is ask me."

"This was something I had to do myself," she said quietly. She found herself lost in the depths of his dark-eyed gaze. The intensity of his regard seared her, leaving her a bit breathless and very much aware of him as a man.

"It had to have been dangerous if you dressed yourself this way. What if something had happened to you? What if everything hadn't turned out all right?" Logan closed on her and lifted one hand to take off her hat, so that he could see her features more clearly in the soft lamplight. When he did, her hair tumbled free in a thick, dark mane about her shoulders, and there was suddenly nothing the least bit masculine about Eden wearing men's attire. Logan stood before her mesmerized, his gaze warming as it traced a path down to the front of her shirt. With an effort, he forced himself to look back up at her face.

"But nothing did happen to me," she protested. Then she added, "But I think Moran and Layton will remember this night for a long time."

"Moran and Layton?" He was shocked.

Eden nodded. "I wanted to teach those Yankees a lesson. I knew no one else was going to stop them, so I had to try. I wanted to make sure they never hurt anyone ever again."

"Eden, those two are very dangerous men. You could have been——" He found himself torn between wanting to throttle her for endangering herself and applauding her for her bravery and determination. She truly was unlike any other woman he had ever known.

"But I wasn't." She smiled at Logan, remembering the sight of the two men in their underwear. "And they didn't look too dangerous when I got done with them."

"What did you do?"

"Considering your vocation, I think the less you know about what happened, the better."

His expression turned fierce. He wasn't feeling very religious right then, and he struggled to act as his own disguise dictated. "Reverend that I am, my vocation calls me to save souls and to worry about innocents who find themselves in trouble."

At his words, she looked up at him. Seeing the intensity of his gaze, her heartbeat quickened, and she found herself remembering the thrill of the kiss they'd shared in the garden.

"You don't have to worry about me," she said in a soft voice, never taking her eyes from his. "I'm not in any trouble. They didn't recognize me."

"Thank God." With a low, guttural growl, Logan reached out and dragged her into his embrace, crushing her against his chest. "And thank God you're safe."

His mouth swooped down to claim hers.

Reason told Logan that this was crazy. This was Eden. She might be his sworn enemy. He told himself, too, that he was supposed to be Reverend Matthews, a man of the cloth, but his desire for her was too powerful. It overruled his meager attempt at logic. Nothing mattered to Logan at that moment except that Eden was in his arms, returning his kiss with equal fervor.

Eden reveled in Logan's embrace. Her heart filled with emotion as she surrendered to his masterful touch. She had gone from terror to ecstasy in a matter of minutes, and the knowledge that Logan had come through that window to rescue her yet another time only heightened the love she felt for him.

Love.

The realization that she loved him shocked her. It was the first time she'd thought of it, but as she lost herself in the heaven of his kiss, she knew it was true. She loved Logan Matthews. Never before had she responded to any man the way she responded to him. He alone could set her soul aflame.

Logan's lips left hers to trail searing kisses down the side of her neck, and Eden gasped at the shiver of sensual awareness that shot through her at his erotic caresses. She closed her eyes and arched back to give him freer access to her throat, reveling in the sensual warmth of his lips.

Logan lost himself in the sweet scent and taste of her. The fact that Eden had been in very real danger that night heightened his need for her. He wanted to hold her close and never let her go. Only when she was safe within his arms could he be certain she was protected from harm.

His lips settled over hers again. This time he deepened the kiss as he parted her shirt and slipped his hand inside to seek out the fullness of her breast.

Eden gasped at the intimate contact. She had never been touched that way before, and yet with Logan there was no thought of resisting. With him, it seemed so right. She responded fully to his explorations, clinging to him, enjoying the rapturous feel of his hard, lean body against her. A deep, abiding ache began to grow within the womanly heart of her. She found she wanted—no, needed—more from him. Hungry to touch him as he was touching her, Eden began to work at the buttons of his shirt and then slipped her hands within to trace the muscled wall of his chest with her fingertips.

Logan reacted passionately to her boldness. He swept her up in his arms and carried her to the bed. There was no thought of leaving her. He only knew that he had to have her, had to be one with her. He lay her upon the softness and then followed her down, covering her body with his. They fit perfectly together, and he braced himself above her on his elbows to gaze down at her passion-flushed features.

"You are so beautiful," he said in a husky voice as he bent slowly to kiss her again.

His words set her heart soaring. Eden had never thought of herself as beautiful. She'd always thought Camille was the pretty one in the family, yet Logan desired her. Logan wanted her. His mouth moved possessively over hers, and she delighted in the power of his embrace. When he drew away from her, she reached out, wanting to pull him back down to her, but he stilled her efforts.

"I want to see you," he told her.

Ever so slowly, he began to remove her clothing. He slipped the shirt from her shoulders and then unfastened the pants and drew them down to reveal her slender, shapely legs. His hands caressed that bared flesh. After stripping away her undergarments, he gazed down at her, committing to memory the glory of her innocence and beauty.

Eden felt shy. She blushed as she tried to cover herself, but Logan took her hands in his and leaned over her to kiss her. When the kiss ended, he stood up and took off his own shirt. He wanted no barrier between them. He saw her eyes widen as she stared at him standing before her naked to the waist, and he realized her truly untouched state. Leaving his pants on, he went back to her and gently gathered her to him. Her naked body was a searing brand against him, and he was hard put to control the need that was driving him to make her his in all ways as quickly as possible.

"Eden, if you want me to go, say so now, for if I kiss you again, I won't be able to leave you." His voice was a hoarse rasp as he fought to rein in his runaway desire.

Eden was on fire with wanting him. She lifted her arms to loop them around his neck and draw him down to her. "Kiss me, Logan," she whispered.

Her words were all the invitation Logan needed. He kissed her hungrily, letting her know by the intensity of the exchange how very much he desired her.

Eden was holding herself a little stiffly against him in her innocence, but as his mouth moved over hers with arousing persuasion, she softened and relaxed.

She wanted this.

She wanted him.

She gave no thought to tomorrow.

Eden only cared that Logan was with her, loving her.

They were alone, and they would not be interrupted.

With the utmost care, Logan began to explore her silken flesh. The fire of his need drove him on. His lips sought her breast, and he pressed heated kisses to that sensitive flesh, drawing a gasp of delight from Eden. She arched to him, offering herself to his arousing, knowing touch. Pleasure filled her and she found herself moving restlessly, seeking something elusive that would put an end to the aching emptiness within her. She began to caress Logan, too, tracing patterns of fire upon his wide, powerful back and shoulders. He shuddered at her ministrations and she felt emboldened by his reaction.

When Logan stopped and pulled away from her, Eden opened her eyes to look up at him. She feared something was wrong, but then realized he had only drawn away to shed the rest of his clothing.

"Do you want me to turn down the lamp?" he asked, knowing she had never seen a naked man before.

"No, I want to see you—"

Logan's gaze caught and held hers as he finished undressing.

Eden watched him with open interest as he stripped away the last of the barriers between them. She had never thought of a man as beautiful before, but Logan was. From the powerful width of his shoulders and chest to his lean waist, he was pure male. She blushed as she saw for the first time the proof of his desire, and it was then that he came back to her, slipping into the bed beside her and taking her into his embrace.

"Are you afraid?" he asked, feeling her trembling as he held her in his arms.

"No—no, I want you, Logan," she whispered, and she kissed him fully on the mouth as she surrendered to his lovemaking.

Logan rolled and pinned her beneath him. It was pure ecstasy as they kissed and caressed each other, seeking only to please one another, driving each other wild with their tantalizing touches. When at last Logan could bear it no longer, he moved over her, ready to make her his own. As slowly as he could, he pressed home the hard heat of his desire for her. Eden opened to him, gasping at that first intimate contact and then accepting the hard heat of him within her.

Logan paused as he reached the proof of her innocence. He had never been with a virgin before and he feared he would hurt her, but Eden urged him on, wanting to be one with him and to know the fullness of his love. With one powerful thrust, Logan breached the barrier and claimed her for his own.

Eden went still as pain stabbed through her, but as Logan continued to move within her, she soon forgot the agony and opened to his rhythm.

Instinctively, she matched his pace and moved with him in exquisite delight.

The aching hunger that had been burning deep within Eden threatened to overwhelm her with the power of its need. She needed something more. As Logan continued to kiss and caress her, the fire within her grew ever hotter until in a moment of pure ecstasy the heights of rapture burst upon her. Sweet agony claimed her as passion's pleasure pulsed through her body. She clung to Logan, trembling in exquisite delight, having never experienced anything so exciting before. She had not known that loving him could be so wonderful.

Logan sensed Eden's release and quickened his pace, seeking his own. The pleasure he found in her body was perfect, and he gave himself over to his desire for her. Ecstasy claimed him, and he held her to his heart.

They lay together, wrapped in each other's arms, their bodies still joined as one. Their hearts were pounding a furious beat as they slowly relaxed.

It was Logan who shifted away from Eden first. He moved to her side, keeping her within the circle of his arms, cherishing the warmth and beauty of what they'd shared.

Eden had never known anything so beautiful, and she lay nestled against Logan, treasuring the closeness. In him she had found gentleness and strength, compassion and passion. As she rested, her exhaustion overcame her and she drifted off to sleep secure in his embrace.

Logan gazed down at her when he sensed she'd fallen asleep, and as he watched her slumber his sanity slowly returned. Eden had given him her innocence. She had come to him willingly, and he had not had the strength to deny himself. Silently, Logan grew angry with himself for his weakness for her. He had wanted her, and he had taken her with no thought of tomorrow. His emotions were in turmoil as he dealt with his own vulnerability where she was concerned. He coldly told himself that he'd just used her to his own end. He told himself that she meant nothing to him, that their lovemaking had only been a physical release for him.

Even as he thought it, though, Logan knew it was a lie. He had wanted Eden as much as she had wanted him.

Logan knew he had to get away from her right then or risk spending the rest of his days and nights making love to her. He carefully slipped from Eden's side, and he was relieved when she slept on, undisturbed. He quickly dressed and then stood over the bed, gazing down at his sleeping beauty. After a long moment, he drew a blanket up over her.

As his reason and logic returned, Logan realized he had an opportunity. It was cold-blooded, considering what he and Eden had just shared, but he had to take advantage of the moment. It was still dark outside, so he knew he had time enough to do a short search of Adrian's quarters and office. He had to move swiftly though, for Eden might awaken at any moment.

Logan silently unlocked the door and left her room. Crossing the hall, he entered the office and closed that door behind him. After quickly lighting a lamp, he turned it down low and began his search. It didn't take Logan long to go through the office and Adrian's rooms. Logan was disappointed that he didn't find anything incriminating, but he was not surprised. Adrian was obviously very good at what he did. A more careless man would have been caught by now.

Logan put out the lamp and returned to Eden's room. He found she was still asleep, and he was relieved. He left the room as he'd come, climbing out the window.

It startled Logan to see that the eastern sky was brightening, and he realized he'd been lucky that he hadn't fallen asleep with Eden in her bed. He got his horse and made the trip back to his hotel room. He had time for a brief rest before he was due back at the Haven to attend church services with Eden and the children in only a few hours.

The thought of sitting beside Eden in church as Reverend Matthews disquieted him as he sought his solitary bed. She believed him to be a minister, yet he had taken her innocence as callously as any rake. In his thoughts, he relived the glory of her loving, and despite his rational misgivings, he knew he would not have changed anything that had happened that night. He just wondered how he was going to keep his hands off her from now on. But he knew he must. He had to concentrate on his mission; he had to find Braden and stop the spies.

Logan found no rest.

Eden awoke as the sun claimed the day. She stirred and started to stretch, then gasped and suddenly sat upright in her bed as she remembered what had happened. She looked around for Logan, but there was no sign of him. It was as if she'd dreamed it all.

But Eden knew she hadn't dreamed his loving. She could never have imagined anything so wonderful. She smiled, believing he'd left her because he'd known he had to get away to save her reputation.

As she thought about it, though, Eden was suddenly overcome by a sense of guilt. Logan was a minister, and she had made love to him without the benefit of marriage.

Logan had come there to save her when he'd thought she'd been in danger, and she had given herself to him as freely as any harlot. She had tempted him, lured him to her bed. He'd even offered to go, and she'd encouraged him to stay. Shame grew within her, even as she realized their lovemaking had been perfect. She did love Logan, but he had not professed any vow of love to her.

The elation that had filled Eden upon first

awakening now turned to caution and humiliation over her own wanton behavior. She wondered what she would say to him when she saw him that morning, and knew she should apologize.

Eden turned back to the bed and saw the proof of her lost innocence. She quickly washed the stain from the sheet. She wondered, though, if she could wash away the memory of his loving as easily, for she knew she could never let it happen again—no matter how much she wanted him.

Chapter Thirteen

Bible in hand, Logan returned to the Haven at the appointed hour that morning. When he knocked on the door, Paul was there to open it for him.

"Good morning, Reverend Logan," the youth welcomed him with a big smile.

"Is it a good morning?" Logan returned, trying to sound as if he were teasing, but in truth he was a bit unsure himself, for he would be seeing Eden soon.

"Yes, sir, it is," Paul assured him. "Everybody's just about ready to go, so we'll be on time today. Some Sundays when we're late, Reverend Miget isn't real happy with us."

"Let's hurry, then," Logan said. "We don't want to get the preacher mad at us."

The two walked together down the hallway to the dining room where everyone gathered once their hair was combed, their faces washed, and they were dressed in their Sunday-best clothing.

Logan followed Paul into the room and looked approvingly over the clean, smiling children gathered there. He'd expected Eden to be in the room, and he was surprised to find she wasn't. Only Jenny was there supervising the children.

"Good morning, everyone," Logan greeted them.

"Good morning, Reverend Logan," they called out, beaming up at him, glad to see him.

"How soon will we be leaving?" he asked Paul.

"As soon as Miss Eden's ready."

"Have you spoken to her this morning?"

"Yes, sir. She's upstairs with Connie. Connie needed help getting dressed," Paul explained.

Logan found he was relieved that everything seemed normal at the Haven. After the glorious night he'd passed in Eden's arms, he hadn't been sure what to expect in the harsh, bright light of day. He wondered if she regretted what had happened between them—if she was sorry they had made love. Try as he might, he couldn't put the sense of unease from him. Logan had just struck up a conversation with Mark when he heard Eden's voice.

"Everyone, it's time to leave," Eden announced as she appeared in the doorway with Connie at her side. She thought the children looked particularly nice this morning, and she was pleased that they were going to be on time for the service. She turned to speak with Connie, and it was then that her gaze collided with Logan's as he looked her way from across the room.

Eden hadn't been sure what to expect this morning. She hadn't even been sure that Logan would show up as he'd promised, but here he was, and just the sight of him so tall and darkly handsome sent a jolt of sensual recognition through her. Her heartbeat quickened as she recalled, in far too vivid detail for her own peace of mind, the pleasure of his touch and the intimacies they'd shared. She tore her gaze away, but as it dropped from his face it settled on the Bible he carried. The disquiet that had troubled her in the early morning hours returned, unsettling her. Again Eden wondered how she could have forgotten herself so completely and allowed herself to make love to Logan. They had only known each other for a matter of days, and yet just looking at him now, she knew it was true— she loved him. He had only to touch her or kiss her and she forgot everything but the wonder of his attention.

Logan had glanced Eden's way when he'd heard her voice, and the sight of her sent a shaft of desire jolting through him. Damn, but she looked beautiful this morning wearing her day-gown with her hair styled up away from her face. Memories of her in other states of dress and undress teased him, and even now he wanted her. Logan fought down his need, but it wasn't easy, for she looked even more lovely to him this morning—if that were possible. Excusing himself from the boys, he made his way to join her.

"How are you?" he asked.

"I'm fine. And you?" Eden couldn't believe she was being so calm and polite when all she wanted to do was throw herself into his arms and never let him go. But she couldn't. His cool politeness only emphasized what she'd feared when she'd awakened to find him gone from her side—last night had meant nothing to him. He didn't care for her as she cared for him.

Before Logan could answer, Jenny's call interrupted them.

"All right, everyone, it's time to leave. Let's line up by twos and make sure you stay together with your partner on the walk to church and during the service."

"Reverend Logan! Will you walk with me?" Connie asked, tugging at his coat sleeve as she gazed up at him.

"Of course," he agreed and went along with her as she drew him away to get in line with the others.

Eden felt bereft, but managed to hide her conflicting emotions as she busied herself with the children, making sure everyone was in line and ready to behave themselves in church. She led the group from the building while Jenny brought up the rear, making sure there were no stragglers who might get lost on the way.

Reverend Bruce Miget was waiting outside to

greet his congregation as they came together for the Sunday morning service. He wasn't a tall man, but the power of his personality more than made up for what he lacked in height. He greeted everyone personally as they entered the church, and all were glad to see him. He was a kind and loving pastor, and they looked forward to his inspiring sermons every week.

"Miss Eden, it is so good to see you and the children," Reverend Miget told her as she led the way up the steps.

"It's good to see you, too."

"What happened to you?" He was shocked to see the fading bruise on her cheek.

Eden quickly told him what had happened. The minister grew grim and angry at the thought of such a lovely lady being attacked by the damned Yankees.

"Is there anything I can do to help you?"

"No, but thank you for offering. Everything turned out all right for us, because Reverend Matthews arrived just in time to stop them from doing any further harm."

"Reverend Matthews?" Reverend Miget looked past her to the man he now saw walking up the steps with the rest of the children.

"Yes. He came down from St. Louis to work at the Haven and to bring us donations from some of the congregations there. He's been quite a godsend for us."

"That's wonderful, and most fortunate that he arrived when he did. Reverend Matthews, welcome, and thank you for taking care of Miss Eden and the children." He went forward and offered his hand in friendship.

Eden introduced them.

"It's a pleasure to meet you, Reverend," Logan said, shaking hands with the clergyman.

"It is our custom to invite visiting ministers to speak to the congregation. It would be an honor for us if you would care to deliver the sermon today," Reverend Miget invited.

Logan was caught completely off guard by his offer. "Oh, no, Reverend, I wouldn't want to try to take your place."

"I won't take no for an answer," the other minister insisted, standing by tradition. "We are privileged to have you here, and we would love to hear some inspiring words from you this morning. Miss Eden was telling me how good you are in your work with the children. Here's your chance to reach them even more profoundly— from the pulpit."

"Well, thank you." Logan was trapped, and he knew it. He managed a smile as he struggled not to panic at the thought of delivering a real sermon to a real congregation. It was one thing to pretend to be a minister working at the orphanage. It was quite another to preach the word of the Lord. He knew preaching was a calling, and it had never been his, seeking justice had been his speciality. "Is there a particular topic you'd like me to address today?"

"Actually, yes, there is. I was hoping to speak

on sin and the pain that not obeying God's word has brought into the world."

"Sin," Logan repeated as he tried not to think of the long list of his own transgressions at that particular moment.

"Come in and I'll show you around before we begin the service," Reverend Miget invited, leading the way inside.

Eden ushered the children into their pews and quietly reminded them once again of the proper behavior for being in church. They were obedient and well behaved as they settled in, and she was pleased. The church was filling up quickly as the time for the service to start drew near.

When Reverend Miget appeared before them, everyone fell respectfully silent.

"Good morning and welcome," the minister said. "We are honored to have as our guest today Reverend Logan Matthews from St. Louis. He has graciously agreed to bring us the word of God this morning. Reverend Matthews." Reverend Miget looked to Logan and waited for him to come out to the pulpit. "Reverend, I'm putting the souls of these faithful followers into your hands." He smiled warmly as he left Logan alone to do his preaching.

Logan stood before the congregation. Never in his life had he felt more inadequate. While he had had a fairly religious upbringing, he had never dreamed he would be called upon to really preach a sermon while on this assignment. He realized he couldn't even use his Bible effectively to quote scripture, for the gun was hidden inside it. Logan managed a smile as he looked out over the crowd of worshipers. They were watching him attentively, waiting eagerly for his words of wisdom. Logan realized he had only one hope. He silently offered up a prayer for divine intervention and divine inspiration. He needed all the help he could get in singing praises to the Lord today.

Sing!

That was it! His divine inspiration.

"Let us open with a hymn," Logan intoned, picking up the hymnal before him. He directed the congregation to a song he was familiar with and led them in singing all three verses.

That done, Logan knew he could delay no longer. He had to preach a sermon, and he had to sound as if he knew what he was talking about.

Well—

Reverend Miget had said he was to speak on sin, and Logan decided with more than a little humor that it was certainly a subject he was familiar with.

"Sin!" he began in a loud, booming voice, wanting to command the children's attention and to keep the grown-ups awake. "Sin is deadly to the soul! Sin is man's conscious and deliberate choice to distance himself from his loving God—"

"Amen!" Someone in the congregation called out.

"The seven deadly sins are just that—deadly. Which one of us has not been tempted? We are human. We all have human frailties. Which one of us has not been angry?" He paused and looked out over the congregation. "If there is one among you who has never known anger, then I say to you, you are a saint—a truly pious person. Do we have a saintly person with us?"

Logan looked out and waited. No one stood. A low chuckle of amusement ran through the congregation.

"So we are all human," he concluded. "What of sloth and gluttony? Do we not all wish in these harsh times to live an easy life, one in which our every need and want is fulfilled? A life where nothing is expected of us except to enjoy ourselves and eat anything and everything we want? How many of you would like to live a life that way? Stand up and be counted."

Everyone stood. The hardships of the war were a reality. The thought of an easy life was seductive.

Logan was impressed. They really were listening to him. Even as it impressed him, the knowledge was intimidating.

"We are human," he repeated. "What of pride and envy and greed? All are deadly sins. Each and every day we make the choice of how we are going to live our lives. Are we strong enough to deny ourselves? Do we feel true happiness when someone else succeeds where we have failed? Do we fight the driving need to always want more than what God has given us? It is good to work to achieve a goal in life, but we must remember why we are striving to attain that goal. We must give the glory to God for our achievements, for we would not be able to accomplish anything without His love."

"Amen!"

Logan was trapped again, and he realized that he had done it to himself. There was one deadly sin left, and it was the one he didn't want to address. But there was no escaping it. If he ignored it, it would be even worse.

"Lust."

He looked out over the crowd. His gaze fell upon Eden, but he didn't allow himself to stare at her for long. He had lusted after her. He had wanted her. He had desired her and he still did. There was no doubt about that. He had made love to her without the benefit of marriage and had taken her most precious gift—her innocence.

"Temptation. Are we strong enough to deny that which calls out to us so enticingly? Can we deny that which tempts us? Look at Adam and Eve. Are we strong enough to control our wants and desires? No! Not without God's help. Only God can save us from ourselves. Every day we are faced with temptation. Every day we must keep up the good fight. We must deny our baser desires and do what is right in the eyes of the Lord."

"Amen!"

Logan did not look at Eden.

"We must turn to our loving God for the strength to live as He would have us live. We must study His Commandments and make them a very real part of our lives." Logan was trying to remember the Ten Commandments and found himself struggling to recall them all. "We must never steal. What right do we have to take another's property? We must not covet another's goods or another man's wife, and we must not commit adultery or kill. These are grievous sins before the Lord. This very day, you have kept holy the Sabbath by coming here to hear the Lord's word being preached to you, and that is a wonderful thing. Love and honor your parents and your God. Never take His name in vain." Logan knew he had missed only one Commandment, and it troubled him as he finally addressed it. "Do not bear false witness. Always be a bearer of the truth, for the truth will set you free."

Even as he spoke of being honest, Logan knew that everything about him and his presence there in the church that morning was a lie. If a lightning bolt struck him down then and there, he wouldn't have been surprised. And he wouldn't have been surprised by where he would have ended up, although his motives for his deceptions were surely pure—he hoped.

Logan paused in his preaching.

He heard no rumble of thunder echoing in the distance.

The day remained sunny.

He felt a bit relieved.

Though he was lying to everyone, Logan could not bring himself to ask for God's forgiveness, for he was not sorry for what he was doing. He was there to try to save his brother's life. If saving Braden condemned him to an eternity in hell, then so be it. If he were to stand by and not try to help his brother, he would have condemned himself to a living hell on earth.

"In closing, know that the Lord is with you always. In difficult times, He will give you the strength you need to overcome whatever it is that is troubling you. All you have to do is ask. Don't let your pride—one of the deadly sins— stand in your way." He paused. "And remember Jesus' words: Love one another as I have loved you. If the world lived by this instruction, there would be no war or hatred. There would be no enemies. There would be only love, and it is true—love does conquer all."

"Amen," Reverend Miget said, coming to Logan's side. "Thank you, Reverend Matthews. You have truly been an inspiration to all of us today."

Reverend Miget took over the pulpit and went on to address issues of the church and to take up the weekly collection as Logan took a seat off to the side.

"We will now offer up our moment of silence," Reverend Miget announced as the service drew to an end, and a hush quickly fell over the congregation.

It had been decreed by the authorities that ministers could not offer up prayers for the Southern Cause or for Confederate soldiers or their leaders. So to avoid trouble, Reverend Miget offered a moment of silence during each Sunday service. He knew, and his congregation knew, that this time of prayer was for the Confederacy, no matter what the Yankees thought.

"May God bless you all and keep you safe until I see you again."

Eden had never been more thankful that a service had ended than she was that day. As she directed the children from their pews, she was overcome with a sense of guilt that would not be dismissed or ignored. Logan was such a wonderful preacher. His sermon had been heartfelt and touching, and she felt completely responsible for what had happened between them the night before. Logan truly was a man of God, and yet she had been the temptation that had led to his downfall—to his sin.

Eden was miserable, but she hid it behind a smile as she concentrated on taking care of the children. She hoped she could find a way to make it up to Logan, but she doubted she could. He didn't love her as she loved him.

"Are you ready to go back?" Jenny asked Eden as they met in front of church.

"Oh, yes," Eden agreed, needing to get away before Logan caught up with them.

"Miss Eden, wait! We can't leave yet!" Connie cried excitedly. "Reverend Logan's coming!"

Leaving the line of students, the little girl darted back to meet him as he came out of the church with Reverend Miget.

Logan saw Connie coming and held his hand out to her in open invitation. She took it without hesitation. He bade the preacher good-bye, and he and Connie moved off to join the rest of the children on their way back to the orphanage.

Chapter Fourteen

Logan and Connie trailed behind the others on the walk back to the Haven. Connie chattered endlessly to Logan as they went along, keeping him entertained with her innocent questions and opinions. They stopped once to watch a bird hopping about in a tree, and another time they paused to peek into a yard and admire the pretty fountain that splashed noisily there. Through her eyes, Logan was seeing the city in a whole new light.

There was no doubt that the tiny blond beauty had won Logan's heart. He hadn't been around many children in his life, and he found Connie's completely unaffected outlook on the world heart-rending. It troubled him greatly that she had lost her parents at such a tender age, and he realized how blessed he was to have had his own parents well into his adulthood.

"Do you have a mama and papa?" Connie asked.

Logan was surprised that she'd seemed to be able to read his thoughts. "No. Both my parents are dead," he answered solemnly.

"So you're an orphan, too," she stated, giving him a sympathetic look.

"I guess I am," he agreed with her logic, although he'd never thought of himself that way before.

"Then are you going to be staying with us at the Haven some more? 'Cause if you are staying some more, I want you to come sleep upstairs with me."

"Some more?" Logan frowned, puzzled. He glanced down at the child, wondering what she was talking about.

"I had a nightmare last night. I was scared and couldn't sleep anymore so I got up. I heard something outside, and I looked out the window and saw you leaving. I was really wishing you'd come upstairs and see me for a while, 'cause I was scared."

"Oh—I didn't know you were up," he said, shocked.

"Well, if you're staying more, we could get an extra bed for you and everything, so you could spend the night with me instead of Miss Eden."

Logan had known seeing Eden today was going to be difficult, but he'd never imagined he would be facing a situation like this. He had thought he'd slipped away without detection the night before. He'd been wrong.

"Did anybody else wake up and sit with you last night to keep you company?" he asked, bracing himself for her answer. He could just imagine what the older children had thought of his sermon about resisting temptation and denying lust if they'd witnessed him sneaking off in the early morning hours.

"No, everybody else was sleeping. That's why I was so scared," she told him honestly.

"Well, if I had known you were awake, I would have come upstairs to visit you." He was glad that she was too young to understand the reason for his question.

Connie smiled up at him. "I love you, Reverend Logan."

Her words touched his heart. "I love you, too, Connie. You are one special young lady."

"You think I'm special?" She beamed at his praise.

"Yes, I do. Can you keep a secret?"

"Oh, yes, sir." She became instantly serious.

"Let's don't tell anybody about my visit with Miss Eden last night, all right?"

"All right. I won't tell anybody! I promise." She didn't know why he didn't want her to tell, but she wouldn't.

"Good girl."

Even as Connie promised never to tell anyone,

Logan knew it was already too late. One accidental, unintentional word from an innocent like Connie, and Eden's reputation would be ruined forever. Before now, he had been unsure how to approach Eden this morning, but now there was no doubt what he had to do. He had no choice in the matter—and neither did she.

They would marry.

Silently, Logan cursed himself for the way in which he'd let the situation develop. Since he'd been caught, as Reverend Matthews he could do no less than offer for Eden's hand in wedlock. It complicated things greatly, but there was nothing he could do about that now, and he had no one to blame but himself.

Logan knew, too, that even if he could turn back the hands of time and relive the night before, he wouldn't change anything. He had charged into the Haven through the open window last night to protect Eden from harm. His motivation had been true then, and in the same way, he would protect her from harm now—harm that, by his own weakness for her, he had caused. He had compromised her, and Connie had seen him leaving in the predawn hours. He would allow no slur upon Eden's reputation. His decision was made.

Logan looked up to where Eden was walking on ahead of them. His thoughts were troubled even as his gaze was warm upon her. He knew he had to get her alone as soon as possible so he could propose to her. They had much to discuss.

A wedding was going to change everything between them—and change his investigation, too, but there could be no avoiding it. He grew grimly determined, for he had a lot of planning to do.

"Eden?" Logan said her name as he came to stand in the doorway of the office a short time after they'd returned to the Haven. "May I come in?"

It seemed ridiculous to him to be so formal after what they'd shared last night, but they were in the orphanage and the children were around.

"Of course," Eden answered, smiling at him.

She tried to appear calm and collected, but just the sight of him standing there in the doorway left her breathless. Her spontaneous reaction to him dismayed her. In spite of all the guilt she'd been feeling, she was still attracted to him. She watched as Logan strode into the office, and she was surprised when he made a point to close the door securely behind him.

"Is something wrong?" she worried.

Logan advanced on her and stopped before the desk. "We need to talk—and I wanted to make sure our conversation was private."

"Oh." She fought to appear cool and composed. "What did you want to talk about?"

Her almost indifferent question left him a bit off balance. Their loving had seemed so perfect and she had been so wonderfully responsive in his arms, yet now she was acting as if those long, passionate hours had never happened.

"Did last night mean so little to you?" The look in his eyes was intense as he faced her.

"Last night—" she repeated breathlessly, mesmerized by the power of his presence, and remembering far too vividly what had transpired.

"I can refresh your memory—if you've forgotten," Logan offered with a bit of a devilish grin.

"Logan—no. I—I'm sorry."

"Sorry?" He paused. He almost felt as if she'd slapped him. "Sorry for what?"

Eden was agonizing as she lifted her gaze to his. She couldn't let him know that the hours she'd spent in his arms had been the most wonderful in her entire life. She couldn't tell him that she loved him.

They had known each other for such a short time that he would never believe her. She had acted the wanton last night, and she regretted it sorely. He was a minister, and she had led him into temptation.

"I'm sorry for the way I acted last night. It was wrong—so wrong. If I could, I would change everything. I'd make sure it never happened. But it did. All I can say is, I'm sorry."

"So you want to pretend that nothing happened between us last night?" Logan had intended to propose to her and then tell her of Connie's involvement, but that was all changing now. He had thought he'd understood Eden's being uneasy around him this morning, and he'd wanted to speak with her and help calm her, but he'd never thought she would be this remorseful about their lovemaking.

"I think it would be best. Don't you?" She was tentative, trying to read his mood and failing miserably. "I never meant for things to go so far. You're a man of God. You're here at the Haven to help the children—and then, last night I acted like some loose woman from the streets."

He suddenly realized the shame she was feeling, and he found himself touched by her emotion. "You were not alone in what happened between us last night, Eden," Logan said gently. "I wanted you as much as you wanted me."

"But it shouldn't have happened. We should never have—"

"But we did." Logan moved around the desk to take her hand and draw her to her feet before him. He had to know the truth of what she was feeling. Without saying another word, he bent and kissed her softly on the lips. "Are you sorry, Eden? Really sorry?"

At the touch of his lips, a thrill shot through her. The power of her reaction to him shook Eden, and she drew back nervously, afraid of the truth. She didn't meet his gaze as she gave a slight shake of her head and whispered, "No."

Logan lifted one hand to cup her cheek. "Eden—there's something you need to know."

At his words, she finally did look up. She saw how serious his expression was, and her eyes widened in apprehension. "There is?"

"There was a witness to what transpired between us last night. I was seen leaving your room."

She went completely still for an instant and then gave a mortified groan. "But it was so late. Who could have—"

"Connie."

"Connie?"

"She told me she'd had a nightmare and had gotten up, scared. She heard a noise and was looking out the window when she saw me leaving."

"Dear God." Eden paled in mortification. She wondered how her life could have become so incredibly complicated so quickly—and all because she loved him.

"As a result, I think it's important that we marry, Eden. The sooner, the better."

Eden had entertained fantasies of marrying Logan and spending the rest of her life loving him. But she hadn't wanted to wed him this way—out of responsibility and guilt. "You're only proposing to me because of Connie."

He didn't deny it. "I won't allow your reputation to be put at risk."

"But the damage is already done," she said quietly.

"Only Connie knows that I was with you, and she promised me she wouldn't tell anyone else. If or when anyone else does happen to find out about last night, I want to make sure you already have the protection of my name."

Her heart sank. His proposal was so cold, so

calculated, so emotionless. Logan had made no mention of love or devotion, of tenderness or caring. He'd spoken only of protecting her reputation—as any good reverend would.

"You don't have to do this," Eden told him, not wanting him to play the martyr and sacrifice himself for her sake.

"I am a man and I am responsible for what happened. I will not let you suffer the consequences of our actions alone. I want to make things right."

"But how do we convince everybody that we've fallen madly in love in such a short period of time?" she challenged. Some part of her hoped that he would respond by saying it was the truth—that he had fallen madly in love with her. If he did say that, she was ready to profess her love for him, too. If only he did love her as she loved him, everything would be wonderful between them.

"Only you and I will ever know the truth behind the reason for our wedding. We'll just pretend when we're in public together," he answered.

Pretend!

The idea of it screamed in her mind. She would not be pretending to love him. She did love him!

"And no one will ever have to find out differently," he went on, "unless Connie accidentally reveals what she saw last night. If that does ever happen, we'll worry about how to handle it then."

All her life, Eden had dreamed of making a love match when she married. But it wasn't going to happen. She might love him, but he didn't love her. Logan was only marrying her out of a sense of duty. That knowledge broke Eden's heart.

Yet, as sad as Eden was about the state of things between them, a slow, angry determination began to grow within her. This was Logan: the man she admired; the man to whom she had given her innocence; the man she truly loved. Somehow she was going to find a way to make him fall in love with her so he would never regret having been forced to marry her.

"Eden, will you do me the honor of becoming my wife?" Logan proposed.

She lifted her gaze to his and answered simply, "Yes, Logan. I'll marry you."

Logan sensed a strange undercurrent of emotion in her. "You won't regret it, Eden."

Silently she prayed that she wouldn't.

"You want me to marry you? Now? Tonight?" Reverend Miget repeated to Eden and Logan.

They had sought him out at his residence in hopes that he would perform the ceremony that very evening. They were seated in his study now after broaching the subject with him.

"Yes, if you would," Logan replied. "It was love at first sight for us, and we don't want to wait any longer to be together as man and wife."

"You're sure about this?" he pressed, looking to Eden.

"Oh, yes," Eden said, her gaze fixed adoringly on Logan.

"Would you like to send for your mother and sister so they can witness the ceremony?"

"You'll do it? You'll marry us?" she asked, surprised and delighted.

"As long as you're both confident this is the right thing for you to do."

"Ours has been a whirlwind courtship," Logan put in, wanting to reassure the minister. "But I've never met anyone like Eden before. I've been very blessed to find her."

"And your mother and sister?" the reverend repeated, looking back to Eden.

"We'll visit them right after the ceremony and surprise them with our good news," Eden assured him.

"Did you tell the children of your plans before you left the Haven?"

"No. We're going to surprise them, too," Eden answered.

"I'm sure they'll be pleased. I could tell they're quite fond of you, Reverend Matthews."

"I'm most fond of them, too."

"Well, give me a moment to get my wife Carla and my son Josh to be our witnesses, and then I'll perform the ceremony for you."

"Thank you."

The reverend left them alone in his study, and they waited in silence for his return. Logan realized then that he didn't have a ring for her, but he made a promise to himself to take Eden out the very next day to purchase one.

In only a few minutes, the reverend returned with his son.

"Carla will be along shortly," he told them after introducing Josh.

When his wife did join them a few moments later, she was carrying a small bouquet of fresh flowers she'd just cut from her garden.

"I am so happy for you, Eden. I wanted you to have these. No bride should be without a bouquet on her wedding day," Carla told her, giving her the flowers. She had known Eden for several years now through the church.

"Thank you."

Reverend Miget was ready to begin.

"Dearly beloved," he intoned.

Eden and Logan fell silent. Their mood turned serious as they prepared themselves to take their vows—sacred vows that would bind them as husband and wife forever. They listened intently as the minister performed the ceremony.

"Do you, Eden LeGrand, take this man, Logan Matthews, to be your lawfully wedded husband? To have and to hold, in sickness and in health, for richer or poorer, for better or worse, until death do you part?"

"I do," she said softly.

"Do you, Logan Matthews, take this woman, Eden LeGrand . . ." He went on to repeat the vow.

"I do," Logan answered firmly.

"Do you have a ring for your bride?"

"No."

The reverend wasn't deterred. He concluded the wedding. "I now pronounce you husband and wife. What God has joined together, let no man put asunder." He smiled at them, genuinely pleased with their union. "You may kiss your bride."

Logan turned to Eden and took her in his arms. His kiss was sweet and respectful.

"Congratulations!" Carla told them in delight after watching them embrace. "You are going to be so happy! You've got yourself a wonderful woman, Reverend Matthews."

"I know," he responded warmly as he slipped an arm around Eden's shoulders to keep her by his side.

"Thank you so much for helping us," Eden said.

"It's so romantic!" Carla said with a sigh.

"I love weddings," the minister admitted. "It's a real joy to bring together two people who truly love each other and who are committed to each other's happiness."

His words caused Eden pain, but her smile never faltered. It was good that the minister believed they really were in love. They had managed to fool him, and she hoped they could fool everyone else as easily.

Logan paid the minister for his services, and they prepared to leave.

"God bless you, Reverend and Mrs. Matthews," Reverend Miget told them as he, Carla, and Josh saw them from the house.

Mrs. Matthews. It sounded so strange to Eden, and yet somehow it felt so right.

"Did you want to go to see your mother and sister now?" Logan asked as they returned to the buggy.

Logan took Eden's arm and helped her into the conveyance, then climbed up beside her and took up the reins.

"Yes, it's best if we tell them our news first. Mother would be devastated if she found out about our marriage from someone else," Eden answered, feeling the heat of his touch all the way to the depths of her soul.

As they sat close together on the carriage seat, every fiber of Eden's being was aware of Logan beside her. Her hip was against his, her thigh was pressed tightly to his thigh. That contact was arousing, and Eden struggled to ignore it, wedding day or not.

Chapter Fifteen

Camille had been sitting in the parlor sulking. She was bored with her life and devastated by the lack of success she was having with Logan. She wanted him for herself desperately. She had flirted with him shamelessly, but nothing she'd tried had worked to win his heart or even his interest. Logan seemed completely oblivious to her.

Camille knew she was pretty. She knew she was charming. Certainly her figure was full enough to attract the attention of any red-blooded man. So she couldn't figure out why Logan seemed so indifferent. Oh, he was polite and gentlemanly when he was with her, but she didn't care about that. She wanted a passionate man.

At the sound of a carriage drawing up out front, Camille rose from the sofa to go look out the parlor window. She was surprised to see Eden arriving with Logan. Camille was delighted to see the reverend, but wished her sister had stayed back at the Haven. She wanted to have Logan all to herself.

"Mother!" Camille called as she hurried into the front hall. "Mother! Eden's home, and she's brought Logan with her!"

Responding to her daughter's call, Francene came out of the back of the house to greet Eden and her guest.

"To what honor do we owe this visit?" Francene asked with a welcoming smile as she and Camille met them at the door. "I hadn't thought we'd get to see you tonight."

"Logan and I had some exciting news we wanted to share with you, and we just couldn't wait," Eden began.

"Exciting news?" Francene was instantly delighted.

"What happened?" Camille asked. It wasn't often that anyone had exciting, good news these days.

Eden and Logan exchanged looks.

"You go ahead," Eden demurred to her husband.

Logan looked to her mother and sister as he slipped an arm about Eden's waist and drew her to his side. "Eden has done me the honor of becoming my wife."

"What?" Francene was shocked. She looked from one to the other in disbelief.

"You two are married?" Camille was devastated by the announcement.

"Yes. We just came from Reverend Miget's home. He performed the ceremony there, and we wanted you to be the first to know," Logan told them.

Francene was completely stunned. She'd had no idea that Eden had any romantic interest in the minister, but looking at her now, she could see how happy her daughter appeared. Eden had never been an impulsive child, so Francene knew that if Eden loved Logan enough to elope with him, she must truly care for the man. "This is so sudden. Why didn't you wait, and we could have planned a big wedding for you?"

Eden looked up at Logan, her eyes shining with happiness. "We didn't want to wait. We love each other, and we wanted to be together."

Francene smiled at them both. "This is wonderful, darling. Logan, welcome to the family." She went to him and kissed him on the cheek. She then hugged Eden as tears of happiness burned in her eyes.

Tears were burning in Camille's eyes, too, but they weren't tears of happiness. Her eyes were wet with tears of rage. She was furious, but she struggled to control that wild emotion as she pressed a cold kiss to Logan's cheek and then looked at her sister.

"I hope you're very happy." In her heart,

though, Camille was livid. She had wanted Logan for herself, but now he would never be hers. Her sister had married him! Camille was certain that she was destined to become a wrinkled-up old maid, while her sister was married to the handsomest man she'd seen in New Orleans since the start of the war.

"Do you have time to join us for dinner tonight and celebrate?" Francene invited. "We were almost ready to eat."

"I would love to, but I promised Jenny I'd get back to the Haven as soon as I could. I don't like leaving her alone too long with all the children. You never know when something might happen."

"Jenny doesn't know about your elopement?"

"No. We didn't say a word."

"Jenny's going to be so happy for you," Francene told them. "Why don't you plan to come to dinner tomorrow night? We can celebrate properly."

"That would be wonderful."

Francene kissed Eden and hugged her close. "Are you happy, darling?"

"Yes, Mother. I am."

"Good. That's all I've ever wanted for you—your happiness." Francene turned to speak with Logan. "I'm entrusting you with the care of my daughter, Logan. Nothing means more to me in life than my children. Please honor her and love her."

"Yes, ma'am. I will do everything in my power

to ensure her happiness," he promised.

"I'll be holding you to that," Francene answered.

"I'm going to get a few things from my room, then we'll have to go," Eden told her mother.

"I'll help you," Camille said quickly, wanting a few minutes alone with her sister.

Camille didn't say a thing until they were upstairs in Eden's room; then she turned on her, her fury evident in her expression.

"How could you!" Camille demanded hatefully.

"How could I what?" Eden asked, surprised by her sister's anger.

"I wanted Logan! You knew that! Yet you went and married him! How could you do that to me?"

Eden wanted to calm her, but she could tell that her sister was too furious to understand reason. "I didn't do anything to you, Camille. Logan and I love each other."

"You couldn't love Logan! You hardly know him!" she argued.

"I know enough about him to know that he's the one man who can make me happy." Eden tried to explain their relationship. "We're in love."

Camille wanted to shriek at her sister that she didn't know what love was, but she managed to control the urge. She'd already made a big enough fool of herself. She retreated sullenly into the hallway to try to compose herself while Eden finished gathering her things. They went back downstairs to rejoin Logan and their mother. Francene and Camille walked the newlyweds from the house and stood together watching as they drove off back to the Haven.

When Francene turned to go back inside, she saw that Camille's expression had changed and tears were streaking down her cheeks.

"What's wrong?"

"You don't know?" Camille challenged.

"No, dear. What is it? What's wrong?" She was worried about her.

"I'll tell you what's wrong! I thought I was going to be the one to marry Logan! I wanted him!" she pouted, stomping inside.

Francene knew how desperate Camille was to find a husband. "You should be happy for your sister."

"Happy for Eden?" Camille gave a sharp laugh. "How can I be happy for her when she's stolen what was mine?"

"Eden didn't steal Logan from you, Camille," her mother advised. "I'm sure there's a man out there for you somewhere. You just haven't met him yet."

"I don't think I'm ever going to get to meet him! This war is horrible! I'm going to end up an old maid!" she cried as she charged up the steps to her room.

Her mother watched Camille go, and while she felt sorry for her, she was also delighted that

Eden had found the man of her dreams. There had been a time when she'd worried that neither Eden nor Camille would ever be happy, but all that had changed now. Eden had married Reverend Logan. He was a good man, an honest, brave man, and she was certain everything would turn out all right for them. They made a handsome couple, and judging from the way they'd been looking at each other, she was sure they loved one another. True, it had all happened very quickly, but there was a war raging, and they had to grab whatever happiness they could when an opportunity presented itself.

Francene said a quiet prayer that Eden and Logan were happy and had a long and prosperous life together. She only wished her husband and son had been there to share the good news.

"Children! I have something wonderful to tell you!" Jenny announced as she came into the dining room where they were all seated enjoying their dinner. Eden and Logan followed after her.

"What?" the children called out, eager to hear what Miss Jenny was so excited about.

"Miss Eden and Reverend Logan were married this afternoon. Isn't that wonderful?"

"You got married?" several children repeated, looking from Eden to Logan in astonishment.

"That's right," Logan answered. "I proposed to Miss Eden, and she accepted. We couldn't see any reason to wait."

"Did you marry yourself, Reverend Logan?" one of the precocious boys called out.

Logan laughed at his question. "No. Reverend Miget married us today."

The children all cheered their happiness.

"Does this mean you'll be staying with us forever just like Miss Eden?" little Connie asked, looking up at Logan, her love for him showing in her expression.

"I'll be here for as long as you need me," Logan promised. Even as he said it, though, he knew it was a lie. He felt the sting of his conscience, but ignored it. He cared about the children, true, but he was there to try to rescue Braden.

Eden was thrilled by Logan's promise. She hadn't worried about where they'd be living before, but now as she realized she was his wife, it suddenly occurred to her that she would have to follow him wherever his ministry took him. The thought of having to leave the children worried her. She loved them and couldn't bear the thought of being separated from them.

They visited with the children for a little longer, then went into the hall. Though it was their wedding night, they had accepted that it would be best if they spent it apart. Eden was needed there at the Haven to help Jenny, so Logan planned to return to his hotel alone.

"What do you mean, you're spending the night here?" Jenny demanded of Eden as she came out of the dining room and overheard a bit of their private conversation.

"I need to be here with you and the children," Eden answered simply.

"That's ridiculous. You can't stay here tonight!" Jenny knew that Eden was dedicated, but there were some things in life that were more important. "This is your wedding night! You pack what you need and go with your new husband right now. We will be just fine without you."

"Are you sure?"

"I'm positive," she insisted. "Go on, and congratulations, you two. This is wonderful!"

Jenny gave Eden an impulsive hug and then couldn't resist hugging Logan, too. "I am so happy for you."

Eden hurried off to pack a few belongings. It didn't take her long. She started to leave her room, then paused, suddenly a little nervous about the night to come.

She was Mrs. Logan Matthews.

She was a married woman.

She was going off to spend her wedding night with her new husband.

Eden's heartbeat quickened as she remembered Logan's heated kisses and caresses from the night before. Making love to him had been ecstasy for her, and now they would have the whole night together—just the two of them with no threat of interruption and no fear of discovery.

It weighed heavily on Eden that Logan had

only married her to save her honor and not because he loved her. Even so, she was his wife and this was their wedding night. A smile curved her lips at the thought of the long, dark, pleasurable hours to come.

As Eden stepped out into the hallway, her gaze fell upon Logan where he was standing, engaged in conversation with Jenny. He hadn't noticed that she'd returned, so she took the opportunity to study him for a moment. There was no doubt about it. Logan was a very attractive man. From his dark good looks to his broad, powerful shoulders and lean, muscular physique, she found him compelling. Everything about him spoke of strength and resolve, of intelligence and determination. He was a force to be reckoned with—and he was her husband.

As if sensing her regard upon him, Logan looked up, and their gazes met across the distance.

Even from this far away, the power mirrored in the depths of his dark eyes moved Eden, and a shock of sensual recognition trembled through her.

Logan devoured her with his gaze. She looked more lovely than ever to him right now, and he found he wanted to take her in his arms and never let her go.

And she was his wife.

"Ready?" Logan asked.

"Yes."

He came to her side and took the small bag she had packed for herself.

"I'll have her back in the morning, Jenny. I promise," he told the other woman with a grin.

"Good night."

Jenny sighed romantically as she watched them go.

Logan escorted Eden to the buggy and helped her climb onto the bench seat. He joined her there, and they started off.

"Where are we going?" Eden finally asked.

"We'll spend tonight in my hotel room. Then tomorrow we can start thinking about where we're going to live when Adrian gets back, and you don't have to stay at the Haven anymore."

Logan's thoughts were racing as he guided the buggy through the streets to his hotel. He was trying to figure out how their marriage was going to change his handling of the investigation, but Eden's presence so close beside him wreaked havoc on his usual logical thinking. There was absolutely nothing logical about his feelings for her.

He wanted her.

He desired her.

She was his wife—

For now.

They would be together until the time came for him to end it. They would be husband and wife, and they would have to find a place to live together.

They reached the hotel, and after seeing that

the horse and buggy were tended to, they started upstairs to their room.

Logan realized he was very lucky that Adrian wasn't back yet. He needed a few days to get things in order. If he and Eden were together all day, every day, he would have no chance to get away and meet with Sam or Jim.

Jim.

The very real possibility that the other operative might be waiting for him in his room tonight jolted through Logan. He knew a moment of true concern as he and Eden made their way down the hotel hallway. There was no way to escape seeing him if he was there, unless . . .

An idea came to Logan, and as he stopped before the door to unlock it, he knew what he had to do. It wouldn't give the other man much time, but it would divert Eden's attention for at least a moment or two, and give Jim the opportunity he needed to escape if, indeed, he was in the room waiting to meet with him.

Logan unlocked the door and left it slightly ajar. Before Eden could walk in ahead of him, Logan swept her up into his arms to carry her across the threshold. As he held her close, he kissed her, full and flaming on the lips.

Logan had meant the kiss to be a distraction for Eden. He had not realized it would distract him, too. The moment his mouth moved over hers, all the powerful emotions that had warred within him the night before returned. He wanted her. He had to have her. And now she truly was his.

Backing into the room, Logan kicked the door shut behind them without interrupting the kiss. As much as he hated to do it, he opened one eye to take a quick look around the darkened room. Relief rushed through him, for there was no sign of Jim. Logan's secret identity would remain just that for now—secret.

Walking straight to the side of the bed, Logan carefully bent down to lay Eden upon its softness. He forced himself to break off the kiss so he could go and lock the door. Her intoxicating kisses had the power to make him forget himself, and if he hadn't left her right then, he might not have left her at all—at least not until the maid walked in on them in the morning.

"Do you want me to light the lamp?" Logan asked as he walked slowly back to the bed.

"No, I only want you," she answered, and she meant it. The pleasure of his embrace had ignited the fires of her passion. She wanted him back with her, his arms around her, his lips upon hers. She wanted to forget everything except that they were together, and they were husband and wife.

Her words sent a surge of excitement through Logan, and he wasted no more time. Stripping off his shirt along with the coat, he joined her on the bed and took her in his embrace. He held her to his heart as his lips sought hers in a rapturous exchange. Each kiss and each caress stoked the fire of their passion. Their souls were aflame in a searing testament to their desire.

It was their wedding night.

They came together in perfect union there in the hot, velvet darkness. Driving passion consumed them through the long, dark hours of the night.

Gentleness surrendered to power, but in surrender, gentleness became the conqueror.

Eden and Logan clung to one another, cherishing the pleasure that had been theirs and would be theirs.

They were one.

In the early morning hours Eden stirred in Logan's arms and slowly awoke. She lay quietly, marveling at the wonder that this man was her husband. Her gaze traced his features. Unable to resist, Eden rose up to press a soft kiss to his lips.

"Be careful," he warned with a chuckle in a low voice. "You're tempting me again."

"Ah, but this is different," Eden told him as she ran one hand over the hard plane of his chest. "A wife can tempt her husband. There is no sin in our loving."

Desire pounded through him at her sultry, inviting words and her touch, but so did guilt over his deception. He had married her, but everything she knew about him was a lie.

If Eden knew the truth—

Logan did not allow himself to dwell on that thought. He turned to Eden and possessed her again. Burying himself deep within the hot, satin depths of her, he sought what forgetfulness he could find through fulfillment in her arms.

Eden clung to him as he took her to the heights of ecstasy and beyond. She treasured the bliss of his touch and kiss, and the joy of being one with him. Though he still had not professed to love her, Eden could not deny her own feelings. She loved Logan.

Chapter Sixteen

Logan lay awake as the coming dawn brightened the eastern sky. He should have been exhausted, for he'd gotten little sleep through the long, passion-filled hours of the night, but he wasn't. The time he'd just passed in Eden's arms had been pure heaven.

Logan savored having Eden slumbering peacefully beside him. He looked over at her, his gaze a visual caress. Eden was such a beautiful, amazing woman. She was brave and intelligent and passionate. His thoughts drifted as he watched her sleep. He remembered the fear that had gripped him when he'd thought she'd been in danger that night at the Haven. His fear for her safety had been real, and as he mentally relived the moment when he'd climbed through the orphanage window to save her, it was even more powerful now.

The fierceness of his emotions startled him. Logan frowned into the darkness as he reminded himself that he was there on assignment. He had a mission to complete. As attracted to Eden as he was, his brother's life was at stake. He didn't have time to get involved with anyone.

Even as he thought it, though, Logan knew it was too late. There could be no denying it. He was involved with Eden. He cared about Eden. He cared enough to have made her his wife, rather than let her reputation be put at risk.

He loved her.

The thought came to him in a flash of insight. *Did he love her?*

His frown deepened. He couldn't afford to love Eden. If it turned out that she was involved with the spy ring, they would be sworn enemies.

But would his enemy have gone to his brother's aid on the riverboat?

"Logan?" Eden said his name softly as she came awake and saw his dark expression. He looked as if something serious was troubling him. "Is anything wrong?"

Logan quickly smiled at her. "No—no, there's nothing wrong."

"But you look so worried."

"I was thinking about your run-in with the Yankee soldiers, and I was worrying because something might have happened to you," he responded, drawing her near. "I don't ever want you to put yourself in danger that way again. I want you to be safe, always."

Eden was touched by his words and pressed her lips to his in a cherishing kiss. Then she nestled back down against him. "I don't think they'll be bothering anybody anymore—or at least, I hope not." A small smile curved her lips.

"What did you do to them the other night?" Logan had to ask.

"Are you sure you want to know?"

"I think I need to know, if I'm going to be able to keep track of my wife."

Eden remembered his sermon and knew she owed him the truth. "I found out the name of a bar Layton and Moran frequented, and I watched and waited for them to come out. When they did, I got them to come into a nearby alley and—"

"You did this all by yourself?" Logan knew how violent those soldiers could be, and he was shocked that she'd put herself in such a dangerous situation.

"I wasn't alone. I had help."

"You did? Who?"

Eden found herself in a quandary. She wondered if she dared tell Logan everything about her involvement with the Confederate resistance. He was her husband, and he did deserve honesty from her, but she wasn't sure just how much honesty she could afford him. She didn't want to put Adrian and the others at risk.

"There are people around who can find out

these things for you and who don't mind helping out a good Cause."

"What did you do once you got them into the alley?"

She told him how she'd made the Yankees shed their pants and then tied them up and left them stranded with the note pinned to them. "I just hope someone took notice."

"And I just hope Moran and Layton didn't figure out it was you. I don't want either one of them coming back to the Haven looking for more revenge."

"Neither do I. But if you didn't recognize me when I was dressed that way, I'm sure they didn't, either. We were very careful that night."

"I pray to God you're right." Thinking about her being in harm's way tore at him. "And thank heaven it's over now, and I'll never have to worry about you doing anything like that again."

Logan kissed her hungrily, wanting to reassure himself that she was safe within his arms. Eden responded fully. She pressed herself against him in open invitation and let him know by her kisses and caresses that she wanted him, too.

As she was loving him, though, Eden struggled with her conscience. Logan's assumption that she would never be part of a risky mission again worried her. She was involved with Adrian's work and she didn't want to give it up. Adrian needed her help. The Cause needed her help. She agonized over whether to trust her new husband. She abandoned all rational thought when Logan moved to make her his own. Eden surrendered herself to his passionate mastery.

Their joining was fierce and powerful, and they reached the heights of pleasure quickly before collapsing, sated, into each other's arms.

As Eden lay nestled against Logan, the memory of his sermon returned again.

The truth shall set you free.

Silently she argued with herself that it would be all right to tell Logan about her involvement with Adrian. Logan was a minister, and he obviously had Southern sympathies, for he had come to the Haven specifically to help the orphans of fallen Confederate soldiers. Logan had saved her from the attack by the Union soldiers, and he had married her to protect her reputation. He had proven himself to be a wonderful man, and there was no reason not to be honest with him. She would swear him to secrecy and confide the truth to him so he would understand how she was trying to help the Cause—and her father and brother—in her own way.

"Logan," she began quietly. "There's something I need to talk to you about."

"You sound so serious."

"I am," Eden said, shifting away from him so she could think more clearly. There was something about being close to him that distracted her.

"What is it?" he asked, surprised by the sudden change in her mood.

"Well, I keep thinking about the sermon you

gave at church and how you believe telling the truth is always best. That's why I think it's important I start off our marriage by being completely honest with you."

"About what?"

"Can I trust you, Logan? Really trust you?"

"I am your husband. You can trust me," he lied.

"I was hoping you'd say that. Now that we're married, there's something else I need to tell you. Something you need to know about me, because I want you to understand." She paused.

"Understand what?" he urged, not wanting her to change her mind.

Eden forged ahead. She hoped that by confiding in him she could possibly win his support. "You know I had help when I went after Layton and Moran."

"Yes." Logan waited. He held himself unnaturally still, willing his body not to betray the surge of excitement that coursed through him. Was there any chance Eden might have information to help him find his brother?

"Well, I'm involved with a group that is trying to help the Confederacy."

"You're working with spies?" Logan had never expected to find out the information he needed so easily. In a moment of cold detachment, he told himself that marrying her had been the right thing to do, for everything she was revealing to him confirmed what Sam and Jim had said. Her testimony would be the proof he needed to bring in Adrian. For now, he pushed aside the disturbing thought that followed: If he used her that way, she would have to be arrested, too, for her involvement.

"I'm trying to see this war ended. I hate all the killing and destruction," Eden told him earnestly. "Look at how the children are suffering—Mark and Paul and Connie and the others, and all because of the war."

"These are very dangerous times, and it's not a good idea for you to be involved." The news didn't sit well with him.

"I know these are dangerous times, and that's precisely why I'm involved." Eden had been afraid he would ask her not to participate in the resistance efforts anymore. "You are my husband, and I respect your wishes, but I can't stop trying to help. I can't quit as long as my father and brother are away fighting. I couldn't go to war with them, but I can help them here. And I will. It's the least I can do until the fighting is finished and they're back home safe and sound."

"But I don't want you putting yourself at risk this way." Logan found as he said it that he truly meant it.

"You don't have to worry. We're always careful."

"Who's always careful?"

"I'm not going to name names."

"Why not?"

"They trust me with their lives, but they don't

know you. It's not my place to reveal anyone else's identity."

Logan fell silent, for there was no point in pressing her any more right then. He didn't know what he would do if she was involved with the spies.

"You're not angry, are you?" Eden asked, his silence troubling her.

"No, I'm not angry, Eden," he answered slowly. "But you are my wife. I want you safe."

"None of us will be safe until this war is over."

"I know. I know." He hugged her close and silenced her with a kiss. She was absolutely right: danger and intrigue did surround them.

"Eden."

She awoke slowly to the sound of Logan saying her name. Opening her eyes, she found him already up and dressed, standing over the bed and gazing down at her.

"Good morning," she said in a sleep-husky voice.

"Yes, it is," he answered as he leaned down to kiss her. "But you might not want to linger in bed too long. I've already gone downstairs and ordered a bath to be brought up for you. The maids should be here shortly."

The thought of a nice hot bath brought her fully awake and made her smile. "Thank you."

Looping her arms around his neck, she drew him closer for a kiss. When she did, the blanket that had been covering her slipped down. Logan needed no further invitation as he sought that silken flesh with a knowing caress. The embrace would have turned into even more if the knock hadn't come at the door just then.

Eden suddenly realized her state of undress and flew from the bed to don her wrapper. Logan waited until she was discreetly clothed to admit the servants.

The maids scurried into the room with everything she'd need for a bath, and they left just as quickly.

Alone once more, Logan was tempted to finish what they'd started, but he knew the bathwater would cool while they were otherwise engaged, and she'd seemed so pleased with the idea of bathing that he wanted her to enjoy it fully.

"Turn your back, please," Eden said primly as she was ready to get into the tub.

Logan couldn't suppress a chuckle. "I've already seen you in many various states of undress, wife."

Eden actually blushed. All their intimate lovemaking had taken place at night. "But it's daylight now."

He gave her a rakish, knowing grin as he turned away. "I'll honor your delicate sensibilities."

He walked to the window to look out at the street below. It was a quiet morning, and that was good. He liked quiet days.

Logan heard a splash behind him and knew Eden had gotten into the tub. He was tempted to turn and watch her, but he controlled himself. Even so, he realized the mirror was close by and he could see the back of her as she bathed. He decided to enjoy the view. Eden had tied her hair up, and Logan watched her hungrily, admiring the graceful line of her neck and the soft curve of her shoulders.

Heat stirred within him.

Temptation lured him.

But he denied himself. He took pleasure in her pleasure, and found he was glad that he'd made her happy by ordering the bath.

"You could have given me no better wedding gift," Eden sighed as she rose from the tub. She quickly dried herself and dressed. She'd been completely unaware of his covert scrutiny.

"My pleasure," Logan told her, and he meant it. "Is it safe to turn around now?"

"Yes."

"Good." He faced her. "After we have breakfast, I want to take you shopping before we go back to the Haven."

"Shopping? What for?"

He smiled tenderly. "A wedding ring. You're my wife now. I want everyone to know it."

A thrill went through Eden at his possessive claim upon her, and her hope grew that she could win his love. She immediately worried about his finances. She knew ministers rarely made a lot of money, and he didn't even have a congregation here in New Orleans. "But can you afford to buy a ring right now?"

"Don't worry. I have enough money put aside to buy you a ring," he assured her.

"Thank you." She gave him a quick, sweet kiss.

Logan cast one last, longing glance at the bed as they started from the room. He wanted to tear Eden's clothes off and lay her down on the bed and make love to her again right then, but he knew they had responsibilities. They were due back at the orphanage that morning. They could afford no delays. Logan knew, too, that if he did give into his impulsive desire, they might not make it to the Haven at all that day. He smiled as he imagined the eyebrows that would be raised if they did not show up for work.

"This one is perfect," Eden told Logan a short time later as she stared down at the elegantly simple gold band he'd slipped on her finger at the jewelers.

The ring was wide and had one heart engraved on it. She had deliberately not looked at the very expensive rings, for she didn't want to embarrass Logan. She'd fallen in love with this piece right away, and she was thrilled that it was a perfect fit.

Logan reveled in the happiness evident in her face as she gazed down at the band, and he turned to the merchant. "We'll take this one."

"Would you like me to put it in a box for you?"

"Oh, no," Eden spoke up quickly. "I'll wear

it." She smiled up at Logan. "Thank you. It's beautiful."

Logan paid the jeweler, and they left the store to return to the Haven.

Chapter Seventeen

"I think it's time I walked the grounds," Braden said as he sat in the shade with Danner and Taylor. The heat of the day was waning but the tree still offered welcome protection from the sun.

"Are you feeling that much better?" Taylor asked.

In the days since his fever had broken, the lieutenant had regained some strength, but Taylor was still concerned that his wound might re-open.

"Yes," Braden answered almost angrily. "I can't stand to just sit here anymore. The sooner I start moving, the sooner we can figure a way out of here." Braden's frustration was great. He was a man of action, and it galled him to be helpless before his captors. "What do you say, Taylor? Don't you think it's time we started planning a way to escape?"

"It's past time, as far as I'm concerned," Taylor responded. "But you still ain't completely healed yet, Lieutenant. So don't go getting too frisky on me. I'd hate to have to start nursing you again."

"I'd hate for you to have to nurse me again, too," Braden growled. "That's not in my plans."

"So you've already got a plan, Lieutenant?" Danner was instantly alert. He was loyal to Lieutenant Matthews and would follow him anywhere.

"Not yet, but I will have real soon." Braden had been watching and keeping track of the guards' activities. The long days in the makeshift prison camp were taking their toll on all of them. There was little in the way of food, and Braden knew that if they waited too much longer, they might not have the strength to get away. "Let's take that walk."

Braden struggled to get to his feet.

Danner was there to help him with a steadying arm. "Are you sure you're ready to try this?"

"There's no time like the present," he told him, his jaw locked against the weakness and pain that swept over him. He was determined not to give in to it. The only way to rebuild his strength was to start getting some exercise and pushing himself to the limit.

The three of them moved slowly out to circle

the grounds. Taylor and Danner matched their pace to Braden's.

The guards kept watch over them, their guns in hand. They were surprised to see that the Yankee lieutenant was still alive. They'd thought he was a dead man for sure when he'd first been brought into camp.

"Is this the usual number of guards for this time of day?" Braden asked.

"Yes," Danner replied. "Near as I can tell, there are six total, and they're all heavily armed."

Braden slanted him a pained grin as his physical exertion began to take its toll. "Think they're expecting us to give them trouble?"

"It looks that way, sir."

"Think we should oblige them, Taylor?"

"I'm looking forward to it." The youth grinned back at him. He was relieved that the lieutenant was feeling good enough to make a joke.

Braden only nodded as pain wracked him again. They trudged on, slowing their pace, yet taking careful note of all the surroundings and the location of the guards. They were almost back to their shaded spot when Braden stumbled.

Taylor was beside him instantly when he grew unsteady, offering a supportive arm around his waist and a shoulder for him to lean on.

It angered Braden that he was still weak, but he accepted the help and leaned heavily on the youth for a moment until he managed to right himself again. It was that simple contact that startled Braden. He looked down at Taylor and scowled, for he had just discovered how skinny the boy was beneath his baggy clothes. There was nothing to him. Taylor was only skin-and-bones and felt downright fragile to Braden. He worried over Taylor's physical condition. If any kind of fever took the camp, and that happened regularly in this climate, the boy wouldn't have enough strength to fight it off.

"You need to eat more," Braden ordered sternly.

"I would if I could, but there ain't a whole lot to eat around here, Lieutenant," Taylor came back at him easily. Though the truth was, Taylor had deliberately been doing without to slip extra portions to the lieutenant and help build up his strength.

They finally reached the shade again.

Braden all but collapsed on the hard ground. He was exhausted from the effort, but already creating an escape plan in his mind. His weak reaction to the little exercise they'd done irritated him, but he wasn't going to let that stop him. As soon as he was strong enough, they would make a run for it. It was his fault that he and Danner had been taken captive, and he planned to make up for it. Braden was still angry with himself for not anticipating the raid on the steamer. He would never let the Rebs catch him unaware again. He just hoped it wasn't too late to redeem himself.

When the time came for the evening meal, the guards brought up a pot of something that was supposed to be stew, but it looked and tasted more like slop to the prisoners. Still, they had no alternative. It was this or starve, so they took as big a portion as they were allowed.

Taylor waited in line, hating the close contact with their captors. The farther away they stayed, the better.

"Hey, you!" a sharp voice rang out.

Taylor ignored it. The guards shouted all the time, so there was no reason to respond.

"I'm talking to you!"

A strong hand grabbed Taylor by the shoulder and jerked the youth forcefully around.

"I was talking to you, Yankee. Pay attention."

Taylor stood silently, glaring up at the tall, mean-looking man.

"I want your chain," the guard demanded, his hold on Taylor's shoulder bruising. He'd seen the glint of gold around the young soldier's neck and wondered how he'd missed seeing it before. Any captive's personal possessions were fair game as far as he was concerned, and a gold chain could bring a pretty penny.

Taylor deliberately slumped a little, trying to keep the chain hidden. "I ain't got no chain, Reb."

"Look, boy, you can give it to me or I can take it. It don't matter. Either way, it's mine, so you might as well just hand it over and save yourself the fight," he sneered, looming over him. The guard was surprised at the defiance the youth was showing, but that didn't matter. In the end, he was going to have what he sought from him anyway.

"I told you, Reb, I ain't—" Taylor never got to finish the sentence.

The guard grabbed Taylor by the shirt front and jerked him forcefully toward him. His rough treatment tore the shirt and revealed not only the chain the youth had hoped to hide, but tight bandages wrapped around his chest. The ham-fisted guard snatched the chain, breaking it as he tore it off. Then he threw Taylor bodily to the ground. The youth lay there stunned for a moment, a look of terror passing over his face.

"You ain't got no chain, huh?" The guard laughed at him as he examined the fine chain and crucifix. "You miserable, lying, little bastard!"

"Give it back!" Taylor demanded in fury, struggling to stand up, ready and willing to fight the bigger man to get the precious chain.

The guard just chuckled and planted a filthy booted foot in the middle of Taylor's chest. Fight as the youth might, the guard's weight was too great.

"Shut up or I'll break a few more of your ribs," he threatened, increasing the pressure of his foot against the boy's bound chest.

Taylor was pinned to the ground, helpless.

"Let the boy up!" Braden commanded fiercely as he came to Taylor's aid.

The guard looked from Taylor to the outraged lieutenant and grinned coldly.

"You're lucky them ribs is all you got broke, boy," he snarled as he pocketed his stolen prize and walked away. He was quite satisfied with himself.

Braden hurried to Taylor's side, concerned.

"I didn't know you were already injured. Are you all right?" He held out a hand to help him up.

Taylor shrugged off his offer of help and stood unassisted, tying the torn shirt closed.

"I will be as soon as I can get my hands on a gun again," Taylor ground out, hating the greedy, sadistic guard who'd stolen the chain and cross.

"You're not the only one who feels that way," Braden sympathized. "Come on. Let's eat. We'll get your chain back before we get out of here, don't worry."

Taylor managed a tight smile at his words. "I intend to do just that."

They got their portions of food and went to sit down. They ate in silence.

Taylor concentrated on eating and fought not to reveal the overwhelming despair that threatened him. This was no time to give in to any weakness.

The rest of the day passed slowly. When darkness finally claimed the land, the prisoners sought what comfort they could in the shelter provided.

Taylor had been sharing Braden's small tent to keep watch over him as he recovered. They bedded down late, and both fell asleep quickly.

The nightmare overwhelmed Taylor.

The fear.

The terror.

The fury.

Visions of the savage battle that had claimed Taylor's brother's life and left Taylor alone in the world and a prisoner of war resurfaced.

In sleep, emotions long controlled were given free rein, unleashed by the cruelty of the guard's assault and theft. Grief and torment roiled through Taylor. Frustration fueled the youth's helplessness. With a cry of rage and grief, Taylor thrashed wildly around, fighting unseen enemies.

"No!"

Braden came instantly awake at the sound of Taylor's cry. He got up to go to the youth, worried that something was terribly wrong. He feared that he might have taken ill. It was dark in the tent, but there was just enough light for him to make out Taylor's tortured features.

"Taylor—wake up," Braden said in a low voice, not wanting to disturb any of the others in the surrounding tents.

Taylor tossed and turned, caught up in the power of the nightmare.

Since he didn't awaken, Braden feared he was feverish. He reached out to take him by the shoulders just as Taylor cried out.

"Charlie—"

It was a soft, mournful, pitiful cry, and the sound went through Braden like a knife in his heart.

"Wake up, you're having a nightmare," he said, touching Taylor's thin shoulder.

"What—?" Taylor sat up quickly, confused by the chaotic nightmare and startled by the lieutenant's touch.

Braden froze and stared down at Taylor. Tears were streaking down the boy's cheeks from the power of the dream, and the torn shirt had fallen open to reveal the bindings around Taylor's chest.

"Oh—Lieutenant—it's you—"

There was something about that voice.

Braden had a vague memory from when he'd been feverish of a soft and gentle voice talking to him. He'd been confused and had thought the voice was that of the woman on the steamer who'd helped him, but now he knew.

It had been Taylor.

The fearsome recognition came to Braden in a sudden shock of awareness as he stared down at Taylor's pale, tear-stained face in the moonlight.

"Dear God."

Taylor went still, realizing with apprehension that somehow, in that instant, the lieutenant knew the truth. He had discovered the secret. No one else had ever guessed, but Lieutenant Matthews had.

"Taylor—" Braden was frowning darkly now, his gaze unwavering upon that tear-ravaged visage. Anger was growing within him.

Was it really possible?

How could he have been so blind?

"What?" Taylor asked tentatively, clutching the shirt together and huddling away from the lieutenant's perceptive gaze.

"Who are you and how the hell did you end up here?" Braden growled in a low voice, not wanting anyone else to hear. He was furious, and he wanted answers.

"I'm Private Taylor, and I—"

"That's not what I mean, and you know it!" He was almost ready to swear.

Taylor had struggled to be strong for so long that she could no longer keep up the ruse. The horror of the nightmare coupled with the guard's attack were her undoing, and she allowed her tears to fall unheeded. She had been living in fear day in and day out. First, she had survived the horror of combat that had left her only living relative, her brother Charlie, dead, killed right before her eyes, and then she had suffered these weeks in this prison camp. With every breath she'd taken since her capture, she'd dreaded discovery. If the guards had learned of her secret, there would have been no telling what she would have suffered at their hands.

Taylor lifted her gaze to meet Braden's. She saw his anger, but she also saw his concern. She considered trying to bluff her way through, but knew the lieutenant was too smart for that.

"What do you want to know?" she asked in a shuddering, cautious whisper.

"Start with your first name," he demanded as he sat back, distancing himself so he wouldn't be intimidating.

"Miranda."

With her answer, his suspicion was confirmed. Taylor was no young boy. Taylor was a female in disguise, and a fine disguise it was. She'd certainly had him fooled all this time. "And who's this Charlie?"

"Charlie's my brother, but he's dead. They killed him." All the agony and torment she felt was mirrored in the depths of her gaze as she answered him.

Braden realized the pain Taylor was suffering. He wanted to offer her solace, but there was no way. His discovery about her true identity was serious, and he had to do everything in his power to make sure no one else learned the truth about her, not even Corporal Danner. He had to keep her secret.

"I'm sorry about your brother." He meant it.

"Thank you."

"But what are you doing here, dressed like a soldier?"

"I *am* a soldier," she replied hotly. "I cut my hair and disguised myself so I could enlist with my brother and fight with him."

"What about the rest of your family? Where are your parents? Surely they didn't approve."

"My pa died two years ago. Ma's been dead for quite a while. I had nowhere else to go, and we wanted to stay together. No one else ever figured it out. You're the only one."

"Was your pa really a doctor?"

Miranda nodded. "He was, and he was a good one, too."

"I know." Braden finally managed a half-smile as he thought of all that had happened to bring them to this point. "If he hadn't taught you well, I'd be dead right now."

Still terrified and unsure of what the lieutenant planned to do with her now that he knew her true identity, she asked, "What are you going to do?"

"About what?" He was deliberately evasive. He had heard that there were women going to war with their menfolk, but he'd never really believed that it happened until now.

"About me," she demanded, expecting the worst.

"Nothing, Private Taylor. The only thing I'm going to do is to try to get some sleep right now. I think we both could use some. It's been a real long day, and tomorrow doesn't look much better." Braden lay back on the pallet that was his bed, seeking what little comfort he could find there.

"But—" Miranda began. His reaction shocked

her. She didn't know what she'd expected him to do, but it wasn't this.

"Good night, Private. Your secret is safe with me."

"Thank you."

"Did the guard hurt you?" he asked, an edge of ferocity in his tone. He wouldn't be able to rest until he was sure she was all right and hadn't been crying because she'd been injured by the violence done to her.

"I'm sore, but it's not too bad."

"All right. Just make sure you figure out a way to fix your shirt by morning," Braden dictated. He didn't want anyone else discovering her secret. He would protect her hidden identity and try to keep her out of harm's way.

Chapter Eighteen

Eden and Logan passed a pleasant day at the Haven. Jenny and the children had planned a celebration for them, and the time went by quickly. That night, Francene prepared a special meal for the newly married couple, and they enjoyed a festive evening, in spite of Camille's bad mood. Eden and Logan returned to their hotel room for a few hours of privacy before he had to escort her back to the orphanage to spend the night.

"How soon would you like to move into our own place?" Logan asked as they made the drive to the Haven.

"As soon as possible," she told him, eagerly looking forward to having their own home.

"We can start looking tomorrow, if you want."

"That would be wonderful, but, Logan . . ."

He glanced over at her, curious, for she sounded so tentative. "What?"

"What are we going to live on? I have a little money saved, but not enough to support us for very long, and you don't have any regular income."

Her family had known hard times these last few years with the war causing so much turmoil, but somehow they'd always managed to make ends meet and keep food on the table. She'd never worried much about money before, but it had occurred to her during dinner that night that Logan didn't have a real job.

Logan smiled easily at her, wanting to calm her fears. "You don't have to worry. I have money put aside that will more than cover our expenses. And besides, the good Lord always provides for His own. Go ahead and find us a place to live. Everything will be fine."

Eden was delighted with the news. "Oh, good. I'll start checking to see what's available first thing tomorrow."

They reached the Haven, and Logan saw her safely inside before returning to the hotel. He was in a good mood as he unlocked the door to his room and stepped inside.

"Had some company tonight, did you?" Jim said from the chair where he was sitting in the darkened corner of the room. He had arrived earlier in the evening and had been waiting on the street, watching for Logan's return so he could speak with him. When he'd seen him enter the hotel with a beautiful woman on his arm, he'd known he'd better come back later. "She was quite a looker."

There was something about the smugness in his tone that irritated Logan.

"Yes, she is very beautiful—and she's my wife," he answered, lighting the lamp before he turned to face him.

"Your wife?" Jim's surprise was real. "I didn't know you'd brought your wife with you to New Orleans."

"I didn't. Eden and I—"

"Eden? Eden LeGrand who works at the orphanage?"

"Yes," he confirmed. "Eden and I were married yesterday."

"Yesterday?" Jim smiled knowingly, believing he understood Logan's motive in taking her as a wife. "Was this a marriage of love— or duty?"

Logan shot him a sharp glance at his question. "I'll have even greater access to Forrester now."

"I wouldn't doubt it. Good—very good," Jim pronounced, believing that Logan had only married the woman to get closer to the spy ring. His respect for him as an operative grew even more.

Logan knew what the other man was thinking, and he offered no argument to the contrary. "I'm glad you came here tonight. Eden spends her nights at the Haven whenever Forrester is away, but once he returns she and I will be together in the evenings, so we need to figure out a different way to meet."

"No problem. Have you heard anything new at the orphanage about Forrester or when he's due back in town?" Jim asked.

"No, nothing." Logan did not tell him any of what Eden had revealed to him about her spying activities. His divided loyalties bothered him, but he told himself he would deal with it when the time came. He wasn't lying to Jim, he was just withholding some information right now. That was all.

"There's a rumor that some kind of shipment is being smuggled in, but we're not sure if it's arms or something else," Jim told him.

"What else could it be?"

"Drugs—maybe morphine or quinine. It's hard to say. Just let us know if you hear anything—anything at all."

"I will. Will you be seeing Sam anytime soon?"

"Yes."

"Then give him the news about my situation. Things won't be as simple as they have been now that I've married, but with the hours that Eden is working at the Haven during the day, I should be able to get away and meet with you both if I learn anything important."

"I'll pass your information along."

When Jim had gone, disappearing into the night again, Logan went to bed. As he lay there, caught up in his thoughts, he found that he missed having Eden by his side. The realization surprised him. He had always considered himself a solitary man who'd never needed anybody. In this business, it was good to be a loner. With work as dangerous as his, it didn't pay to have any lasting ties. But now Eden was changing all that. He wasn't sure if the change was good or bad, but he was going to enjoy what time he had with her—*for as long as it lasted*.

Logan pushed that last, troubling thought away. He would live every day to the fullest where Eden was concerned, enjoying each moment with her as much as he could, but he would not let her distract him from his mission. As soon as Forrester returned, he expected to bring an end to the man's days of spying, and in the process find out where Braden was being held prisoner.

Betrayal.

The thought jarred him. He wondered if he would be betraying Eden or his duty. Logan wrestled with his conscience as he closed his eyes to seek sleep.

The following days passed quickly. Eden found a small apartment not too far from the Haven. It was partially furnished and clean, and that was all that mattered to them. Logan moved in right away.

Eden spent as much time with him there as she could. She had never thought she would be so eager for Adrian's return, but she could hardly wait. She wanted to be with Logan not only during the days, but during the nights as well.

Memories of Logan's sweet loving stayed with her, and there were moments during the day when she found herself daydreaming about him and wishing they could escape the Haven for a while and find some time alone. Eden never revealed her longings, but she did enjoy fantasizing about them. When Adrian returned, she and Logan would have plenty of time to make up for what they'd been missing—and she planned to do just that. That thought left Eden smiling as she turned back to her work.

Adrian didn't think he'd ever been so glad to see New Orleans as he was right now. It had been a difficult trip, but it was finally over. He found grim satisfaction in the thought as he watched the crew tie up the steamer and lower the walkways for the passengers to disembark. Soon, very soon . . .

After leaving the ship, Adrian waited for his trunk to be unloaded. Once that was done, he looked around to hire a carriage for the trip to the Haven. It was then that he saw the small group of Union soldiers coming his way. He tensed and pretended to ignore them.

"Adrian Forrester?" the officer leading the group asked as they stopped before him.

"Yes, I'm Adrian Forrester."

"I'm Captain Cory Berry, and I need you to come with us, please." His tone was cordial, but his hand resting on his sidearm left no doubt that he was serious.

Adrian was suitably shocked by his request. "Why? Is something wrong, Captain Berry?"

"There will be time for questions later, Mr. Forrester. Please follow us." The officer ordered his men to bring Adrian's belongings with them, and they moved off toward a warehouse nearby.

"What is the meaning of this?" Adrian demanded. He used his anger to disguise the fear that was eating at him. He had worked so hard on this mission. It couldn't end like this! Not now! "Why are you doing this?"

The officer didn't respond until he'd ushered him into a small office inside the warehouse.

"We have reason to believe that there is a smuggling operation going on. We're going to search your belongings for possible contraband. If we don't find anything, you will be free to go."

Adrian was furious, and he hoped it came across as outraged anger. "I have nothing to hide from you. Here's the key to my trunk." He handed him the key.

"I appreciate your cooperation. You won't mind if we search you, too, then will you?"

"Of course I mind! But there's nothing I can do about it. You're in charge, Captain Berry."

Captain Berry had Adrian empty his pockets, and he went through all his papers. Finding nothing incriminating on his person, the officer went with his men to open the trunk. They found only his clothing, personal belongings, and some toys.

After emptying the trunk completely, they examined the lining, but there were no secret compartments.

"I see you've brought toys back for the children at the orphanage," Captain Berry remarked, lifting one of the dolls and one of the balls to examine them.

"Yes, I always try to find something for the children when I'm away, so they'll know I was thinking about them," Adrian explained. "Are you finished checking everything? May I go now?"

The Yankee put the toys back. He was still eyeing him suspiciously, but he had no reason to hold him. Whoever had given them the information that Adrian Forrester might be a smuggler had been wrong, and the captain didn't like getting bad intelligence.

"Yes. You may go."

"Thank you." Adrian moved to repack his luggage.

The officer sent one of his men to get a carriage for him. A short time later, Adrian's trunk had been loaded up and he was finally on his way to the Haven.

Adrian's mood was black as he made the trip. Somehow, some way, the Yankees had found out about his operation. He was relieved that he had made it through their search this time without being found out, but that didn't mean their suspicions about him were over—not by a long shot. He would have to be even more careful in the future. He realized it would probably be wise to stop all his activities for a while, since they were getting this close to him.

It wasn't until he saw the Haven in the distance that Adrian finally allowed himself to relax a bit and let his guard down. It was good to be back. When the carriage came to a stop before the orphanage, Adrian climbed awkwardly down from the vehicle, his wooden leg making the descent difficult. He finally managed, though, and headed up the walk with the driver following, carrying his trunk. He unlocked the front door, and he and the driver went in.

Eden was just starting down the stairs when she saw Adrian come into the front hall.

"You're back!" Eden called out and hurried forward to welcome him. "Children! Mr. Adrian's back!"

Adrian looked up to see her coming toward him, and he couldn't help smiling. Eden had a way about her that always seemed to make the day a bit brighter.

"I take it you missed me?" Adrian asked.

"We all missed you!" she replied as the children came running down from the second floor, followed by Jenny, to welcome him home.

Adrian quickly paid the driver and directed him where to put the trunk in his private quarters. When the driver had gone, Adrian turned his attention to the children as they surrounded him in a loving rush. He spoke to each child, telling them how glad he was to be back. He noticed a new boy standing off away from the others, looking on.

"And just who do we have here?" Adrian asked, turning to Eden.

"This is Mark. He's just come to stay with us," Eden offered. "Mark, I'd like you to meet Mr. Adrian. He's the director of the Haven."

"Hello," Mark said a bit shyly.

"Hello, Mark," Adrian said, going to him and shaking his hand. "Welcome."

Jenny came to join them then, and after allowing everyone to visit for a moment, she ushered the boys and girls back upstairs to class.

Adrian and Eden were left alone together in the hallway.

"So everything ran smoothly while I was away?"

"There were a few problems," she replied, her tone more serious.

After what he'd just gone through in disembarking, he was instantly concerned. His gaze narrowed as he asked, "Did something happen here?"

"Yes, and I'll tell you all about it in a minute, but first, let's get you settled in. How was your trip?" Eden asked as she accompanied him into the office. She was eager to find out if everything had worked out the way he'd hoped.

"It all went very well," he told her. "Until I reached the riverfront today."

"What happened at the riverfront?" Eden saw

his expression darken now that they were in the privacy of the office.

Adrian waited to answer her until he'd closed the office door behind them.

"I was detained and searched by the Yankees. Luckily, nothing was discovered, but it was close." He drew a ragged breath as he went to sit at his desk. "Too close."

"But they didn't find anything," she repeated, breathing a sigh of relief as she sat down in the chair before him.

"No. The shipment is here, and it's safe," he told her in a low voice.

"That is wonderful!"

"All I have to do is see it forwarded on, and I'm going to take care of that right away."

Out in the hall, the sound of some of the children calling out excitedly interrupted Adrian.

"Reverend Logan! Reverend Logan! Guess what? Mr. Adrian finally got back!"

Adrian looked up at Eden. "Reverend Logan? Who is Reverend Logan?"

"He's my husband," she answered simply, expecting Adrian to be shocked by her words.

She was not disappointed.

Chapter Nineteen

Logan smiled as the children approached him in the hall, but there was nothing pleasant about the way he was feeling. Forrester had not seen him where he'd been working in the side yard when he'd arrived, so Logan had been able to follow him inside undetected. He had come to stand just outside the closed office door, so he could eavesdrop on Forrester's conversation with Eden, and things had just gotten interesting as Forrester had begun to speak about the shipment when the children came running up calling his name.

"I was detained and searched. Luckily, nothing was discovered, but it was close. Too close."

"But they didn't find anything."

"No. The shipment is here, and it's safe."

"That is wonderful!"

"All I have to do is see it forwarded on, and I'm going to take care of that right away."

Logan had missed the rest of what Adrian was saying, and he was frustrated.

"I know Mr. Adrian's back," Logan told the children. "That's why I came inside. I wanted to meet him."

Even as he spoke, the office door was thrown open and Adrian stood there. He was a big, tall man of imposing presence, and his blue-eyed gaze was coldly assessing upon Logan.

"Hello," Logan spoke up first. "I'm Reverend Logan."

"So I heard," Adrian bit out as he eyed him. Eden had married this man, true, but he didn't look like any minister Adrian had ever seen. Adrian thought he looked more like a common workman than a preacher, standing there in his shirtsleeves.

Eden came to Adrian's side, smiling up at Logan as she made the introductions. "Adrian, I'd like you to meet my husband, Logan Matthews. Logan, this is Adrian. He's finally returned to us."

"I saw the carriage pull up while I was outside working and thought it might be you. That's why I came in," Logan explained. "It's nice to meet you. I've heard a lot about you."

They shook hands.

"Come into the office with us, Reverend," the director of the orphanage invited. "Eden was just beginning to tell me everything that happened here last week. It sounds like I missed a lot—especially your wedding. Congratulations." Outwardly, Adrian made the effort to seem cordial, but he was not feeling very trusting toward anyone right now.

"Thank you."

As Adrian turned to lead the way back into the office, he got a good look at Eden's cheek for the first time and saw the faint shadow of the bruise there. He stopped to stare down at her. "Eden—what happened to your face?"

She touched her cheek self-consciously. The bruise had faded a lot over the last days, and she had been putting some powder on it to try to cover it even more. "That's part of what I have to tell you."

Adrian sat down at the desk while Eden and Logan took chairs before him.

"Now, what went on here while I was gone?" he asked intently, still trying to come to grips with the news of Eden's marriage and now the discovery of her injury.

"It's a long story," Eden began. She quickly recounted how the Union soldiers had invaded the Haven trying to get to Paul. "And that was when Logan showed up." She looked over at her husband. "Logan saved us that day. If it hadn't been for him, I don't know what would have happened to me and the children."

"Thank you, Reverend. It's a true blessing

that you arrived here when you did," Adrian told him.

"That it was," Eden said, and she quickly explained why Logan had been coming to the Haven in the first place—how he had raised money for them, and how he had rescued Mark from the streets.

"You heard about us in St. Louis?" Adrian was surprised.

"Oh, yes. The Homeless Haven Orphans' Asylum is a model for orphanages everywhere. The people in the congregations I visited to raise funds for you were most impressed with what you've accomplished here."

"Which congregations were those?" Adrian asked astutely, deliberately putting him on the spot.

Logan quickly named several churches and their pastors that he had checked on before coming to New Orleans. He was glad now that he'd done his research. Adrian had just proven he was not a stupid man. He was a more than worthy adversary.

"And your wedding?" Adrian asked, looking at Logan. "You must have swept Eden right off her feet to have convinced her to marry you so quickly."

"It was love at first sight for us," Eden spoke up. "He seemed like a guardian angel to me the way he threw those Yankees out of the Haven."

"Yes, it was love at first sight," Logan added. "Eden is wonderful. I was honored that she agreed to become my wife after only knowing me for such a short time."

Eden's heart soared at his declaration. He had never said he loved her before.

Adrian had never known Eden to be impulsive, but looking at her now as she gazed at her new husband, it was obvious that she honestly was in love with the man. That still didn't mean he trusted this preacher. He was going to do some checking into Reverend Matthews's background. Adrian's line of work demanded he be suspicious of everyone. And the stranger's arrival there seemed too convenient. Not to mention the fact that, considering what had happened on the riverfront earlier, Adrian wasn't about to take anyone's word for anything any more. There was too much at stake to trust him blindly, minister or not.

"It's wonderful that everything turned out as well as it did. I'm happy for you both. And since the building is still standing"—he changed the topic with a grin—"I take it the children didn't behave too badly while I was gone?"

"They've been wonderful, and very accepting of Mark, too. He's made his transition smoothly."

Adrian looked at Logan. "That was very kind of you to assist the boy that way."

"He's had a hard time of it, but with the right influences, I believe he'll be fine."

"You've been quite a help to us here, Reverend—"

"Please call me Logan."

"All right, Logan. Welcome to the Haven. We're delighted to have you with us."

"And I'm delighted to be here," Logan said, and he meant it. By Forrester's own statement, the shipment was there—somewhere close. All he had to do was find it.

Logan went back outside to finish the job he'd been working on. He was in a hurry to complete it so he could make a quick trip to the bank. He had to meet with Jim right away and let him know the latest information regarding the spy ring.

Eden and Adrian stayed in the office. Once he was sure that Logan had gone outdoors, Adrian closed the office door so he could speak to Eden privately.

"The fact that you're now married changes everything," he said sternly as he sat back down at the desk.

"It does? How?"

"You won't be helping us anymore."

"Why not?" Eden was truly surprised by his dictate.

"What would you tell your husband? Especially on those occasions when we have to make a move at night?"

"I've already told him that I—"

"You've already told him what?" Adrian demanded sharply, wondering suddenly if there was a connection between Logan's arrival there and his being detained coming off the steamer. "How much does he know?"

"Logan's a minister, for heaven's sake!" Eden protested. "He would never do anything to cause trouble. He came down to New Orleans to help us."

"Or so he says," Adrian countered. "What did you tell him? It's important. I need to know."

"Nothing, really," she hurried to assure him. "I just told Logan that I'm involved in trying to help the Cause. I didn't mention any names or details."

"You've told him too much already. He's your husband, and I'm glad you're happy, but that doesn't mean I want him involved in our plans. You're out."

Eden was growing angry because Adrian didn't trust her judgment where Logan was concerned. "You really don't want my help anymore?"

"There is no way you can be effective now that you're married. I'm sure you love him or you wouldn't have married him. But I don't know your husband, and it takes me more than five minutes to trust someone enough to involve them in a life-or-death situation."

She felt the sting of his words. She'd always trusted Adrian's judgment, but she knew he had to be wrong not to trust Logan. Logan was wonderful.

Adrian saw the change in Eden's expression. He hadn't set out to hurt her feelings, but he didn't have the luxury of being able to trust her instincts. Lives were at stake, and the circumstances surrounding the arrival of her "husband" struck Adrian as just a little too convenient not to be suspicious. If this Logan was so supportive of the Haven, he could have just sent the money. He didn't have to come in person. It all seemed a little too coincidental for Adrian.

"It's too dangerous right now," he continued. "Look at how I was stopped and searched coming off the steamer. The authorities may be on to us, so we have to be more careful than ever. After this shipment, there's only one last thing I have to do before we can quit and lay low for a while."

"Isn't there some way I can still help?"

"No. Our secrecy is everything. From now on, as far as you're concerned, we don't exist."

Eden returned to her work with the children, saddened. She realized Adrian was just being honest with her, but it bothered her that he didn't trust Logan. Logan had been nothing but a blessing to everyone at the Haven—and to her. He would never do anything to cause them harm. She was certain of that.

Eden argued with herself about whether to tell Logan that she would no longer be involved with spying. She knew he would rejoice at the news, for he had been insistent that she stop. Still, she held out hope that she might find some way to convince Adrian to let her work with him, even if only in small ways. Anything she could do to aid the Cause, she would.

Logan worked quickly to finish his job outside. His thoughts were on the shipment, and he was anxious to do what he could around the orphanage to help find it. If he couldn't locate it, though, he would have to leave it for Jim and Sam to do tonight. This was his and Eden's first night together in their new home, and there was no way he could come up with an excuse good enough to explain his absence from their marriage bed.

When his repair job was finished, Logan got cleaned up. He sought Eden out to let her know that he would be leaving the Haven for a while to run an errand and would meet her back there before it was time to quit for the day.

Logan made the trip to the bank.

"Well, Reverend Matthews, what can I do for you today?" Jim asked in a professional manner, playing his role to perfection.

"I wanted to speak with you about setting up an account."

"Fine, tell me what it is you need, and I'll do everything in my power to get it for you."

They pretended to be filling out paperwork as Logan told him what had transpired at the Haven.

"There's a shipment passing through town even as we speak. Adrian was searched on the riverfront as he disembarked, but nothing was found on him or in his possessions. I'll see what

I can do at the Haven, but I won't have access to his quarters."

"What about tonight? Can you get away?"

"Not without some kind of emergency, and if that happened, Eden would want to go along, too."

Jim nodded. "All right, we'll take it from here."

"What about your boss? Have you found out anything there?"

"He returned to town this afternoon, too."

They shared a knowing look.

"Good luck," Logan told him.

"Thank you for your business, Reverend Matthews."

"It's been a pleasure."

Logan was deep in thought as he headed back to the Haven. He was trying to figure out how Forrester was going to move the shipment. The trip passed quickly. He arrived at the Haven to find the children filing into the dining room, but there was no sign of Eden.

"Paul—Mark—have you seen Miss Eden?" he asked the boys.

"I saw her outside with Mr. Adrian a while ago," Paul told him.

"Thanks."

Logan went back out, looking for Eden. He circled the house and heard the sound of two voices coming from the flower garden, but he couldn't make out what they were saying. As he drew near, he heard Eden laughing, and he watched as she threw her arms around Adrian and hugged him.

A shaft of some foreign emotion stabbed at Logan at the sight of her in the other man's arms.

Eden was his wife!

Eden and Adrian were not aware of his presence as he looked on. Eden ended the embrace quickly and moved away from Adrian, still laughing at something he'd said. There had been nothing lewd or romantic about the hug, but the feeling that had rocked Logan was powerful. He remained where he was for a moment, coming to grips with his reaction.

Was he jealous?

The thought startled him, and he had to admit that it was true. He scowled, troubled by the dangers he faced where Eden was concerned. She was the enemy—yet he had fallen in love with her. The realization tormented him.

Only when he was certain he could play Reverend Logan Matthews convincingly did he venture forth to speak with them.

Chapter Twenty

Adrian was glad when Eden and Logan left for the night. He had a lot of work to do, and he didn't want to risk being interrupted. He watched and waited until the cook was busy serving the children their dinner; then he retrieved the empty milk bottles in a small wooden carton outside the back door and took them to his office with him. No one would ever miss them. He had planned this perfectly. Adrian locked the door behind him and drew the drapes.

His trunk had been stowed in his bedroom off the office, and Adrian went there now to get the precious shipment. With utmost care, he opened the trunk and took out the dolls. There were eight of them, one for each girl at the Haven. Adrian smiled. Each girl would have her own new doll, but not until he was finished with them.

Taking the dolls back to his desk, Adrian set to work. He gently pried the china head from a doll and carefully took out the small package that was hidden inside the doll's hollow body. His smile broadened. The Yankees had been so close to catching him, but he'd outwitted them. No one would have suspected that they would be smuggling morphine in children's toys. The idea was brilliant—and it had worked.

Adrian continued to work, carefully removing the stowed medicine from inside the dolls. He was glad that none of the pouches had torn. When he had emptied all the dolls, he stuffed the packets into the milk bottles and then put the heads back on the dolls so no one would suspect.

Adrian set the small case of milk bottles outside the back door again, making sure that no one saw him. When the milkman came by that evening, he would be able to find them easily, and just in case some Union soldiers were watching the house, nothing would be suspicious about the routine. A milkman did come to the Haven every night. Tonight, though, it was going to be a different milkman. No one would know that except Adrian.

Returning to his office, he got the dolls for the girls and the balls for the boys and made his way to the dining room to present them to the children. They were thrilled with the unexpected gifts, and they all hugged him with loving devotion.

Little Connie had never had her very own doll before. She clutched it to her lovingly as she gazed up at Adrian.

"Thank you, Mr. Forrester," she told him, her eyes filled with joy.

Adrian knelt down beside her and gave her a hug. "You're welcome, Connie. I hope you like her."

"Oh, I more than like her," she said solemnly. "I love her."

Adrian stood and, satisfied that everything was fine at the Haven that night, he went into the kitchen to get his dinner. While he was eating at the table, he saw the milkman coming up the back walk. Their gazes met through the open kitchen window, but neither man spoke. The milkman simply did his job. He took the carton of empty bottles and got in his vehicle and disappeared.

No Yankees came out of hiding to try to stop him. All was quiet.

Adrian was relieved and delighted. He passed a very pleasant evening indeed.

Their apartment was small, but it didn't matter to Eden and Logan. They took great delight in their privacy.

Eden prepared dinner for them, and they sat together at the table enjoying the meal and each other's company.

"You're a good cook," Logan complimented her.

"You can thank my mother for that. She insisted Camille and I learn when we were very young."

"I'll be sure to do that. She did a fine job. I think I'll thank Adrian, too."

"For what?"

"For finally getting back in town, so I can have you all to myself tonight. I didn't like all the competition I was having for your affections."

"Paul and Mark?" she asked with a laugh.

"To name only two."

"Ah, but I'm jealous of you, too," she said with a knowing smile. "I know for certain that there's another woman who really owns your heart, Reverend."

"You never have to worry about me being unfaithful," he protested with a grin. But even as he was promising to be true to her, his conscience troubled him. Everything Eden believed about him was a lie.

"Oh?" Eden countered, enjoying the exchange. "This young lady is blond and beautiful, and I know she loves you, for she told me so herself."

Logan's smile broadened. "It's good to know that whoever she is, I won her over with my considerable charms."

"That you did, and Connie is not easily won over. But she's not the only one you've charmed," Eden said in a soft, alluring voice.

"There's someone else?" he asked, his gaze darkening as he looked at her across the table.

Eden was so beautiful. She was wearing her hair up tonight, and he longed to pull the pins from it and free the heavy, silken mane to his caress. The memory of her in Adrian's arms in the garden that afternoon returned, and again he felt the strong sting of jealousy.

She gave a throaty laugh as she teased, "Yes. My mother and my sister."

"They are two lovely ladies who are obviously very astute judges of character."

Eden grew serious as she realized how little she really knew about Logan. "Tell me about your family. You know about mine, but you've never said much about yours."

"There's not much to tell you, really. My parents are dead."

"Don't you have any brothers or sisters?" She was truly interested.

"I have one younger brother."

"What's his name?"

"Braden."

"Where is he now?"

"He's in the army somewhere in Louisiana, the last I heard from him, but it's been a while."

"I hope he's all right," she said innocently.

"So do I."

"I'll be glad when the war is over and everyone gets to come home to their families. I know my mother hasn't heard from my father or my brother for weeks and weeks. It's so hard for her, and for us, never knowing where they are—if they're safe—or even if they're still alive."

"I understand," Logan said, and he did, more than she would ever know. His concern for Braden was always with him, haunting him. He silently hoped that he was getting closer to finding a way to rescue him.

They were quiet for a moment.

"You never have told me how you came to be a minister," Eden said. "I think it's so wonderful that you have a calling to bring God to people. When did you know you wanted to preach?"

Logan had always known that this moment would come. He hated lying to Eden, but he supposed he was as prepared as he would ever be to elaborate on the deception already in place. "I wasn't as young as some ministers are when I realized my calling."

"But how did you know?"

"It suddenly seemed the most important thing in the world that I try to help others." *My brother*, he thought.

"But you could have taken any number of jobs if you just wanted to help people. I mean, you could have been a doctor or a lawyer—"

"It was more than that. I wanted to bring people the good news of freedom and salvation." Logan was certain Braden would have been thrilled with his freedom right then.

"That is so special. You're very blessed, you know."

Logan looked up at Eden. "I know."

Across the table, their gazes met. It was a quiet moment of revelation.

"I know I'm blessed to have you," he finished.

Her heart sang at his words. "You are?"

Logan rose and moved to stand by her. He reached down and drew her up to him. "I am."

His lips captured hers in a gentle, yet hungry kiss. His whole life with Eden was a lie. Everything she believed about him was untrue, and yet Logan knew one thing: he loved her. In this short amount of time, she had come to mean so much to him.

A vague and distant memory of the sermon he'd given tormented him.

And the truth shall set you free!

Logan knew the truth would completely destroy the happiness and joy they had found together. He pushed the thought away and deepened the kiss. He wanted to erase all the torment and worry from his soul for at least a little while as he lost himself in Eden's loving.

Eden gave a soft moan as he kissed her with a sudden, hungry desperation. The fierceness of his embrace surprised her even as it excited her. Any thoughts of Adrian's doubts about him vanished as she clung to him, looping her arms around his neck and offering herself to him fully.

This was Logan—her guardian angel.

He was her husband.

She loved him.

Caught up in the power of his need, Logan crushed her to him and held her to his heart. He broke off the kiss and told her in a husky voice, "I love you, Eden."

She gasped as she looked up at him. It was the first time he'd professed his love. She caressed his cheek and stood on tiptoe to press her lips to his in sweet surrender. "And I love you."

Logan gave a low growl as he swept her up in his arms and carried her to their bed.

They fell upon its softness together, their hands racing to help strip away the clothing that kept them apart. They wanted each other— needed each other.

As if in slow motion they began the mating dance. Kissing, touching, arousing. His hands traced patterns of fire upon her willing flesh, and his lips followed the trail he'd blazed. Eden arched against him in pure ecstasy, reveling in the excitement he stirred within her.

With eager caresses, they came together, man and woman, joining to become one. They moved wildly in love's age-old rhythm as the power of their passion drove them on. Pure rapture burst upon them, and they clung to one another, cherishing the thrill of their union.

Sated, they lay together, wrapped in each other's arms.

Eden was resting with her head on his chest, and she could hear the powerful, steady beat of his heart. *Logan loved her!* The knowledge filled her with joy.

"You're beautiful, you know that?" she told Logan, running a bold hand across the hard-muscled width of his chest. She caressed him possessively and then moved her hand teasingly lower, deliberately wanting to excite him.

"Men aren't beautiful," he protested, completely enjoying her daring. She had never been so forward with him before, and he wanted to encourage her to keep it up.

"Well, I think you are," she insisted. She rose up to press herself fully against him.

"I'm glad," Logan said before completely losing control of his desire.

They made love in furious delight, eagerly seeking to arouse and satisfy one another until ecstasy claimed them, and they collapsed together.

Logan savored the moment as he held Eden in his arms. He knew he would never have a love more perfect than what he shared with her right then. At the thought, all that he'd been trying to deny came back to him with a vengeance. He hadn't meant to fall in love with her. He realized that caring for her this way was his heaven right now, but it would soon become his hell—and there was no way for him to escape that ultimate fate.

Logan saw that Eden had fallen asleep, so he slipped out of bed and went to stand at the window and stare out into the night. Somewhere out there, Jim and Sam were trying to locate and stop Adrian's smuggled shipment. He hoped they were successful, so he could give up this charade and go find Braden.

Turning away from the view of the city, Logan came to the bed and to his wife. Eden was beauty and honesty and gentleness. She was strong and determined and fierce in her devotions. Logan knew that when the truth finally came out she would despise him forever. He wished with all his heart that there was some other way to accomplish what he needed to do, but there wasn't. Everything was set in motion. It was only a matter of time.

Logan drew her to him. She stirred but didn't awaken, and he was glad. He wanted to treasure the serenity of the moment as she nestled against him. He wanted to cherish this memory and keep it in his heart, for he did not know where the future would lead him.

Adrian was up and out of the orphanage early the next morning. He arrived at the bank as they were opening and immediately went in to speak with Nathaniel Talbott in his private office.

"Good morning, Adrian," Nathaniel greeted him with a smile.

"Yes, it is, my friend," he agreed. "Everything went smoothly last night, I take it."

"Indeed it did."

"Good." Adrian was pleased and relieved to know that the morphine had been transported safely out of town. "There were a few moments when I was worried, but it's good to know that all went well."

"Yes, I heard about the difficulties you had upon arriving. That was dangerous."

"And that is why I've come to see you this

morning." Adrian leaned forward, deadly serious. "There's someone I don't quite trust, and I want to do a little checking into his background."

"Who?"

"The good Reverend Logan Matthews."

"Who's he?" Nathaniel had not heard of him before.

Adrian quickly told him about the minister.

"Has he done something in particular to arouse your suspicion?"

Adrian frowned. "No—not really. It's just a feeling I have that something about him isn't quite right. Can you make some inquiries for me and see what you can find out? From what I understand, he's from St. Louis."

"Of course, but it will take some time. Our communications aren't as fast or as reliable as they were."

"There's not a lot of time left, but whatever you can find out will help. As dangerous as things are getting to be, I want this to be our last job."

"I think you're smart there. It's a shame you can't stop now."

"The munitions shipment that is due to arrive in town this week, is big—really big. We'll destroy it in the warehouse. It won't help our troops directly, but it will keep the arms out of the Yankees' hands."

"Just let me know when and where, and I'll get the word out. And, if I hear anything at all about your Reverend Matthews, I'll let you know."

They shook hands and parted.

Adrian was as satisfied as he could be as he left the bank. He hoped Nathaniel could get him the information about Logan quickly, before they acted to destroy the warehouse holding the munitions. He wanted to make sure no one was going to interfere in their work.

Inside the bank, Jim had kept careful watch over the two men. He regretted that the door to his boss's office had been closed, but it was obvious that something exciting was either happening or about to happen. He and Sam had had no success last night in trying to stop whatever shipment Adrian was moving, and he wondered now what had gotten the man so excited that he'd shown up at the bank so early this morning. He hoped they found out soon.

Chapter Twenty-one

Logan heard nothing from Jim or Sam the following day, so he realized Adrian's shipment had made it through unscathed. Frustration ate at him. Logan was a man of action. He wanted to bring down the spies and find out what had happened to Braden. Being forced to bide his time was wearing on him.

Eden had made no further mention of helping the Cause. She was with him most of the day and definitely all of the nights, so he knew there were no activities going on—right then. He could only wonder how much longer it would be before things finally started to go his way.

As confident as Logan was that he could bring Adrian down, he also he knew what his actions would do to his relationship with Eden. Nothing she believed she knew about him was true. She thought him a man of God—he was her enemy, a Yankee. She thought he'd come to help the Haven—he'd come to destroy Adrian. She professed to love him, but Logan knew that when she learned the truth her love would be put to test. He wondered if it would be strong enough to endure.

The thought drove him from the Haven.

Logan went outside to walk in the garden for a while. He had just reached the side yard when he heard a child crying. Looking around, he found Connie sitting by herself on a bench, tears streaking down her face as she clutched something in her arms. He couldn't make out what she was holding, but he knew it had to be important to her for her to be so despondent.

"Connie? Are you all right?" he asked as he went to her.

She looked up at him, teary-eyed. "No."

"Can I help you?" She sounded so pitiful that he wanted to try to make things right for her.

"It's my new doll. Mr. Adrian just gave her to me yesterday, and I broke her." She sniffed loudly as she held her doll out for him to see. Its head was missing.

"What happened to it?"

"I was just playing with her, and it fell off. I didn't hit her or drop her or anything," Connie told him miserably. She had been very careful, for she'd never had such a beautiful doll before.

"Do you still have the head?"

She nodded.

"Want me to try to fix her for you?" Logan offered.

"Could you, Reverend Logan?" Suddenly the child brightened.

"I can try."

Logan sat on the bench next to her, and she gently lay the doll's head and body in his lap. He picked them up to examine how they fit together, and it was then he discovered they were both hollow. He frowned as he stared down at the doll, and in that instant, he realized what Adrian had done. He had used the dolls to smuggle in his contraband.

"Did everybody get a new doll, Connie?" Logan asked easily.

She nodded. "All the girls did, but not the boys. The boys only got balls to play with."

"They probably wouldn't have wanted a doll anyway."

Logan knew there were few things that would have fit inside dolls this size, and probably the most needed would have been drugs, possibly morphine. It all made sense now, and it was so simple.

"Is something wrong, Reverend Logan?" Connie asked, wondering why he was just sitting there staring at her doll.

"No, Connie, everything is fine. Just fine."

"Can you fix her?"

"I think so. What's her name?" He began to

work at fitting the doll's head back onto the body.

"Her name is Margaret."

"That's a pretty name. Why did you pick Margaret?"

"That was my mother's name."

Logan successfully reattached the head and handed the doll back to Connie.

"Thank you, Reverend Logan!" She beamed up at him and threw her arms around him to give him a big hug.

"You're welcome, Connie. You and Margaret have fun playing."

"We will," she told him with confidence, and she was almost dancing as she hurried back inside.

Logan watched her go, and he couldn't help smiling. Though all he'd seen in the years of the war had left him jaded, the innocence of the children still had the power to touch him.

"I thought I saw you come outside," Eden said as she came up the path toward him. "Were you here with another woman?" she teased, having passed Connie on her way inside.

"You caught me," he told her with a grin. "Her doll was broken, so I fixed it for her."

"It looks like you're not only my guardian angel but Connie's, too." Eden went to him and, knowing they were alone for a moment, she kissed him sweetly.

"My pleasure, ma'am," Logan replied.

They went back inside together, but Logan

was already planning to get away later in the day so he could reveal what he'd just discovered to Sam.

"There's another munitions shipment due in tomorrow," Sam told Logan as they met that afternoon.

"Then I'll keep an extra careful watch on Forrester's comings and goings. He seems to have a fondness for arms shipments—and for drugs."

Sam shook his head, annoyed that the morphine had gotten past them, but fully understanding the South's need to smuggle it in. Their field hospitals were desperate for it.

"That was smart, very smart. The guards would never have thought to search toys meant for orphans. They won't get past us again," Sam vowed. "This next arms shipment is a big one, and it's going to be stored right there in this warehouse." He nodded toward a building nearby.

"Will there be extra guards posted?"

Sam smiled confidently. "If Forrester and his men decide to show up, we'll be ready and waiting for them."

Forrester and his men—

Sam's words tore at Logan. If Eden was involved with Adrian's group, she would be caught in the middle of all the action. He wanted to keep her safe. He had to find out if and when Adrian was going to try anything, and he had to make sure Eden wasn't there. His divided loyalties ate at him.

"I'll let you know what I can find out," Logan promised as he left Sam.

Much later that night, Logan lay in bed with Eden in his arms. Fear for her safety threatened to consume him. He wanted to warn her about the danger she would face if she dared try anything with the group she'd told him about, but he knew he couldn't broach the subject. He had to maintain his silence or risk revealing his true identity.

Eden seemed to sense that something was troubling him, and she lifted a hand to caress his cheek. "What's wrong? You're so quiet tonight."

"Nothing's wrong. I guess I'm just tired," he lied, savoring her nearness and wondering how long their elysian ecstasy would last. Would it be weeks, or was their time together running out? Would it end in only a matter of days?

Eden gave a throaty chuckle. "I didn't notice you were too tired a little while ago."

They had come together in a passionate rush when they'd first retired for the night and he'd shown no hint of weariness then.

"You wore me out, woman," he said, trying not to give in to the need to smile at her.

"That's too bad. I was thinking about how handsome you looked when I found you in the garden this morning, and I was jealous that you'd been with another woman."

"You were jealous?"

"Extremely."

"I'm glad," he growled, drawing her down for a deep kiss.

It was a soul-searching exchange that was poignant and breathtaking, and it ignited the fire of their desire again. Logan knew that as long as there was life in his body he wouldn't be able to get enough of Eden. He made love to her with a desperation born of fear this time, taking her quickly and powerfully. Time was running out for them—but only he knew it.

Much later, Logan awoke in the middle of the night. He lay there staring into the darkness, haunted by what he knew was to come and by the knowledge that he couldn't stop it. Eden slumbered peacefully beside him, unaware of his turmoil.

"You made it," Steve said as Adrian finally joined him at a table in the back of the tavern on Gallatin Street.

"It isn't easy to get away some nights," Adrian said as he sat down next to him and ordered a whiskey from the bargirl.

They were silent as the girl served his drink, and she left them quickly when they showed no interest in purchasing anything else from her.

"From everything I've heard, it should be arriving tomorrow."

"Do you want to make our move tomorrow night?"

"Can you be ready?"

"We're ready now," Steve assured him. "This is going to be different than taking the *Bayou Belle*, but we'll handle everything just fine."

"Don't be too sure of yourselves. They may be watching for us, so we'll have to be extra careful."

"I heard you were searched when you got back from your last trip."

"They didn't find a thing," Adrian said with a cold smile.

"So maybe they aren't worried about you anymore."

"I'd like to think that, but if anything, I'm afraid it made them even more suspicious."

"Well, it won't take us long once we're sure the shipment has arrived. The hardest part will be getting inside the warehouse. Once we're in, it will take only a matter of minutes."

Adrian managed a tight smile. "I hope it goes as easily as you think it will."

Steve lifted his glass in salute. "I do, too."

They shared a look as they each took a deep drink.

"I'll send word to you through Nathaniel tomorrow if everything is to go as planned."

"We'll all be waiting to hear." Steve leaned back in his chair. "I can't wait to see the warehouse go up in flames."

They smiled at each other, confident that they would succeed.

*   *   *

Dawn found Logan already up and dressed. He had gotten little sleep that night and could see no reason to linger in bed. This promised to be a long day—a very long day. Eden was still asleep, so he took his Bible into the small kitchen and opened it to check on his gun. It was loaded and ready. His expression was serious as he closed the Bible. He sat there staring down at it for a time, his thoughts racing to the dangerous hours ahead. Somehow, some way he had to keep Eden safe. He knew what he had to do that night, and he prayed that everything would turn out all right.

"Good morning," Eden said from the doorway, smiling softly at him. She'd just awakened and had come to find him. He sat with his Bible closed before him on the table, looking thoughtful. "Were you praying? You look so serious."

"As a matter of fact, I was," Logan answered honestly.

"That's a nice way to start off your day."

He got up and went to kiss her, wanting to distract her from his Bible. "I can think of another way that's nice."

"Oh?" Eden asked archly.

"Want me to show you or tell you?"

"You could do both, just like I do with the children when we play 'show and tell,'" she told him, laughing in delight as he swept her up in his arms and carried her back to bed. "Speaking of the children—we do have to get to the Haven sometime this morning, you know."

He didn't bother to respond as he started to "show" her how to start her morning with a smile. He wondered, as he made her his own, if he'd ever get the chance to love her this way again.

Eden truly believed she'd found her heaven in his arms.

They made it to the Haven on time—just barely.

The day passed quickly. It was early afternoon when Logan left the Haven on the pretext of paying a visit to Reverend Miget. He did actually stop to see the minister for a while, just in case anyone checked on him; then he headed to an apothecary. He was about to enter the store when he saw Paul and Mark coming up the street.

"Where are you two heading?" Logan asked. It was a rare occurrence when the children were sent on errands without an adult accompanying them.

"Mr. Adrian needed us to go to the bank for him and then to the store to get some flour," Paul told him.

"Want some company?"

"Sure," Mark spoke up, always glad to have time with the minister. He had come to greatly admire Reverend Logan. He was certain the man had saved his life by finding him a safe place to live at the Haven.

"What do you have to do at the bank?" Logan

asked casually. "Anything I can help you with?"

"Just give this note to a Mr. Talbott," Paul answered.

"Well, I tell you what. Why don't I deliver that for you while you two get some candy at the store?"

They smiled at his conspiracy, but knew they shouldn't. "Mr. Adrian only gave us enough money for the flour."

"Here." Logan took a few coins from his pocket and handed them to the boys. "Just don't tell him I was spoiling you. I'll get in trouble."

"Thanks!" Mark was delighted. He hadn't had candy in ages.

"Here." Paul handed over the missive without a thought.

"Wait for me a minute. I have to get something here at the apothecary and then I'll be ready to go with you."

The two boys waited on the sidewalk while he went inside. He returned a short time later.

"All right, we can go now. Do you two want to run on ahead to the store, and I'll meet you there after I drop this off at the bank?"

"Sure."

"Was Mr. Talbott supposed to get the note?"

"That's right."

The boys darted off full of excitement. Logan watched them go, feeling a different kind of excitement as he stared down at the envelope he held in his hand. He couldn't be sure right then, but he had a feeling that his luck had just changed for the better. When the boys were out of sight, Logan moved into a quiet alleyway and carefully opened the envelope. He made sure that it didn't tear so he'd be able to seal it again without Talbott discovering that it had already been opened.

"*Midnight tonight.*"

That was all the message said. Logan smiled and returned the piece of paper to the envelope. Walking on to the bank, he found that Talbott was not at his desk. He delivered the missive to Jim to be passed along to the other man.

"Thanks, Reverend Matthews. I'll make sure Mr. Talbott gets this."

"I appreciate your help," Logan said as they shook hands. Then in a quiet voice for Jim only to hear, he advised him, "It's midnight tonight."

"Tell everyone at the Haven hello for us," Jim responded easily.

"I will."

Logan went on to meet the boys at the store, and they started back to the Haven together after Paul and Mark had eaten all their candy.

As they came up the walk, Logan happened to look up and saw Eden watching them from a second-floor window. She was so beautiful and innocent in so many ways. He paused to smile up at her. The smile cost him dearly, for he knew that within a matter of hours their lives were going to be changed forever. He was going to do everything in his power to keep her safe and out of trouble. He only hoped that when she finally learned the truth about him, she could understand his motives in deceiving her. He was tense as he followed the boys indoors, for he knew that, after today, nothing would ever be the same.

Eden had been passing by the window when she'd seen Logan outside with Paul and Mark. She had paused to watch them together, thinking how blessed they all were that the reverend had come into their lives. Logan was everything she'd ever dreamed of in a husband. He was honorable and kind, gentle, yet fiercely protective when he had to be. She couldn't imagine anyone more perfect for her than Logan.

When he had stopped to smile up at her, Eden's heartbeat had quickened and she remembered how wonderful their lovemaking had been that morning. She didn't know what the future held for them, but she was looking forward to spending the rest of her life loving him.

Chapter Twenty-two

Adrian had been watching, too, anticipating the boys' return. When he saw them coming back up the front walk with Reverend Logan, he grew instantly suspicious. It wasn't until later, though, that he managed to get Paul alone.

"Did everything go all right when you were running the errand today?" Adrian asked.

"Yes, sir. Everything went fine."

"Good, good. Where did you run into the reverend?"

"We met him when we were at the store, and he walked back with us," Paul told him, without lying. He wasn't about to reveal the candy the preacher had bought them.

"That was nice of him to walk back with you. Did he go to the bank with you, too?"

"No, sir," Paul answered, again not lying, for they hadn't been with him at the bank.

"Well, thanks for your help, Paul. I appreciate it." Adrian dismissed him then, relieved. He would have worried if Logan had been at the bank with the boys when they'd delivered the note to Talbott. Now, it was just a matter of a few hours. His excitement grew.

Paul left the office feeling quite pleased with himself that he had told the truth.

The hours passed far too quickly for Logan. Soon it was evening, and he and Eden were settled in at their apartment for the night. Eden was busy preparing their dinner while Logan poured them each a cup of coffee. With the utmost care, when she wasn't looking, he tore open the packet he'd purchased that day at the apothecary and poured the contents into her cup, then stirred it in until it had dissolved completely. Logan knew he should have felt guilty doing it, but at that moment he was only feeling relief. He had to make sure Eden didn't show up at the warehouse tonight. He had to know she was safe here in their home. He would protect her—even from herself.

"Delicious," he complimented her after they'd eaten and were relaxing over their coffee. He was watching carefully to make sure she drank it.

"Thank you," Eden sighed, taking a sip.

They lingered at the table for a while. Logan drank his coffee and got a refill, while Eden drank slowly, making hers last. Logan couldn't decide what was worse—anticipating the night to come or anxiously wanting her to drink the whole cup so she got the full dose of the sleeping compound he'd added to the brew.

"I think I'm ready to call it a night," Eden said wearily as she got up to pour out what was left of her coffee.

"You're that tired already?" he asked.

"I really am," she sighed.

Logan watched as she dumped out almost a third of her coffee and started toward the bedroom. He hoped the amount of the drug she'd imbibed would be powerful enough to keep her in a deep sleep long into the night.

Knowing he had to follow what had become their normal routine, Logan got ready for bed, too. He slipped under the covers beside her and gathered her near. Eden seemed as eager as ever to make love, and there was no way he could even consider denying himself.

Logan gathered her to him and worshiped at the altar of her body. Anguish filled him, for he knew this might be the last time she came to him fully and without reserve.

"I love you, Logan," Eden whispered in a sleep-husky voice as he moved over her to possess her fully.

He did not answer, but kissed her passionately in response, telling her by that intimate embrace what she meant to him. She welcomed him, opening to him, taking him deep within her and matching his rapturous rhythm.

Logan was lost in a haze of pure sensual pleasure. For that moment in time, he allowed himself to believe that there were just the two of them in a world all their own, a world where there was no war, no hatred, no Yankee or Rebel—there was only love.

United as one, they sought and crested the heights together. They clung to each other in ecstasy's delight as waves of excitement washed over them. They lay quietly together in the aftermath of their loving, neither speaking, merely savoring the glory that was theirs.

Logan did not move away from Eden. He wanted to make sure she was deeply asleep before he left her. He was to meet Jim, Sam, and the others who would be working with them that night at 10:30 on the levee near the warehouse. He could not risk waking Eden when he left, so he remained quietly in bed until he couldn't delay leaving any longer.

Moving carefully so as not to disturb her, Logan left the bed and dressed. He gently drew the blanket back up over her, then went to the table in the kitchen and sat down with pen and paper. He wrote a single sentence that he believed expressed everything she needed to know. He folded the note and left it on the table where she would find it easily. After getting his gun out of the Bible, he checked once again to make sure it was loaded and put it in his coat pocket, then closed the Bible.

He returned to the bedroom and leaned down to press a tender kiss to Eden's cheek. Relief swept through him when she didn't stir.

Without looking back, Logan left the apartment. This was the night he'd been waiting for. They were going to trap Adrian and his men, and then he would find out the location of the camp where Braden was being held. Filled with grim determination, he got his horse and rode for the meeting place on the riverfront. He hoped that by this time tomorrow he would be on his way to rescue Braden.

Shortly before midnight, Adrian met with Nathaniel, Steve, and the others as had been arranged. They made certain they had the supplies they needed to set the warehouse on fire; then they made their way to the riverfront. The men kept a careful watch as they went.

"If you see anything unusual, say the word, and we won't go in," Adrian warned them on the trek down.

A few blocks from the warehouse, they split up and circled the area to make sure all was quiet. They noticed nothing strange. There were no Union soldiers around, just the usual number of drunks, some passed out, some staggering, along the levee. There were dock workers still laboring in the night, too, but no sign that anyone was aware of their plan.

Adrian's confidence grew as he and Nathaniel closed in on the back of the warehouse. There were numerous windows there, and they forced one open. They were grateful when it made little noise. It was dark inside, so they believed the element of surprise was theirs. They planned to get in and out of the building before anyone had any idea of what was going on. The other men joined them there. Darrell was posted to keep watch at the end of the passageway, and Adrian was going to stand guard outside the window because of his leg.

"All right, let's set see what kind of fireworks we can set off tonight," Adrian encouraged them in a low voice.

Steve led the way as they climbed inside. They wanted to destroy the munitions and disappear undetected into the night.

Logan was hiding in the darkened recesses of the warehouse with Jim and the Union soldiers who were backing them up. The soldiers had supplied Logan with a sidearm, knowing his derringer wouldn't be enough protection if a fight broke out. They were waiting and watching from their vantage points as Adrian's men started to enter the building. Logan knew that Sam and several of their men were outside, lying in wait for the Rebs, so they had Adrian and his men effectively surrounded already. All they had to do was bring them in.

Logan and Jim shared a knowing look as the

men climbed in the back window. They silently signaled the Union captain. They were ready, and it was almost time.

Steve, Nathaniel, and the others crept inside the building. They knew they couldn't light any lamps, so they had to move carefully around in the dark as they prepared to sabotage the warehouse.

Logan knew that the moment they were all inside was the time to take action. They couldn't risk giving them the chance to plant any explosives or start any fires. He was angry that Adrian had remained outside, but knew the man wasn't going to get away from them tonight. Adrian's days of spying and sabotage were over.

They waited only moments longer before making their move. As soon as all the Rebs were inside, Logan called out.

"Stop where you are and drop your weapons! You are all under arrest!"

Shooting erupted instantly at his order.

Steve and Nathaniel fired in the direction of his voice as they all dove for cover. The soldiers hiding in the warehouse returned the fire, pinning them down.

Outside, Adrian heard the commotion and drew his gun, ready to go to their aid, but before he could climb in the window, one of the soldiers who'd been hiding nearby started to close in on him.

"Adrian! Look out!" Darrell shouted as he saw someone coming up behind Adrian. He'd heard the shots being fired and was running to help. He managed to get off a round at the man, but it went wide.

The man returned his fire. His aim was true, and Darrell was wounded and fell. The soldier had no time to go check on him; he had to stop Adrian.

Adrian realized to his horror that he had led his men into a trap. Swearing, he turned and got off several rounds in the direction of the Yankee as he shouted to his men inside, "Get out of here any way you can! It's a trap!"

The soldier dodged Adrian's shots and returned fire. Adrian screamed as one of the bullets hit him. He fell, his gun flying from his hand.

The fighting raged on inside the warehouse.

Nathaniel had scrambled away from the heaviest of the shooting, wanting to start a fire in the back of the building and provide his men with enough cover to escape. He was working to start the blaze when he felt the cold metal of a gun pressed against the back of his neck.

"Stop what you're doing right now," Jim ordered.

"Jim?" Nathaniel was completely shocked, and he went still. Adrian had suspected it was the minister who'd betrayed them, but all along it had been Nathaniel's own employee who'd been after them!

"That's right. Just back on away from what you were doing. It's over. There's not going to be any more trouble here tonight."

Nathaniel was furious, but he did as he was told. There was nothing else he could do. If he tried anything—anything at all—he would be a dead man.

Jim quickly searched him and took his gun.

"I'll see you in hell for this!" Nathaniel swore.

Jim smiled tightly but said nothing. The shooting had ceased, so he knew the fighting was at an end. He directed the banker back to the rear of the building. By the time they reached the area, the lamps had been lighted, and he could see that Logan and the others had everything under control.

"You *were* one of them! You bastard!" Nathaniel cursed when he saw Logan standing over the other members of their group who had already been disarmed and bound, hand and foot. Several of the men had been wounded.

Just as Nathaniel finished speaking, the door opened and Sam and a Union soldier came in half carrying and half dragging the wounded Adrian. The other soldiers who'd been hiding outside followed them.

When Logan saw they had Adrian, he rushed to help carry him.

"There was another one out there standing guard. I took a shot at him and thought I wounded him, but when I went looking for him he was gone," the soldier said as he and Sam laid Adrian on the floor.

Adrian was conscious, but bleeding from his wound. He looked up to see Logan come to stand over him. Hatred shone in his eyes as he glared up at him.

"I was right about you all along, *preacher-man*." He said the word with pure venom in his tone. "You were just using Eden. Does she know what a lying bastard you are?"

Logan felt the stab of his words but didn't respond. He looked at the captain. "Get these men out of here, and somebody go get a doctor for him."

The soldiers took over. A wagon was brought up, and Adrian, Nathaniel, Steve, and the others were loaded into it and taken off to be locked up under military guard. Several soldiers stayed behind to stand guard over the warehouse.

Logan, Jim, and Sam went looking for the missing Reb, but they could find no trace of him.

"Whoever he was, I don't think he'll be causing us much trouble anymore. Forrester and his men are finished," Jim said with satisfaction as they returned to the warehouse to check it over one last time. "Good job, Logan."

Logan was feeling some sense of satisfaction, too, but he was not finished. "I'm not through yet."

"What do you mean? We've just brought down Forrester's whole operation." Jim didn't know what more needed to be done.

"Now that we've got Forrester and Talbott, I need to have a personal talk with them."

"Why?" Sam asked.

Logan looked at the two men. "Because the

Union guard who was wounded and taken prisoner on the *Bayou Belle* was my brother. I'm no longer on assignment for Cotlar—my job for him is done. Now I'm working for myself. I want to find my brother and bring him back to New Orleans."

"God only knows where they could have taken him," Jim said.

"God—and Forrester and Talbott," Logan said grimly. "I intend to find out what I need to know from them tonight."

"Are you going after your brother alone?" Sam asked.

"Yes."

"You won't stand a chance by yourself. I'll go with you," Sam volunteered.

"Thanks, Sam." Logan truly appreciated his offer. He needed all the help he could get. "But first I've got to get the information out of one of them."

"Let's go to headquarters. They'll have them locked up there," Jim said.

They left soldiers in charge of the warehouse and headed off to confront the leaders of the spy ring.

Eden came awake in the darkness of the night. She was feeling strange, a little light-headed. She stretched, reaching out for Logan, wanting to touch him and feel the quiet strength of him beside her. When her hand touched only the sheets, she was startled by his absence. Eden told herself he'd probably just now gotten up from the bed and that was what had roused her.

"Logan," she called softly, wanting to draw him back to her side.

Silence was her answer.

Eden frowned, trying to make sense of her jumbled thoughts. Surely Logan had to be there somewhere. Maybe he just hadn't heard her.

"Logan?" She tried again, this time calling a little louder, but still she got no answer.

Slipping from the bed, Eden drew on her wrapper and made her way from the bedroom. She noticed she was a little dizzy, so she moved cautiously. After looking in the sitting room for him, Eden moved into the kitchen. She lit a lamp and turned it up so she could look around. It was then she saw the note on the table. She grabbed it up, fearful that something terrible had happened and he hadn't wanted to wake her to tell her about it.

> Eden—
> *Just know that, no matter what, I truly do love you.*
>
> *—Logan*

A chill ran down Eden's spine as she stared down at the note in her hand.

What did *"no matter what"* mean?

Struggling to concentrate, she looked around the room. She frowned as she saw Logan's Bible on one of the chairs. It was then she realized that something was wrong—very wrong. He would never have gone off without his Bible unless he'd been in a hurry.

Worry consumed Eden. She sank down in a chair, wondering where her husband had gone. She picked up his Bible and ran her hands lovingly over the leather binding. This Holy Book meant a lot to Logan. She'd never had a chance to look through it before, so she opened it, intending to read some scripture to calm her fears.

Eden gasped as she stared down at the book. The center of its pages had been cut out in a strange shape, leaving an opening that could be used for hiding something—

Like a gun.

A myriad of emotions stormed through her.

Had Adrian been right?

Horrible suspicions tore at her heart. Logan was a minister—wasn't he? He was a preacher who had come to the Haven to help the children. But if Logan was really a preacher, why would he need to carry a gun hidden inside his Bible?

She thought back over her time with him. Had she been fooled? Had he used her to his own ends? Had his declarations of love been lies? Where had he disappeared to in the middle of the night without a word?

Eden had to find out. She would go to the Haven. If Logan was there taking care of a crisis of some kind, she would know that her worries and fears about him were wrong. But if she got to the Haven and Logan wasn't there . . .

The possibility sent a shaft of pure pain through her heart.

Determined to learn the truth, Eden quickly dressed and left the apartment.

Chapter Twenty-three

"Where's Adrian Forrester?" Logan asked Captain Shawn Valint after he, Jim, and Sam arrived at the jail where the men had been taken and identified themselves.

"Forrester's been taken to the hospital."

"Is he under guard?" Logan did not trust Adrian, even wounded.

"Yes, and he will be the whole time he's there."

"Good. I have one request, I need to speak with Nathaniel Talbott alone, somewhere private."

"Yes, sir."

Captain Valint showed Logan into a small, windowless room off the main office. It was furnished with only a table and chairs. The Captain lit the lamp on the table, then left Logan alone while he went to get the prisoner.

Sam and Jim waited outside in the office. Captain Valint brought Talbott through, his hands tied before him. Talbott shot Jim a hate-filled look but didn't speak.

"Here you are, sir. I'll be right outside if you need anything," the captain told Logan.

"Thank you, Captain." Logan turned to the banker after the officer had left and closed the door behind him. "Please, have a seat."

Nathaniel considered refusing on principle, but went ahead and sat down. He didn't speak right away. He simply sat there watching Logan, wondering what he was up to. He realized what a fool he'd been to have been so completely deceived by Jim—and by Logan, too.

"I need your help," Logan began.

"Go to hell, *Reverend*," Nathaniel responded coldly.

"I need some information," Logan went on, undeterred by his attitude.

"Why don't you pray on it?"

"I don't have time to play games with you, Talbott. As I said, I need some information that I think you can provide. If you choose not to, well—prison camps aren't known for their comfort, and the guards aren't especially fond of spies." Logan noticed that the man's expression paled a bit at his unspoken threat.

"Who are you?" Nathaniel's gaze narrowed as he studied Logan.

"I'm an agent for the United States government. If you choose to cooperate with me, I'll see what I can do to help you."

Logan had deliberately chosen to approach the banker, for of all the men they'd taken captive, he was the one who would be most affected by serving time in prison.

"What can you do for me—and for the others?"

"That depends on what kind of information you give me," Logan stated flatly.

Nathaniel went silent for a moment, considering his options. He was furious that they'd been trapped and taken prisoner. Adrian had assured him that everything had been set. He'd believed that they would be able to pull off the raid on the warehouse as smoothly as they'd handled the *Bayou Belle*. But it was over now, and the failure was just as much his own fault as it was Adrian's. He had never suspected that Jim was there at the bank to spy on him. The future looked very bleak for him and for the others who'd been involved.

"What do you want to know?" Nathaniel felt safe enough asking, for he didn't believe he had information that could harm anyone else.

"The raid on the *Bayou Belle*," Logan began.

Nathaniel made certain to keep his expression unreadable as he listened.

"I want to know what happened to the two Union soldiers who were guarding the shipment. One of them was wounded during the encounter, and they were both taken prisoner. Where are they? Where did you take them?"

"What's it worth to you?" Talbott countered shrewdly.

"No, the question is, what is it worth to *you*?" Logan smiled thinly at him. There was no trace of warmth in his gaze. He felt no sympathy for this man or for any of the men working with him. "This is war, Talbott. Spies can be hanged for their offenses."

Nathaniel regarded Logan coldly. As much as he despised the man, he respected his intelligence. He hoped that if he revealed the location of the prison camp, Logan would find some way to help him and the others.

"There's a prison camp . . . It's small . . ." He went on to give Logan the location of the camp where, the last he'd heard, the two Union guards were being held.

Logan nodded, satisfied. "If what you've told me is true, when I get back, I'll do what I can for you."

Nathaniel wanted to protest, to argue that he needed some kind of payback or assurance now, but he had no power. There would be no negotiating. He said nothing as Logan went to open the door.

"Captain, I've finished with the prisoner," Logan called to Captain Valint.

Logan stood aside as Talbott was led away. Their gazes met, but neither man said anything more. When Talbott had gone, Logan went into the main office and looked at Jim and Sam.

"Did he know?" Jim asked.

"Yes."

They all shared a smile.

"And I'm leaving right away," Logan went on. "It's been too long already."

"I'm going with you," Sam spoke up. He looked at Jim. "Send word to Cotlar that I'm going to be off-duty for a while."

"Good idea," Jim agreed.

Logan couldn't believe that Sam wanted to help. He was grateful for his offer. "Thanks. I can certainly use your help."

Sam smiled at him. "I was wondering how you thought you were going to do it alone."

Jim spoke up. "I'll take care of everything here while you two are gone. Be careful. It won't be easy. And, Logan—"

Logan looked at him questioningly.

"I hope your brother's all right."

"So do I," he said, his tone serious. "Let's go, Sam. We've got a lot to do before we can head upriver."

"Logan—what about your wife?" Jim asked. "Don't you want to go—"

"No." Logan glanced at him, his expression carefully blank. "I left her a note. There's no point in going back tonight after all that's happened. I'll see her when we return."

"Do you want me to take her any kind of message?"

"No. She'll learn the truth soon enough." Logan's thoughts were bitter as he spoke, for he could well imagine what her reaction was going to be.

Jim said no more as Logan walked out. Sam followed after him.

Logan and Sam hurried to get the guns, clothes, and supplies they needed for their trip; then they were ready to head out.

When Eden reached the Haven, it worried her to find the building dark. If it was quiet, that meant Logan wasn't there. And if he wasn't at the Haven with the children, where had he gone? Her doubts and fears about him threatened to overwhelm her, so she pushed them aside.

Silently, Eden climbed down from her buggy and tied it up out front, then hurried inside. She had to go to Adrian and tell him that her husband had disappeared, and warn him about the deceptive Bible Logan had been carrying with him all this time. Shutting the door behind her, she went into the office and closed that door, too, for she did not want to disturb the children.

Eden knocked quietly on the door to Adrian's private quarters. She waited anxiously for him to respond, but she heard nothing from inside his room. She knocked again, this time calling his name in a low voice. Still, there was no answer. Desperate and worried, she tried to turn the doorknob and found that the door was unlocked. Brazenly she pushed it ajar.

"Adrian—it's Eden. I need to speak with you. It's important!"

Again there was no answer, so Eden boldly stepped into the bedroom ready to rouse him from his sleep. If someone found her there, she no longer cared. This was not the time for social sensitivities. This was an emergency. Walking into the darkened room, Eden went straight to the bedside where Adrian appeared to be asleep.

"Adrian—"

When he still didn't awaken, Eden reached out to touch his shoulder. She gasped at the discovery that all that lay under the covers were more covers, piled up to look like a sleeping man.

Adrian was gone! He was missing! Just like Logan!

Behind her, Eden heard what sounded like the office door opening and closing. She hurried from the bedroom, believing it was Adrian returning.

"Adrian—I was—" Eden began as she entered the office, but she stopped and stood staring across the darkened office in shock at the tall male figure staggering toward her. Even in the shadows she recognized Darrell immediately. "Darrell!"

"Eden—" He said in a weak, hoarse voice.

She rushed to his side and realized he'd been wounded. "Let's get you in here."

Eden put an arm around his waist and helped to support some of his weight as she guided him into Adrian's room. Darrell sat down heavily on the side of the bed with her help.

"What happened? How were you hurt?"

"They knew about us! They knew everything. They were waiting for us—"

"Who was waiting for you? Where? What was going on?" she demanded as she went to the bureau to light a lamp and then hurried back to see to his wound.

"Tonight—we were going to blow up the munitions in the warehouse, but the Yankees were already there." He grimaced as he leaned back to allow her to tend to the wound. "I was standing guard, and so was Adrian—"

"Where is Adrian?"

"I don't know. He was shot, too. I managed to get away and hide. They were looking for me, but they couldn't find me."

"Who were 'they'?"

Darrell looked up at her. Adrian had told the others working for the Cause all about how Eden had married the minister so quickly while he'd been away on his trip, and how he'd forbidden her to work with them anymore because of the minister. Darrell knew how terrible the truth was, yet he had to be the one to tell her. "It was your husband, Eden. It was the minister. He was one of them."

"Oh, God—no." She began to tremble as her worst fears became reality. "It can't be. Not Logan—"

"He was there. I saw him myself."

Fury raged through Eden as she realized what she'd done. By accepting Logan completely and without question, she had betrayed her friends. Logan had been such a wonderful actor, he'd fooled everyone—and she had proven to be the biggest fool of all! She had fallen in love with him!

Guilt followed her anger.

Adrian had been right. Everything he'd suspected about Logan had been true. And yet, Eden couldn't deny that the feelings she had for Logan were real.

Again Eden realized what a fool she'd been.

Logan had used her.

Their marriage was a sham.

Then Eden remembered the note Logan had left her.

Just know that, no matter what, I truly do love you.

Bitterness rose like bile in her throat, and she shoved all thoughts of her husband aside. There was only one thing that mattered right then. It was too late for her to save Adrian, but she could do everything in her power to see that Darrell made it to safety.

"Do you think you can travel anymore?" Eden asked as she continued to press the cloth against his wound, trying to stop the bleeding.

"Yes, if I have to," he answered with grim determination.

"Good. We have to get you out of here. If the Yankees are searching for you, this will be one of the first places they'll come, since they know about Adrian's involvement. Keep this on your wound, and I'll try to help you walk."

Slowly and unsteadily, Darrell got to his feet. Eden slipped an arm around his waist and together they moved carefully and silently out of Adrian's room, through the office, and out to the buggy. It wasn't easy, but Darrell managed to pull himself up into the vehicle. Eden rushed back to straighten everything up and then locked the Haven as she left. That done, she climbed in beside Darrell, and they rode away into the night.

Eden knew where she had to take Darrell. There was nowhere safer than her mother's home to hide him. Darrell had helped her in her hour of need; she could do no less for him.

"Where are we going?" he asked weakly.

"To my mother's house. You can stay there with my mother and sister."

"But I'll be putting them in danger," he protested, not wanting Eden or her family at risk because of him.

"Don't worry. It'll be fine, and you'll be safe. Save your strength. You're going to need it once we get to the house."

He fell silent as Eden drove them on. When at last they reached her home, she drove around to the back entrance, where there would be less chance of being seen. After tying up the horse, Eden went to help Darrell down. Supporting as much of his weight as she could, she guided him inside and helped him to sit down at the kitchen table. She lit a lamp, then started from the room to wake her mother and tell her what had happened.

"Wait here. I'll get help."

Darrell nodded and half smiled in spite of his pain. She didn't have to worry; there was no danger of him going anywhere.

Eden rushed upstairs to her mother. She slipped into her bedroom as quietly as she could, for she didn't want to wake Camille. The fewer people who knew Darrell was there, the better.

"Mother," she whispered going to stand by the bed.

Francene awoke instantly and sat up.

"Eden?" Seeing her daughter there, she immediately feared the worst. "What is it? What's wrong?"

Eden quickly told her everything she'd learned.

Francene got out of bed and took Eden in her arms to hold her for a moment. Until that second, Eden had not allowed herself to cry, but her tears fell unheeded as she clung to her mother for strength.

"It's all my fault. I loved Logan and I trusted him—"

Francene could offer no words of consolation. She just held her daughter close. She understood the power of Eden's pain. She, too, was heartbroken over the revelation, for she had thought the world of Logan and had truly believed he was a minister. The news of Adrian being injured and arrested with the rest of his men devastated her, too. These were terrible, terrible times.

Eden drew away after allowing herself the moment of weakness. "I have to take care of Darrell."

"I'll help you."

"Can we hide him here until he's healthy?"

"Of course." Francene was firm in her commitment to offer any aid she could. "Is he strong enough to reach the attic? He can stay there. No one will ever know."

"I think so, if we help him."

Francene donned her robe and followed her daughter from the bedroom.

Camille had heard the sound of a carriage drawing up outside her bedroom window and had looked out to see that it was Eden's. She'd wondered what her sister was doing there at that ungodly hour and realized it had to be important.

After putting on her wrapper and lighting a lamp to take with her, Camille had hurried out of her room. Her mother's bedroom door was closed, so she went downstairs. As she reached the front hall, she could see light coming from the kitchen. Camille assumed it was Eden, so she left her lamp on the hall table and hurried on to the kitchen.

"Eden? What are you doing here? It's so late—" Camille began as she entered the room.

Darrell had heard someone coming and instinctively reached for his gun. At first he'd thought it was probably Eden returning, but then he heard another woman's voice calling Eden's name, and he knew he was about to be found out. He still had enough energy to get up and try to hide. Pain wracked him. He managed to take a few steps toward the back door, but the woman appeared in the kitchen doorway before he could make his escape.

Camille stopped, startled by the sight of the tall stranger standing with his back to her, alone in the kitchen.

"Who are you?" Camille asked in a whisper. She was intrigued by his presence, for he had come in Eden's buggy, yet there was an edge of fear to her intrigue, for she could see no sign of her sister anywhere.

Darrell realized he was caught. There would be no running or hiding. He slowly turned back to answer the woman. It was then that he saw Camille for the first time. Darrell thought he must be dreaming or hallucinating, for before him stood the most beautiful woman he'd ever seen—and she was wearing only her nightgown and wrapper, and her body was silhouetted by the lamplight behind her.

"I'm—" Darrell began.

"Oh, my God!" The words were torn from Camille as she saw his blood-soaked shirt. Without another thought, she ran to his side. "Let me help you."

Camille didn't worry about the blood. She could see the pain etched in his face, and she only wanted to help him. Putting her arm around him, she supported him as they made their way back to the chair at the table.

"Did Eden bring you here?"

"Yes."

At that moment, Eden and Francene appeared in the doorway to find her hovering over the wounded man.

"Camille!" They were surprised by her presence. They'd thought she was still asleep.

"Mother, he's been shot!" she said, aghast. She looked at her sister. "What happened to him?"

"Darrell was trying to help some men blow up a Yankee warehouse tonight."

Camille gasped, shocked at the news. "How do you know about it?"

"That doesn't matter. Right now, all that's important is that we hide him and keep him safe from the authorities. We have to get him upstairs to the attic. Will you help us, Camille?" Eden asked, looking her sister straight in the eye. She and her mother had deliberately never involved her in any of their plans before, but there could be no more protecting her now.

Camille looked down at the wounded man, his features gray and grim, blood staining his clothing. She saw, for the first time up close, the true horror of the war, and she was deeply moved.

"Yes," Camille answered. "I'll help you. Let's move him."

Chapter Twenty-four

Dawn would be coming soon, and Camille and Francene were worried as they waited nervously in the kitchen for word of Darrell's condition. After they'd hidden him upstairs, Eden had rushed to the home of Dr. Craig Unger, a close friend of Adrian's who could be trusted completely. She'd convinced the physician to come to the house and treat Darrell. He'd returned with her, and they were upstairs with the young man now.

Once Camille and Francene had turned his care over to the good doctor, they'd returned to their own rooms to get dressed for the day. They'd been waiting impatiently in the kitchen ever since, hoping and praying that the news would be good and Darrell would make a full recovery. Francene had confided all that had happened that night on the riverfront, and the truth about Logan's cruel deception. Camille had been shocked and horrified, for she had believed in Logan, too.

They heard footsteps in the hall, and Camille hurried out to find Eden coming toward her.

"Is Darrell going to be all right?" she asked, her concern for him real.

"Dr. Unger got the bullet out," Eden told her as they walked into the kitchen to join their mother.

"That's wonderful," Francene said, having overheard their conversation.

"Is the doctor going to be much longer?" Camille cast a glance back toward the hallway. While the bullet might be out, that still didn't mean Darrell was going to be fine.

"I don't think so. He was putting the bandage on him when I came down."

"How serious is Darrell's condition?"

As Eden was about to answer, Dr. Unger appeared in the kitchen doorway. He had his bag with him and looked tired but satisfied as he went to the sink to wash up.

"Your young man's lost some blood and is weak, but if he stays quiet, rests for a few days, and gives himself time to heal, he should make a full recovery," the doctor explained.

"Thank heaven," Eden said, relieved and delighted with the news. Now all she had to do was keep Darrell safely hidden from the Yankees until it was time to sneak him out of town.

"And thank you, Dr. Unger," Camille added with heartfelt sincerity. She didn't know why Darrell had affected her so deeply, but she found she really was very worried about the man.

"How much do we owe you, Dr. Unger?" Francene asked. She didn't have a lot of money, but she would find a way to pay him whatever he asked.

"I expect no payment for my services tonight, ladies. You put yourselves at risk by bringing him into your home and nursing him. The least I can do is offer my help to you and to a fine, brave young man. I wish him well. If you find you need me for anything—if his condition worsens or he develops a fever, let me know immediately," Dr. Unger said.

"We will, Doctor," Francene promised. "And thank you again."

"I'm ready to go, if you can take me home now, Eden. It's going to be a long day for all of us," he said. "One of you ladies should stay with Darrell for the next twenty-four hours or so, just to make sure he doesn't think he's well enough to get up too soon. He needs all the bed rest he can get."

"We'll keep watch over him," Camille promised.

Eden left with the doctor, wanting to get him home before daylight, leaving Francene and Camille alone. They were glad that Sarah, their servant, had slept through everything in her quarters over the carriage house. They would tell her what had happened later, for they knew they could trust her implicitly.

"Let's go up and make sure he's resting quietly," Francene suggested.

They made their way back up the steps to the attic. The room was cramped, with one small window. Eden had hung a dark cloth over the window so no one outside would know there was any activity going on up there during the night. Francene and Camille entered the room to find Darrell lying with his eyes closed on the narrow cot they'd set up for him. The blanket was drawn up only to his waist. His shirt had been discarded, and his chest was wrapped in bandages. He looked very pale, and Camille clutched her mother's hand, suddenly fearing that his condition had worsened. When they saw the steady rise and fall of his chest, they realized he was sleeping.

Camille sighed in relief and stepped outside the room with her mother to talk for a moment. They spoke softly so they wouldn't disturb him.

"I'll stay with Darrell for now, Mama, if you want to go back to bed and try to get some sleep," Camille offered, seeing how exhausted her mother looked. It had been a long, traumatic night for all of them—from Darrell's unexpected arrival, to the horrible news about Logan's involvement, to the doctor's secret visit.

"I suppose it would be best if I did rest for at least a little while," Francene agreed. "Will you be all right up here alone?" She worried about her youngest daughter, for Camille had never been the most nurturing of souls. She usually recoiled from anyone's pain or suffering, preferring to ignore the ugliness of life.

"I'll be fine. If anything unusual happens with him, I'll come and get you immediately," she assured her mother, surprised at how calm and capable she suddenly felt.

"All right, darling. Thanks." Francene went downstairs to her bedroom to seek what ease she could.

Camille entered Darrell's room and closed the door. She sat down in a chair by the bedside to watch over him. As she did, she studied his features, visually tracing the lean strength of his jaw, the straight line of his nose, and the dark arch of his brows. He was not a classically handsome man, but she was drawn to him in some elemental way. She wondered if it had been the pain she'd seen mirrored in his eyes or the fierceness of his will to survive.

Camille sat back and tried to relax. There was nothing more she could do for him right now except maintain her vigil and pray he recovered fully. She would do both.

Eden took the doctor home and dropped him off just as dawn claimed the land. When he'd gone inside, she sat in the buggy for a long moment, trying to decide what to do next. Overnight, her marriage had been completely destroyed. The trust she had placed in her husband had been shattered, and her heart felt as though it, too, had been broken into a thousand pieces. Her life had become a living hell, and somehow she had to find a way to deal with all that had happened.

Eden's anger returned as she thought of Logan, and it gave her the strength she needed to act. She knew it couldn't be avoided, so she decided to return to the apartment right then and be done with it. Her plan was simple. She would collect all of her things and move into the Haven. Adrian would not be returning, so she had to find a way to continue to care for the children.

The possibility that she might find Logan at their apartment troubled Eden, but she girded herself for the possible confrontation. It was bound to happen some day, so she had to be ready for it. In truth, she hoped she didn't see him, for she wasn't sure how she would react. Her emotions were in complete turmoil. She hated her husband, yet she couldn't deny that a part of her still loved him—still cared about him.

Eden thought back over their relationship as she made the trip to the apartment. It was clear to her now why he'd been so concerned about marrying her to "save" her reputation. He had seen the marriage as an opportunity to get closer to Adrian, and he had. Their marriage on his part had been a sham from the beginning. The memory of his note slipped into her thoughts, but she pushed it away. Eden hoped and prayed as she made the trip to the apartment that Logan would not be there.

Eden's prayers were answered. The apartment was exactly as she'd left it. It didn't take her long to pack her clothes and gather her few belongings. She paused by the table where Logan's note lay next to the Bible, and her heart ached at the deception that had destroyed her life and her happiness.

Allowing herself a moment of sadness, Eden longed for the days when she'd believed Logan to be the wonderful, heroic reverend. He had saved her from harm. He had made love to her. He had married her. She had thought he cared about her, but he'd been acting the whole time. He'd been there to bring down Adrian, and for no other reason. Falling in love with her hadn't been a part of his plan, so she had simply been discarded as soon as she had become inconvenient for him.

For a moment, Eden considered taking his note and Bible with her. Then her anger took over again. She turned her back on both items and walked away. She did not look back as she locked the door and headed for the Haven. She didn't know where Logan was, and she didn't care. That part of her life was over.

Camille had been keeping watch over Darrell. When he began to stir restlessly and moan slightly in his sleep, she grew worried that his condition was worsening. She went to his side and reached out to touch his forehead, checking to see if he was running a fever.

At her touch, Darrell's eyes few open, and he reacted swiftly, reaching up to snare her wrist.

"Oh!" Camille gasped as she found herself staring down at him and fearing the momentary look of madness that shone in his eyes. "Darrell—you're awake—"

"Awake?" he muttered, frowning as he focused on who she was and where he was. When reality returned, he let his hand drop away from her, but not before he'd noticed how fragile she had felt to his touch.

"You've been sleeping since the doctor left," she explained, wanting to calm him.

Darrell tried to move, but pain savaged him.

"Don't," Camille ordered. "Dr. Unger said we were to keep you quiet and make sure you rested."

"But I have to get out of here," he insisted desperately. "The Yankees will be looking for me. I can't stay here."

"Oh, yes, you can, and you will," she dictated.

"But if they find me here . . ." He was worried about protecting Eden's family. They had been kind enough to help him, and he didn't want the fact that he was a fugitive to put them in danger.

"They won't find you. We'll keep you safe. Don't worry." She put a restraining hand on his shoulder.

Darrell nodded, wanting to believe her. He drew a ragged breath. The touch of her hand was calming, and because of it and the soft, soothing sound of her voice, he let himself relax.

"Thank you," he told her.

"Don't thank me. Thank Eden. She's the one who managed to get you here safely, and she's the one who convinced the doctor to come and take care of you."

"I will thank her when I see her again, but you're the one who's taken me in," he said. "I don't want to cause you any trouble."

"Mother and I are more than glad to help you. My father and brother are off fighting, and I'd like to think that someone would help them if they were in trouble."

He nodded and closed his eyes against the pain that was ravaging him again.

Camille returned to her chair. She would not leave Darrell alone, but would stay by his side until her mother came back.

Eden was not looking forward to the coming scene at the Haven. Somehow she was going to have to explain Adrian's absence—and Logan's. She considered telling the children the truth, but they had already suffered so much trauma and loss in their lives that she wanted to avoid it if she could.

"Miss Eden! Need some help?" Paul asked as he saw her coming through the front door with her arms full. He was on his way into the dining room for breakfast, but was more than willing to go to her aid.

"Yes, thanks, Paul."

"Come on, Mark."

The two boys went to help her, taking up her bundles.

"How come you're bringing all your things back?" Paul asked, curious. Mr. Adrian had returned, and when he did, Miss Eden always went home to live.

"I'm going to be staying with you for a while again," she answered him.

"Mr. Adrian's gone?"

"Yes, he had to leave last night," she offered.

"What about Reverend Logan? Is he coming here to live with you?"

"No. I'll be the only one staying, and, in fact, Reverend Logan was just called away, too. He might not be back for a while."

"That's all right," Paul told her with a big grin.

"Yeah, we like having you here best," Mark put in.

Her heart broke as she gazed down at the boys.

"It's nice to be wanted." She managed a smile for them, but it did not touch the sadness in her eyes. She was glad the boys were too young to notice.

"Have you got anything else you need us to bring in?"

"As a matter of fact, I do. Come on, we'll go get it together."

The three of them went outside to finish emptying out the buggy. It didn't take Eden long with the boys' help, and soon she had everything inside in her room. She made short order of stowing things away, then went to join the children for breakfast. She didn't feel much like eating, but she would make a show of it and then announce to everyone that Adrian had been called away.

As Eden entered the dining room, she wondered what kind of story she should tell them about Logan. She had no idea where he was, and no idea if, or when, she would ever seen him again. Tormented, she tried to keep up a smiling front for the children, but she knew that sometime that day she was going to have to confide in Jenny all that had happened.

The time came sooner than she'd hoped. They had just sat down to eat breakfast when someone knocked loudly at the Haven's front door.

"Excuse me, children. I'll be right back."

Eden went to see who was there, and she was shocked to find a Yankee officer and several soldiers standing on the porch. She stepped outside and closed the door behind her to keep the children from seeing them or hearing what they had to say.

"Good morning, ma'am," the officer spoke up. "I'm Major Anderson. These are my men. I'm here to inform you that Adrian Forrester has been arrested for spying, and we're here to make a complete search of the premises."

"Adrian was arrested? For spying?" Eden hoped she seemed truly shocked by his revelation. But beyond her acting, she knew true terror as she waited for him to arrest her, too. This man was a Yankee, and if Logan had revealed to him her part in working for the Cause, she would be arrested and taken away by these soldiers right now. It took every ounce of her self-control not to panic.

"Yes, ma'am. Last night Mr. Forrester and his men were caught in the act of trying to sabotage a warehouse of munitions near the riverfront. One of his men was wounded and managed to escape. We're here to conduct a search to see if we can find the fugitive."

"You think this fugitive might be hiding here? But this is an orphanage—" Eden protested.

"Yes, ma'am, but Adrian Forrester ran this place, did he not?" the major insisted.

"Yes—yes, Adrian does—did." She was suddenly tremendously relieved that she had made sure nothing had been left lying around to reveal Darrell's unexpected visit last night in Adrian's room.

"Then we're going to look around. If you'll excuse us?" The major started to move past her to open the door.

"Wait!" Eden said quickly, sounding as nervous as she was.

Major Anderson gave her a suspicious look.

"No—I have nothing to hide. I just want to let the children know that you're coming in, so they won't be frightened by your presence. You can come with me and listen to what I have to say if you don't believe me, but, please, Major, let me speak with the children before you begin your search."

"That will be fine," he agreed to her terms.

Eden led the way indoors. They went straight into the dining room.

"Children, we have visitors this morning." She introduced the major. "Major Anderson is here to take a look around the Haven. So, let's give him a warm welcome, shall we? Everyone. 'Good morning, Major Anderson.'"

The children greeted him with her. Eden watched them carefully to make sure no one looked frightened. She saw angry looks on the older boys' faces, but everyone else seemed calm.

"Thank you, Major. Can I be of any help to you?" Eden offered graciously.

"No." His answer was terse as he directed his men to begin.

Eden remained in the main hall watching and waiting to see what they were going to do. Jenny came to join her, looking more than a little nervous.

"What's going on?"

"Adrian's in trouble. I'll tell you more later when the Yankees are gone, but don't let on to the children that anything's wrong. I don't want to frighten them," Eden advised her.

It didn't take the major and his men long to go through the building, but they found nothing except her father's gun in the dresser drawer.

"Major Anderson, that gun is my personal

property. It belongs to my father, and I keep it with me here in case of an emergency," Eden told him.

The officer handed over the gun to Eden. "If you should see or hear from a man named Darrell Ankarlo, report him to us right away."

"I will, Major."

"Thank you for your cooperation, ma'am."

With that, the Yankees left, and Eden felt like collapsing into a heap on the floor. She'd never known she could be so tense.

A sense of relief swept through her. It seemed certain that Logan hadn't turned her in as a possible spy. Surely, if he had, the major would have arrested her and then searched her apartment and her mother's home as well.

Eden gave silent thanks that Logan had not betrayed her. Even as she thought kindly of him for a moment, the reality of all that had happened returned, and she angrily denied any kinder feelings for her husband. He meant nothing to her. What had existed between them was finished.

Pulling herself together, Eden returned to speak with the children. It was time to let them know that Adrian and Logan would be gone for a while.

Chapter Twenty-five

Adrian's expression was bleak as he and Nathaniel sat on their cots in the jail cell. He had been brought to the jail only a short time after being treated at the hospital.

"How are you feeling?" Nathaniel asked.

"It hurts like hell, but the doctor said it's not life-threatening." Adrian gave him a twisted smile. "Of course, the Yankees have been known to hang spies, so I guess that doesn't matter much."

"They're not going to hang us," Nathaniel said, sounding quite certain.

"How can you be so sure?"

"Because I talked to Logan. He said he'd help us."

"He said he'd help us? Why would he?"

Adrian was stunned, and instantly suspicious of any deal Logan might have offered Nathaniel. He knew firsthand that Logan couldn't be trusted.

"It turns out that the Union guard who was shot on the *Bayou Belle* was his brother. Logan's a government agent, and he came down here to find him. He said he would help us if I told him where the prison camp was."

Instant fury raged within Adrian at Nathaniel's betrayal of the Cause. He knew it was a good thing that he was too weak to act upon his anger, for had he been stronger, he would have physically attacked the banker. "You fool! What the hell were you thinking?"

"I was trying to save our lives!" Nathaniel insisted.

"You were trying to save *your* own life! Whose side are you on? You just sent that bastard off to kill more of our men!"

"Logan said—"

"I don't care what he said! He's a Yankee! He'd lie and tell you anything—promise you anything—just to get what he wanted out of you!"

"But—"

Adrian would not let him speak. "Look what he did at the Haven. He disguised himself as a minister and seduced Eden. And you made a deal with him—a deal with the devil—just to save yourself!" Adrian cursed him in disgust.

Nathaniel was angered by Adrian's attack and

countered, "What does it matter? Logan will probably be shot long before he can get anywhere near the camp."

Even as he said it to shut Adrian up, though, Nathaniel knew that he didn't want Logan dead. The man had promised him nothing for the information he'd given him until he returned from freeing his brother.

"I hope you're right, but don't count on it," Adrian snarled at him, his fury growing because there was nothing he could do to change anything. He was a prisoner himself now and helpless before the Yankees.

"Forrester, you have a visitor," the guard announced as he came into the cell area.

Adrian looked up to see Eden being ushered in. In spite of her strained expression, she looked lovely to him as she always did, and he was thrilled to see her. He'd been worrying about her, wondering if she'd heard the news and wondering, too, how she'd reacted to the discovery of her husband's true identity. Gathering his strength to stand, Adrian moved unsteadily to face Eden through the bars of his cell.

"Eden—"

She greeted him and Nathaniel and the others before addressing him solely.

"Adrian, how are you? A Major Anderson came to the Haven and told me you'd been arrested." She didn't add that she'd learned about his wound from Darrell. "But the major didn't say you'd been shot—"

"I'll be all right."

"Oh, Adrian. I'm sorry. So sorry." Her words were a hoarse whisper. Her misery was real.

Their gazes met, and Adrian could see from the pain reflected in her eyes that she had learned the truth about Logan.

"It wasn't your fault," he told her quietly so the guard who was still in the area couldn't overhear him. "There was another man involved, too. He was undercover, working at the bank."

Though Logan had been a part of it, Adrian knew that Eden had been an innocent in what had happened. Logan had used her, coldly and callously.

"I didn't know." She was shocked by his disclosure. "But what's going to happen to you—and to Nathaniel and Steve and the others?" She looked toward the men in the cells beyond his.

"We don't know yet. I'm sure that in time there will be a trial of sorts." He'd been trying not to think about the future—or his lack of one.

"How can I help you?" Eden asked, truly wanting to do something to save him. "What can I do?"

"Just take care of the children for me," Adrian told her. His expression was serious as he spoke. He wanted her to stay out of this. "Make sure they're safe and happy. What did you tell them this morning?"

Eden explained how she'd told everyone he was away on another trip.

"Good. They've suffered enough. They don't

need to know the truth of what is happening. What of Logan? Has he been back to the Haven yet?"

"No. I haven't seen him or heard from him since late last night. I don't know where he is."

Adrian could see how torn she was. "Remember, Eden, Logan used you. The only reason he came down here was to stop me and find out what happened to his brother—"

"His brother?" She was startled by his statement. "I didn't know his brother was involved in any of this."

"The guard on the *Bayou Belle*—the one who was shot. He was Logan's brother."

"Oh, my God." She paled at the news, remembering their conversation about the raid, and their later discussion in which he'd told her his brother was in the army somewhere in Louisiana and that he hadn't heard from him in a while. She saw now how carefully worded his statement had been. "Where is Logan now? Do you know where he's gone?"

"He probably left town to free his brother. Nathaniel told him where the prison camp was," he said harshly.

The thought that Logan would have left without talking to her tore at Eden, even as she told herself she was glad she hadn't seen him again.

"Protect yourself, Eden," Adrian cautioned. He cared deeply about her, and he could tell how devastated she was by all that had happened. He knew it was too late to change anything, but she must be prepared for the future.

Before she could say anything more, the guard interrupted them.

"Ma'am, it's time for you to go."

"Adrian, I'll come back and see you as often as I can," Eden promised, then asked, "Is there anything you need?"

He nodded. "I need you to let the children know I love them. That's all."

"I'll tell them."

Devastated, Eden left the jail. The responsibility of the Haven rested squarely on her shoulders now. Somehow she had to find a way to keep it running—to keep food on the table for the children. Too many lives depended on her. She couldn't let them down. She would do whatever she had to do to keep the orphanage going.

Eden started back to the Haven; then, haunted by what she'd just learned about Logan, she changed her mind. She switched directions and drove to the apartment. Reining in before the building, she sat there for a moment, arguing with herself about going in. She'd planned never to return to the home they'd shared, but a part of her desperately needed to know if Logan had left the city to search for his captured brother.

Girding herself, Eden got out of the buggy and went inside. It angered her that a part of her was hoping Logan would be there. She told herself that she was only going in because she needed to know what to tell the children about him. If

343

he didn't return to the Haven for days or weeks—or possibly never, now that she knew the truth about him—she had to have a believable story for the children.

Quietly Eden unlocked the apartment door and went in. She only had to step into the room to discover that Logan hadn't been there since she'd left. Nothing had been touched or changed. All of his personal belongings were still there. Both relieved and hurt by the knowledge that she'd meant so little to him, Eden left the apartment. She'd hoped to get away undeterred, but met the landlord on her way out.

"Hello, Mrs. Matthews. How are you today?" Ben Colvis greeted her in the hall.

"Busy," she told him with a smile, not wanting him to suspect anything might be wrong. "I'm going to be staying at the Haven for a while, and my husband was called out of town, so we won't be around for a few days."

"I'll keep an eye on everything for you."

"Thanks. I—we appreciate it."

With that, she left, certain she would never be back there again.

Eden longed to know how Darrell was doing, but didn't want to go to her mother's home just yet. The search by the Yankees that morning had left her nervous and edgy, and she didn't want to risk creating any suspicion where her mother and sister were concerned. She would return to her normal routine at the Haven when Adrian was away, and keep praying that somehow she would manage to make everything turn out all right.

It was during dinner that night that she stood up to announce that Logan had been called away. She had already spoken with Jenny, telling her everything that had happened, and they had agreed that the less the children knew about what had transpired, the better.

"Children, there is something I need to tell you." When she had all their attention, Eden began, "As you know, Mr. Adrian has had to make another trip, and he'll be away for a while. I told Mark and Paul earlier that Reverend Logan was called away, too, and I've just learned that he's going to be gone from us for some time, also."

"Oh, Miss Eden—not Reverend Logan," little Connie cried out in heartbreak.

"I know, Connie. I feel the same way, but he was called to move on, so he has."

"When's he coming back?" Paul asked.

"I don't know, but as soon as I hear from him, I'll tell you what he says."

"We'll miss him," Connie said sadly, knowing her days were going to be long and empty without Reverend Logan. She loved him.

Eden didn't mean to say it, but she did. "I know."

When they'd finished eating and the children had gone to bed, Eden left Jenny in charge while she made a trip to check on Darrell. Her fear that someone might be watching her kept her alert, but she saw nothing unusual around the

Haven or her mother's house. Only then did she begin to relax her guard a bit and believe that Darrell would truly be safe there.

"How is he?" Eden asked Camille once she was inside.

"He did manage to get some rest today. Mother and I have been taking turns sitting with him to make sure he didn't try to get up or anything. She's with him now," Camille told her.

"Good," Eden said, looking at her sister in gratitude. Camille seemed to have grown up a lot in the last twenty four hours. Her willingness and ability to help the fugitive cast her in a whole new light. Eden touched her arm. "Thank you for your help."

Camille smiled sadly at her. "You're welcome. I'm just sorry all this had to happen. And, Logan—the more I think about it, the angrier I get."

"I know." It was a flat statement.

"How could he have used you that way?" Camille was outraged for her sister, and deep in her heart she was thankful now that he hadn't been interested in her.

"I just found out today that the guard who was shot on the *Bayou Belle* was Logan's brother. Logan came down here wanting to stop Adrian and find out where they'd taken his brother prisoner."

"His brother was the man you helped on the steamer?" Camille repeated, startled by the revelation.

"Yes."

"No wonder he wanted to talk about the *Bayou Belle* that first night when he came to dinner. Do you think his brother is still alive?"

"I don't know, but for Logan's sake, I hope so."

"You do?"

"Yes." Eden found she really meant it.

They went upstairs to find Darrell awake, talking with their mother.

"Eden." He smiled in welcome.

"You are looking much better tonight." She was glad to see that he had some color in his face.

"I'm feeling much better, thanks to your mother and Camille. They've been taking very good care of me." He gave them a grateful look, his gaze lingering a moment longer on Camille. Then he asked, "Have you heard anything more about what happened at the warehouse or how Adrian is?"

"Yes. In fact, some Yankees showed up at the Haven this morning and searched the place looking for you."

"I'm sorry. I should never have come to the Haven and put you and the children in such danger."

"They would have come there anyway, since they knew about Adrian. Luckily, they didn't find anything. I've been watching for them the rest of the day, but they haven't been back. I think everything is fine. No one suspects anything about you being here."

347

"That's a relief. And how is Adrian?"

"He's going to recover." She told him about her visit to the jail to see him.

Darrell was glad to hear that Adrian would be all right.

"As soon as you're well enough to travel, we'll make arrangements to get you out of New Orleans."

"Thank you."

"It's the least I can do, after the way you helped me with Layton and Moran," she told him, deliberately trying to lighten their mood. "I'll come to see you as often as I can while you're here, but I have to get back to the Haven right now. I know I'm leaving you in good hands."

"I know you are, too. Your family is very special." He was grateful for all their kindness.

Eden left the room with her mother while Camille stayed on to keep Darrell company for a while.

"Who are Layton and Moran?" Camille asked him innocently, wondering what Eden had been talking about.

"Well . . ." Darrell hesitated for a moment, unsure whether he should tell her or not. Then he explained, "They were the Yankees who attacked Eden in the Haven."

"They were? What did you and Eden do to them?" This man was becoming more heroic to her with every passing minute, and all the things she was learning about her sister were surprising her.

Darrell told her what they'd done and was amused by her expression of pure astonishment.

"And you left them there, tied up that way?"

"We did."

"What happened to them?"

"The last I heard, they had been transferred out of the city. We haven't seen or heard anything about them since, and that's good, as far as I'm concerned."

"I hope they're out in the fighting now."

"So do I."

"I can't believe everything you're telling me about Eden. I knew she spent a lot of time at the Haven, but I had no idea she was involved in anything like all this."

"You should be proud of her. There aren't many women who could do the things she's done."

"I am proud of her," Camille said, and it was a bit of a revelation to her. She'd never realized just how much she loved her sister before.

"It's not going to be easy for Eden from now on. With Adrian gone, the orphanage will be all hers to run."

"And then there's Logan, too. I wonder if he'll ever come back."

"Logan was very good at what he did. He had to be, to fool Eden so completely."

"There's nothing 'good' about Logan Matthews! He's a Yankee, and I hate him!" she said with pure disgust. She had no idea what Eden was going to do about her unfortunate marriage to the vile man.

"I hope we'll never have to see him or deal with him again."

"That would be good. The farther Logan Matthews stays away from my sister, the better."

Darrell watched Camille as she was speaking. He saw the fire flashing in her eyes and knew she was every bit the woman her sister was—she just hadn't discovered it yet.

Darrell smiled to himself and wondered if he would be around when she did.

Chapter Twenty-six

"Taylor—"

The soldier's call from outside their tent in the middle of the night woke Taylor and Braden from a sound sleep.

"What is it?"

"It's Johnson. He's real sick," the soldier explained. "He's down with a fever. Can you come and take a look at him? You did such a good job on the lieutenant here, I thought you might be able to help him, too."

"Sure." Taylor didn't hesitate. Without another word, she left the tent and went with him to do what she could for the sick man.

They had no lanterns, but Johnson's tent was close enough to the campfire so Taylor had enough light to see. She was horrified by Johnson's condition. He was burning up with fever, and dysentery had ravaged his body. She knew how deadly the combination could be and she set to work, hoping to save his life.

Taylor fought for hours to bring down Johnson's fever, but had little success. His dysentery was so severe she feared it would ultimately kill him.

"How's he doing?" Braden asked, coming to check on her shortly after sunup. Since discovering the truth about her identity, he rarely let her out of his sight.

"Not good. Not good at all," she told him sadly as she glanced back at him over her shoulder without leaving the sick man's side.

"Is there anything I can do to help you?"

"No. He needs a real doctor. I think I'll go talk to the guards," Taylor told him as she came out of the tent, frustrated and worried. "I don't know if it will do any good, but I have to ask them. I can't just let him die."

"I'll go with you."

They started toward the main guardhouse. Taylor let her gaze wander over the camp and the prisoners as they went. She was looking forward to the day when Braden was healthy enough for them to try to escape. She hoped it would be soon, for this was a miserable, filthy place. Close to forty men were being held in the fenced area that wasn't even a full acre of ground. The guards had told them that they were to be sent back north in exchange for Southern prisoners, but they had not said when the trade would happen. So they suffered through little food and terrible sanitary conditions, living on the hope of one day going home. Some of the prisoners were forced to sleep in the open, for there weren't enough tents for everyone.

"I wonder if hell could be much worse than this," she remarked sadly, looking up at Braden.

"Not much," he agreed.

"Of all the places I thought I'd end up when I enlisted with my brother, I never thought it would be a prison camp somewhere in Louisiana."

"I don't think any of us planned to end up here. We just got lucky, I guess."

"If this is the kind of luck I've got, remind me never to gamble," Taylor came back at him.

"I'll do that, just as soon as we get out of here."

She nodded, then told Braden, "Wait here. I'll go talk to the guards alone."

Braden didn't like the idea of her approaching them by herself, but he knew she was right. The two of them together would look more like a threat. They had been ordered not to come within ten feet of the perimeter or risk being shot.

"Be careful."

"Don't worry. I will."

Squaring her shoulders, Taylor moved forward alone.

Braden couldn't believe what a brave woman she was. Taylor had suffered and endured so much, and yet she still wanted to do all she could to help the other prisoners. He knew he owed her a lot—even his life for the way she'd doctored him. He was feeling much better now and his strength was returning—slowly but steadily.

The guard came out of the building and without a word of warning fired at Taylor. The shot hit the ground in front of her, stopping her in her tracks.

"Keep your ass back there, Yank!" the guard snarled. He was tempted to go ahead and shoot the damned prisoner for daring to come that close to the guardhouse.

"I need to talk to you," Taylor called out to him. "It's important. One of the prisoners is very sick. He needs to see a doctor."

The guard came forward, sneering at the youth. "What are you? Stupid? You think there are doctors out here in the middle of nowhere?"

"He could be dying," she insisted.

He laughed cynically. "Good, then there will be one less Yankee bastard I have to worry about."

"You've got to do something!" she insisted. "You can't just let the man die!"

"The hell I can't. Watch me."

"Where's the captain?" Taylor demanded, starting past him toward the guardhouse. A man's life was at stake. She couldn't give up, and she wanted to speak with his commanding officer.

The guard grabbed Taylor forcefully by the

shoulder and shoved her away. "Get the hell back where you belong!"

Braden tensed as he watched the exchange between them.

"I'm going to speak to the captain!" she said defiantly, starting past him again. It was life or death for Johnson, and she would never be able to live with herself if she didn't do everything in her power to save him.

"Like hell you are!" He brought his gun to bear, ready to shoot. He felt no qualms about making an example of this youth. If the soldier dared to defy him, he'd die for it.

Braden was ready to go to Taylor's aid. Unarmed, he knew he'd be little help against the armed Reb, but he wouldn't stand by and let the young woman come to harm.

"What's going on, Private?" Captain Gibson came out of the guardhouse.

"This one's giving me trouble, Captain."

The officer eyed Taylor, seeing the anger and defiance in the prisoner's expression. "A little time in solitary might change his way of thinking."

"Yes, sir." The guard grinned. "It sure might!"

"But one of our men is dying!" Taylor argued, wanting to plead with the officer for help.

"Lock him up," the captain ordered, ignoring the protest.

"Don't!" Braden was furious, and he started forward, determined to help.

The captain drew his sidearm and turned on

him. "Stop right there or you're both dead."

Braden froze. He was furious in defeat and looked on in frustration as the guard roughly shoved Taylor toward the small, windowless building that served as solitary. Only a few men had been in there in the time he'd been at the prison, but from what they'd told him about it, it was a true hellhole.

Taylor fought against the Reb's bruising hold as he all but dragged her toward the building.

"Stop fighting or I'll shoot you right here," he threatened, tightening his grip.

She ceased struggling against him, knowing it was pointless, but anger raged within her. "You have to take care of the soldier—"

"Sure, I'll take care of him for you. I'll bury him once he's dead," he laughed as he shoved Taylor through the door and slammed it shut, then locked it securely.

Braden watched from afar, the captain's gun still trained on him. He turned his hate-filled glare on the officer.

"Why are you punishing Taylor for trying to help a dying man?" he demanded.

The captain looked him straight in the eye and smiled thinly. "This is war, Lieutenant. You would do well to remember that. Now, get back. With good behavior, we might let Private Taylor out in a day or two."

Braden backed away, hate for the officer exploding within him. He glanced once to the building where Taylor had been confined, then back at the two Rebs. Silently he vowed to find a way to rescue her and escape this place.

Logan and Sam traveled for more than a week. The first part of the journey upriver was by steamer, and then they headed west on horseback into Rebel territory.

Now that Logan knew where his brother was being held, he was like a man possessed. Nothing was going to stop him. He'd thought of Eden often during the trek, missing her, wondering how she was, and wondering, too, how she'd taken the news of his betrayal. He was certain she knew everything by now, and he was equally certain she despised him. He had considered going to see her before he and Sam left New Orleans, but had decided against it. He had left her the letter at the apartment. There had been nothing more to say. He would face Eden—and her anger—after he'd brought Braden to safety. For now, Logan wanted to concentrate only on the task at hand—freeing his wounded brother from prison.

Logan and Sam had continued on across the countryside. Though the danger had grown with every passing mile, their luck had held. They had not encountered any Southern troops. The few people they did meet, they passed themselves off as master and slave and were never questioned.

It was early in the afternoon of the eighth day when they finally located the prison camp. No one had seen them, so they were able to hide in the wooded area nearby and keep watch. They wanted to learn the routine of the guards so they could plan their rescue. There were only the two of them, so the attempt had to be timed perfectly or all would be lost. After everything Logan had been through to get to this moment, he wasn't about to fail. Braden was nearby. Logan knew it, and he was going to get him out. They maintained their surveillance in silence, readying themselves for the night to come.

"There! That's him! Thank God! Braden's alive!" Logan told Sam in an excited whisper when he saw Braden emerge from one of the tents. He could tell that his brother had lost a lot of weight and was moving slowly, but he was alive! That was all that mattered.

"Good," Sam said. "Now all we have to do is figure out how to break them out. It looks like there are six guards, and they're all heavily armed. How many prisoners do you think there are?"

"At least thirty, maybe more," Logan answered. "If we could find a way to lure the guards away from their posts, we might be able to capture them one by one without the others noticing right away. That would improve the odds."

Sam nodded. "The way the Yankees are stationed, especially by the guardhouse, it would be hard to get them all if we tried a frontal assault. They might start shooting the prisoners then and . . ."

They shared a knowing look. Whatever they

did, they would have to be accurate and deadly.

"Let's plan on going in late, when things are quiet. The more relaxed the guards are, the better our chances to surprise them."

They checked their weapons and sat back to wait. Logan tried to keep an eye on Braden so he would know where his brother was when the time for their attack came.

It was almost midnight when they made their move. They had planned it carefully and were ready. Circling to the back of the camp, they managed to surprise the guard posted there, jumping him from behind and knocking him unconscious. Logan took the guard's hat and coat; then they bound and gagged him. In his new disguise, Logan was able to approach the next guard without arousing suspicion. Only too late did that Reb realize he'd been tricked. Before he could call out a warning, Sam struck him from behind. They took both guards' weapons with them, and they stayed out of sight as best they could as they headed for the main guardhouse.

"We've got to do something and soon," Braden told Danner as they sat together before his tent.

"I'm ready whenever you are," Danner said, prepared to do whatever he had to do to escape.

"It would be a lot easier if Taylor wasn't in solitary."

"You're planning on taking him with us?" Danner was surprised.

"I can't leave him here." Braden's concern for

Taylor grew with each passing hour. It had been three days since she'd been locked away, and he wanted her safe with him.

Danner looked disapproving. "That is going to make it a lot harder for us. It's one thing for the two of us to try to sneak out. It's something else for us to try to break Taylor out and get away ourselves."

"We can do it." Braden was firm in his resolve. He wouldn't leave without Taylor. "We know when the guards are patrolling. We just have to plan things carefully. Watch out the back there. Any minute, Hawkins will be passing by. He's always on time."

They watched and waited. Hawkins paced regularly at the rear boundary, making sure no one escaped. They were surprised when, after a time, there was no sign of him.

"Where is he? I've never known him to be late. He's always there."

Braden was frowning. "I'm going to take a walk in his direction. The minute he sees me, he'll come out. Then we'll know what he's up to."

Braden got up and started toward the back of the camp. As he went, he caught sight of a slight, furtive movement out of the corner of his eye. He stopped and glanced that way into the cover of darkness, but could discern no one there. He moved on, suddenly wondering where Hawkins was. It wasn't like him not to be vigilant in his duty. He'd observed him every night, and the man was always there, keeping watch, guarding the prisoners, so there was little chance for them to escape undetected.

Braden almost made it to the back of the compound when shots rang out near the guardhouse. He turned and ran for cover, uncertain what was happening. He knew one thing for sure—it had to be good if someone was shooting at the Rebs.

A roar of excitement swept through the prison camp as Logan and Sam began their attack. Their first shots felled the two guards who were standing outside the guardhouse, but the two remaining guards were holed up inside. They began firing wildly from the windows of the small building, not caring if they hit the ambushers or the prisoners. The prisoners hit the ground as shots were exchanged. They didn't know who their saviors were, and they didn't care. They just wanted out of the prison.

Logan kept working his way closer to the guardhouse. When one of the guards showed himself in the window, Logan fired off a round. The guard's scream rent the night as a bullet found its mark.

"Give it up!" Logan shouted to the remaining guard. "You're the only one left. You keep fighting, you're a dead man!"

Silence reigned for a moment, and then the man threw his gun out the window. "I'm coming out!"

Logan and Sam grabbed the soldier the minute he came outside. They quickly tied his hands and gagged him, throwing him down on the ground where they could keep an eye on him.

"Logan!" Braden had heard the shouting and recognized his brother's voice instantly.

"Braden! You're alive!" Logan threw open the gate.

Braden rushed forward to greet him.

"I can't believe you're here!" he said as they hugged.

"It wasn't easy, but Sam and I made it." Logan introduced Braden to Sam.

"Thanks." Braden shook the other operative's hand.

"Let's get everyone out of here. I don't know how much time we have. Someone might have heard the shooting, so we'd better hurry," Logan told him.

"Danner! We're free! Tell the others!"

Danner hurried to round up all the prisoners, while Sam claimed two of the guards' horses. Braden started off away from Logan.

"Where are you going? We have to get out of here."

"Not yet—not without Taylor!"

"Without who?"

Braden didn't answer. He was already running toward the building where Taylor was confined.

"Split up! Travel in small groups," Logan ordered as the prisoners crowded around him. He took all the guns and ammunition from the guardhouse and passed them out to the men as they disappeared into the night; then he went after his brother. He had his gun in hand in case there might be more trouble.

"Taylor! Stand back!" Braden shouted as he stopped before the door to the shack where Taylor was being held.

With one violent kick, he broke down the barrier. He rushed inside to find Taylor cowering in a corner.

"It's all right! Come on! We're free!" Braden went to help her stand.

"What happened?"

"We've been rescued. Let's go."

He helped her to her feet, and they came out of the building just as Logan reached them.

"Taylor's been locked up in here for quite a while," Braden quickly explained. "Taylor, this is my brother, Logan."

She looked from Logan to Braden and even in the darkness of the night she could see the family resemblance. "You came for us?"

"I couldn't just leave you here," Logan told them. "Now, let's head out. There isn't a lot of time."

Sam was waiting for them with Danner by the horses.

"There's one more thing I've got to do," Braden said fiercely.

He went to the guard who was tied and gagged inside the guardhouse, the one who'd abused Taylor. When he emerged from the building a few minutes later, Braden approached Taylor.

"Here." He handed her the chain and cross.

She looked up at him, fighting desperately not to cry. "Thank you."

He only nodded; then they joined the others, mounting up. Braden insisted Taylor ride double with him.

Taylor was thrilled to be free again, but as they started to leave, she suddenly grabbed Braden's arm.

"Lieutenant, we can't leave without Johnson! Where is he? We can put him on one of the horses. He can ride double with someone," she told him, her exhilaration at being released suddenly tempered by concern for the sick soldier.

Braden looked down at Taylor, hating what he had to tell her. "I'm sorry, Taylor. Johnson died."

"When?" she asked in barely a whisper.

"The day after you were locked up," he answered solemnly.

She didn't say a word. Her heart was heavy as she mourned the loss of the young man who could have been saved. Together, they rode away from the horror of the prison camp.

Braden felt an overwhelming desire to comfort Taylor in her sorrow, but he knew he couldn't. Not here. Not now.

As they rode away into the night, Braden found himself wondering what he was going to do about Taylor. The thought troubled him. He had never cared about anyone this way before, but no matter what happened, he knew he would protect Taylor with his life—for she had certainly saved his.

Chapter Twenty-seven

There was much that Braden wanted to tell Logan, but no time to talk. They were in Rebel territory and needed to get back to New Orleans as quickly as they could. The next few days were going to be very dangerous—and possibly deadly if they weren't careful.

They rode away from the prison, racing through the long, dark hours of the night, trying to put as much distance between themselves and the camp as they could. Once the breakout was discovered, there would be an extensive search for them, so they had to get far away.

"How did you and Sam find us?" Braden asked Logan as they sat together in the predawn darkness after stopping to rest the horses.

"It wasn't easy," Logan answered. "We've

been working with another operative named Jim in New Orleans trying to bring down Adrian Forrester and his men. They're the ones who stole your arms shipment."

"Did you get them?" Braden asked anxiously.

"We got them," Sam affirmed.

"How did you do it?"

"Logan here makes one fine man of the cloth," Sam chuckled. "He had a whole lot of people fooled about his true calling."

"You were disguised as a minister?" Braden was surprised, although he knew he shouldn't have been. Logan was one of the best operatives the government had, and he'd just proven it again by breaking them out of prison.

"Forrester ran the Homeless Haven Orphans' Asylum in New Orleans. I needed a way to get to him and win his confidence. Becoming the 'Reverend' Matthews seemed the easiest. Very few people would suspect a minister of being an undercover agent, and I was able to pass through the lines without question."

"How did you finally trap him?"

"I was working at the Haven, and I intercepted a note from Forrester to his partner, Nathaniel Talbott. They were planning to blow up a munitions warehouse, so when the time for the attack came, we were ready for them—along with quite a few soldiers. We arrested them before they could do any damage."

"I'm impressed," Braden told them. "Those men were smart and dangerous."

"I was impressed with the way it turned out, too," Logan admitted. "Everything worked perfectly. After we had them locked up, I managed to convince Talbott that it would be in his best interest to tell me where they'd taken you. Once I'd learned the camp's location, Sam volunteered to come along. We managed to find our way to you without incident." He deliberately avoided speaking of Eden. He would tell his brother the tale of his marriage later—in private.

Danner looked at the men who'd saved them. "Sam—Logan—we can't thank you enough."

"I'm just glad we got you out of there safe," Logan said, his gaze meeting his brother's.

"Now all we have to do is make it back to New Orleans," Danner added.

"We will. We'll just keep going for as long as we can without making camp. The next few days are going to be hard ones," Logan said. "Now tell me what happened to you. How did they steal the shipment from you?"

Braden explained all that had happened on the boat, taking full responsibility for the loss. "I couldn't let them commandeer the guns without a fight, so I managed to work my hands free and went after one of their men. I almost had his gun, too, but then I was shot."

Braden's mention of being wounded brought unwanted thoughts of Eden to Logan. He'd been trying not to think of her these last few days, but she was always there, hovering in his thoughts and in his heart. "You were lucky you weren't killed that night."

"I know. There was a woman who helped me for a while, but the Rebs ran her off."

Logan knew exactly who that woman was, but he said nothing right then. Later, there would be time to tell his brother everything that had happened.

Braden went on, "I am lucky to be alive, I know that. Taylor took care of me in camp."

Braden looked at Taylor in hopes that she was ready to reveal her secret. He didn't see any reason for her to continue her disguise once they made it to the city. She could become herself again and forget about ever going back to war with the troops.

"Taylor?" Braden said her name quietly, encouraging her to be open with them.

Taylor knew what the lieutenant wanted her to do, but she felt a bit uneasy about it. She had played the role of a boy for so long now, she'd forgotten what it was like to be a lady.

"It's all right," he urged. "You're safe with us."

Logan looked at the boy and wondered what the youth could be so worried about.

"The lieutenant wants me to tell you that"— she paused, trying to think how to phrase it— "I'm not what you think I am."

All but Braden looked at Taylor in confusion. They were at a loss as to what she was about to say.

She managed a wavering smile as she confessed, "When my brother enlisted, I signed up to fight with him because I didn't want to be left behind all alone. Our parents were dead, and we had no close relatives. So, I cut my hair off, and I never used my first name because—it's Miranda."

"Miranda?" Danner repeated, staring at her, stunned. "You're a girl?"

She nodded, giving him an almost shy smile. "Yes."

Logan, too, was amazed at her revelation. "And you went to war with your brother? You actually fought with the men?"

"Yes, I stayed with my brother the whole time. I was with him when he was killed. That's when I was taken captive and brought to the prison camp."

Sam was as shocked as the others. "You are one brave woman. I can't believe the whole time you were in camp, no one knew."

"Only the lieutenant figured it out, but he kept my secret for me." She looked at him and smiled gratefully.

"What do you plan to do now that you're free?" Logan asked, wondering about her future.

"I don't know." Miranda said slowly, having never given much thought to the prospect that she would ever regain her freedom. She had been living day to day, hour to hour for so long that planning for the future seemed quite frightening.

Braden took charge. "Until we get to New Orleans, she's Taylor." He turned his head to meet her gaze. "Once we're there, you can figure out what you want to do."

Taylor was relieved that no quick answer was necessary, for she couldn't have given them one.

The horses were rested, so they mounted up again and rode off into the night. They could waste no time, for there were many miles to cover. The trip was difficult, but they didn't care. They stayed on the move, avoiding contact with people as best they could.

The closer they got to New Orleans, the blacker Logan's mood became. He would soon be facing Eden again, and he knew their reunion was not going to be a happy one.

Late one night, long after they'd made camp and bedded down, Logan was still awake. He got up and moved off, away from the campsite, needing some peace. Thoughts of Eden were haunting him. He loved her, and yet he had betrayed her trust in him. Nothing she'd believed about him had been real—except his love for her. He didn't know if he would be able to convince her of that, but he had to try. And that hour was coming soon.

"Logan?" Braden had awakened to find him gone and had gotten up to look for him. "What's wrong?"

"It's a long story."

"I've got the time," Braden told him. He'd sensed a change in his brother and wondered what was troubling him.

371

They moved a little farther away to talk privately.

Logan was honest with him and began at the beginning, telling him of his first tumultuous encounter with Eden at the Haven and how he had confronted the drunken soldiers. He told him of how he'd married her after he'd been seen by one of the children leaving her room one night.

"It wasn't supposed to happen, but I fell in love with her," Logan admitted.

"Your Eden sounds very special."

"She is—and you would know." At his brother's questioning look, he explained, "She was the woman on the *Bayou Belle* who went to your aid."

Braden was amazed by the coincidence. "You did very well for yourself, Brother. The woman who helped me on the steamer was beautiful."

"Yes, Eden is very beautiful." There was sadness in his tone. "But I'm sure she hates me now."

"Has she told you so?"

"No. I haven't seen her since I left her the night of the warehouse raid. I didn't go back to confront her. I left to come after you immediately after talking to Talbott."

"Maybe it won't be as bad as you think." Braden tried to be encouraging.

"It will be. I'm a Yankee," he said flatly.

"But if you love each other—"

"Eden loved Reverend Logan. Not me."

Logan fell silent. He'd faced many dangerous

situations as an operative, but none had challenged him the way Eden did. He knew she would believe that everything he said and did now was a deception. Somehow, he had to convince her of his love.

The time had come.

Darrell's wounds had healed enough to make travel possible. Eden had secured a mount for him earlier in the day, and as the midnight hour neared, he was preparing to disappear from New Orleans.

With Forrester and the others all in jail, there was nothing to hold Darrell there—nothing except the feelings he'd come to have for Camille. He was tempted to stay, but he wasn't sure if the Yankees had learned his identity. It was best that he go.

The knock sounded at the door to his attic room, and Camille entered at his bidding.

"So you're ready," Camille said in a soft voice, her gaze hungry upon him as she realized he really was leaving her.

"Yes." It wasn't often that Darrell found himself at a loss for words, but this was one of those instances. He hadn't understood until that moment just how much Camille meant to him. Not only was she the most beautiful woman he'd ever seen, but during this time he'd spent recuperating under her roof, he had come to eagerly anticipate her visits and companionship.

"You'll be careful," she urged.

"I will."

"I'm going to miss you," Camille admitted, unwilling to let him leave without telling him how much she'd come to care for him.

Her simple confession was all the encouragement he needed. He moved solemnly toward her, his gaze trapping and holding hers.

"I'm going to miss you, too."

The moment was magic as they stood staring at each other. They were tempted by their attraction, yet hesitant to reveal what they were feeling.

Darrell realized he might never see her again, and unable to resist, he bent to her and claimed her lips in a flaming exchange. It was a kiss that left them both breathless in its intensity. The power of it surprised Darrell, and he broke it off and deliberately moved away from her, needing to put a distance between them if he was going to keep to his plan and leave.

Camille opened her eyes to stare up at Darrell. She couldn't believe the shivers of delight that had coursed through her at the touch of his lips.

"Don't go," Camille pleaded in a voice barely above a whisper.

He was tempted, oh-so-tempted, to stay, but he couldn't, no matter what his heart told him. "I want to stay with you, but I can't, Camille."

"I may never see you again!" she protested.

"You'll see me again. Don't worry about that," he promised.

"When? How soon?"

"As soon as I can arrange it and make sure that everything is safe for you."

Camille wanted to launch herself into his arms and hold on to him and never let him go, but somehow she controlled the need. She had to be strong for him.

Francene came through the door right then, wanting to make sure everything was all right. "You're ready to go?"

"Yes, ma'am, and I wanted to thank you both for all you've done for me," Darrell told her.

"We were glad we could help you, Darrell. Be careful on your travels, and Godspeed." Francene went to him and gave him a warm hug.

"Tell Eden I said thank you, too."

"We will," Francene promised.

They left the attic and made their way outside where the horse was tied, saddled and ready for him.

He mounted, then looked down at Camille. The tears he saw in her eyes touched him. "Good-bye, Camille. Mrs. LeGrand."

"Take care," Francene said, wishing him safe passage.

"Darrell." Camille said his name gently. "I'll be waiting for you."

He nodded. Without another word, he rode off into the night.

"He's one very special young man," Francene said to Camille, her tone soft in understanding as she gave her daughter a gentle smile.

"Yes, Mother, he is."

Chapter Twenty-eight

"Miss Eden?" Connie called out as Eden passed by her table at the noon meal.

"Yes, Connie, what is it?" Eden stopped to speak with her.

"Have you heard anything from Reverend Logan yet?" she asked hopefully.

Eden smiled sweetly at Connie even as her heart was breaking. Every day the little girl asked about Logan, and every day Eden had to give her the same answer. "No, I haven't heard from him yet, but I'm sure I will soon."

As always, Connie's expression turned to one of deep disappointment. "I miss him, Miss Eden."

"I know."

And Eden did know. For all that she kept herself busy by day, at night she lay alone in her bed at the Haven, arguing with herself about her conflicting feelings for Logan. There were moments when she missed him and longed to be in his arms. The memory of their first night of passionate lovemaking in that very bed taunted her and would give her no rest. Yet as soon as she allowed herself the luxury of remembering how sweet his loving had been, thoughts of his betrayal returned and vanquished the memories.

"When do you think he'll be back, Miss Eden?" Paul asked from a table nearby.

"I'm not sure. It could be any day, or a month. There's no way of knowing."

The boy nodded and seemed to accept her answer. She was glad when he didn't ask any more questions, for she truly didn't want to think or talk about Logan. It hurt too much.

New Orleans.

It had been a grueling trip, but they'd made it! Sam wished them good luck and left the group soon after they reached the city. Danner went off to report in to headquarters and tell them of their escape from the prison camp. Braden planned to report in, too, but first he wanted to make sure that Taylor was taken care of.

"Where are we going?" Taylor asked.

"I have an apartment here. I thought we'd go there first," Logan answered.

Since Adrian had been arrested, he was certain that Eden was spending most of her time at the Haven. It would be safe for them to go to the apartment and get cleaned up before they decided what they were going to do. They reached the building and went in.

As Logan opened the door to the apartment, a part of him wanted everything to be as it had been before he'd left. But when he walked in and saw his Bible and the note he'd written Eden lying discarded on the table, he knew. He checked the bedroom and had his suspicions confirmed. All of Eden's things were missing. Eden was gone.

The men decided to get cleaned up first and then Braden would go and buy Taylor some clothes while Logan went to find his wife.

"So Eden is your wife?" Taylor asked. The two men had not spoken of Eden before in front of her.

"Yes. She's probably been staying at the Homeless Haven with the orphans since I've been gone."

"I'm sure she'll be glad you're back," she told him.

Logan wished that were true, but he knew better.

Logan and Braden bathed and changed clothes, then went to join Taylor in the sitting room. Her eyes widened a bit as she saw Braden coming toward her. She had always thought the lieutenant nice-looking, but now he appeared most handsome. That realization startled her.

"You look like a regular gentleman, Lieutenant."

He grinned at her. "I won't for long. As soon as I report in, I'll be back in uniform."

"Should I report in, too?"

"No. I'll take care of things for you. Right now, though, I'm going to go out and get you some clothes. I'll be back as soon as I can."

"But I don't have any money to pay for anything," Taylor said, embarrassed.

"That's all right. My brother's buying," Braden said, still smiling at her.

"I'll pay you back," she promised Logan.

"There's no need for you to pay me anything. You helped Braden when he needed it. This is the least I can do for you."

She was touched by his generosity and kindness. "Thank you."

"Will you be all right here by yourself?" Logan asked, for he was ready to leave and find Eden.

"I'll be fine."

"If there's anything you need. Help yourself."

Logan and Braden left the apartment, each one a man on a mission.

As soon as they'd gone, Taylor got fresh water and treated herself to her first bath in what seemed like forever. She scrubbed herself until her skin was rosy, wanting to feel clean again; then she washed her hair, too. She realized after she'd dried herself that she had nothing to put on except her dirty uniform, and there was no way she was going to don those filthy garments again. Logan had told her to help herself if she needed anything, so she wrapped herself in the sheet from the bed and lay down to await the lieutenant's return.

Braden had been gone longer than he'd intended, but at last he made it back to the apartment with clothing for Taylor. He was surprised when he entered the apartment and she didn't come to greet him immediately. He saw the closed bedroom door and knocked.

"Taylor, I'm back and I've got some clothes for you."

"Oh, thanks. Just leave them outside the door, please."

He did as he was told and went into the kitchen to wait for her to come out. As he was sitting at the table, he saw the door open a crack and a bare, slender arm reach out to grab the bundle of garments.

Braden had always wondered what took women so long with their toilettes, and he was wondering anew as he sat there. He hoped he'd gotten something that would fit. He hadn't been sure of her size, and so had simply eyed the garments hoping they would fit her. After quite a while, he heard the bedroom door start to open and he watched with interest as Taylor emerged—no longer the army private.

Taylor found for some reason that she was very nervous as she left the bedroom to face the lieutenant for the first time as her real self. It had been a long time since she'd felt like a woman.

Braden's eyes widened in startled appreciation when he saw Taylor. She had washed her hair and, though short, it crowned her head in a tumble of soft curls. The dress he'd bought her was a sedate daygown, and she filled it out perfectly. He noticed, not even meaning to, that the bodice was a bit tight on her. The discovery amazed him. She was beautiful, and yet she had lived among the men as one of them and no one had noticed.

"How do I look?" Taylor asked quietly, unsure how to read the look on his face.

"You look wonderful," he told her, his voice deep and sincere.

She almost sighed out loud in relief.

"There is one other thing."

"What?" She feared she'd forgotten something.

"I know the guard broke your chain, so I bought you a new one." He presented her with a small jewelry box.

Deeply touched by his thoughtfulness, she hurried back into the bedroom to retrieve the cross and broken chain from the pocket of her dirty pants. Braden followed her and, taking the cross from her, threaded it onto the new chain. When she presented her back to him, he fastened it for her. Taylor touched it reverently as she turned to smile up at him.

"Thank you."

"You're more than welcome, Tay— No, you're not Taylor anymore. You're Miranda now."

"It's been a long time since anyone called me that."

"Well, I don't think anyone will ever forget again. Not looking as pretty as you do right now," he complimented her. "I went to headquarters and told them everything. You have no obligation to the military anymore. Do you know what you want to do? Where you want to go?"

"I'm not sure. My family's all dead. I guess I'll have to find a job of some sort to support myself."

"I'm being stationed here in New Orleans because I haven't fully recovered from the wound yet. I can ask around and see what I can find for you. Until you're financially able to take care of yourself, I'm sure it will be all right with Logan if you to stay on here."

"Oh, but this is his home—"

"He may not be moving back in," he said, but did not explain further. "So you would be welcome to stay here."

"Thank you, Lieutenant."

"Since I'm no longer your commanding officer, I think you can start calling me Braden," he teased her.

Miranda smiled, truly smiled for the first time. "Yes, Braden."

Something about her smile touched the very heart of him, and Braden knew he would stay in

New Orleans for as long as he could to keep watch over Miranda.

The children were in class with Jenny upstairs, and all was quiet in the Haven. Eden decided to take advantage of the lull in activity and go outside for a few minutes. Things had been so complicated since Adrian's arrest that she hadn't had any peace. She sought that now, going alone out to the garden so she could lose herself in the heavenly scent of the flowers for a little while.

Wandering slowly along the path through the flowering shrubs, Eden closed her eyes to savor the solitude. She paused as the memory returned of the time Logan had kissed her there in the garden. A great sadness filled her at the thought of all that had been lost. Disturbed by memories of Logan, the peace she'd longed for proved elusive, so Eden went back inside to lose herself in her work.

She was pleased that things were still quiet inside. She walked straight into the office, only to come to a complete stop at the sight of Logan standing there before her.

"Hello, Eden," he said quietly.

The sound of his deep voice sent a thrill coursing through her, but Eden fought to deny it. She fought to deny, too, the part of her that longed to throw herself into his arms. She stiffened, her gaze hardening as she stared at him.

"What are you doing here?" she demanded, her tone cold as she circled around him to go and stand behind the desk. For some reason, she felt safer having the desk between them.

"I came to see you," he answered simply.

"Well, I could say it's a pleasure to see you again, but it's not."

"Did you get the note I left at the apartment?"

She gave him an icy smile. "I found your note, and I found your Bible, *Reverend*."

"You're my wife, Eden."

"Our marriage was a farce from the very beginning. It was meaningless. You only married me so you could get close to Adrian!" she challenged.

"If our marriage was a farce, why are you still wearing your wedding ring?"

Eden looked down at the ring on her hand that marked her as Logan's wife. "I wear it for the children. They don't know anything about what happened—not about Adrian and not about you! I kept it all from them, and if you leave right now before anyone sees you, we can continue the charade until I can find the right way to tell them the truth."

"What will you tell them? That I was a government agent who came to New Orleans to try to find my brother? The same man you helped to save on the *Bayou Belle*." His gaze caught and held hers.

"You know—"

"Thank you, Eden. I wanted to thank you before, when you talked about what happened that night, but I couldn't—not until now. Braden's here, Eden. I want you to meet him."

"No. I don't want anything to do with you or your brother. You lied to me! You betrayed me! Everything you ever told me about yourself is probably a lie. Is your real name Logan Matthews, or are you somebody else?"

"I am Logan Matthews, and you are my wife," he said slowly, then added in a more conciliatory tone, "Eden, I had a job to do. I had to get my brother out of the prison camp."

"Good for you," she said coldly. "You saved your brother's life. You came here to rescue him and you did. So now you can leave! Go on! Go!"

Pain stabbed at Logan. "If that's what you want, Eden, I'll leave. I have to report in, in St. Louis, but I want you to come with me. You're my wife, and I love you."

"I don't want to cross the street with you, let alone go to St. Louis with you!"

Her words spurred him to action. He wanted only to prove to her that what they'd shared was real; he strode across the room and took her in his arms and kissed her. His kiss was a hot, passionate possession that told her without words how he felt.

Logan ended the kiss abruptly and stood looking down at her. "I'm going now, Eden, but don't think for a minute that this is over between us."

Eden's emotions were in complete turmoil. The power of his kiss had ripped away any shred of pretense that she wanted nothing to do with him. He had only to touch her and any thought of hating him vanished. Eden was furious and humiliated. She glared up at him in defiance and turned her back to him, standing rigidly, wanting him to go.

Logan stood there for a moment longer. He wanted to take her in his arms and tell her of his love. He wanted to somehow find a way to erase all the heartache he'd caused her and make things right between them again. But he couldn't change the past. He could only control the future. Without another word, Logan left Eden, hoping and praying that he could find some way to reach her.

Eden heard him leave the room and close the door behind him. She had been crying silently as he'd stood behind her, and once he'd gone, she wiped angrily at the tears that revealed her true torment.

She loved him.

But how could she love the man who was her sworn enemy?

Eden stared down at the ring on her hand. She had told Logan that she'd continued to wear it because of the children. The truth was, Reverend Logan had placed that ring on her finger and made her his wife, and she had never thought of taking it off.

Epilogue

Early Summer, 1865

Logan was tense as he reined in before the Haven and dismounted. He started up the walk to the front door, ready for the confrontation to come. The long months he'd been apart from Eden had taken their toll on him, but the war was over now. He had resigned from his job with the government and had returned to New Orleans with only one thing on his mind: He was going to find a way to win over his wife. The battle was about to begin, and he had no intention of being defeated.

During the time he'd been away, Logan had heard nothing from Eden. He had gotten a letter from Braden shortly after he'd left New Orleans all those months ago, telling him that he had gone to visit Eden to thank her for helping him on the steamer. She had talked with him and had accepted his thanks, but had not encouraged any further contact between them. Logan had continued to write to her regularly and had even arranged for money to be sent to the orphanage from other sources, so she wouldn't know the funds were coming from him. As he looked the Haven over now, it seemed in good condition, and he was glad. He had only wanted the best for Eden and the children.

Logan stopped at the door and knocked. After a moment, Jenny answered.

"Reverend Logan—er, I mean, Logan!" Jenny said, shocked to see him. "You're back!"

"Hello, Jenny. Is Eden here?"

"Well . . ." Jenny looked awkward, not sure what to say. Realizing she had no choice, she told him, "Eden's in the garden."

"Thank you."

Logan wasted no time on small talk. There was only one woman he wanted to speak with, and that was his wife. He hurried around the side of the building, looking for Eden.

Jenny watched him go, and knew this was going to be a very interesting day. She went back to the children, but was anxious to see how everything turned out.

Eden was sitting on the bench in the garden, holding her son on her lap. Michael Logan Matthews was a little over a year old, and she loved him with all her heart and soul. Every time she looked at him, she was reminded of his father. Michael was going to grow up to be a strong, handsome man just as Logan had been.

At times like this when she found herself thinking of Logan, Eden grew sad. What they'd shared had been beautiful, and it had ended far too soon. There were still days when she regretted having sent him away, but even if she had the chance to live it over again, she would have done the same thing.

They had been enemies.

Her allegiance had been to the South.

But now the war was over.

Her mother had recently received a letter from her father telling them that he and her brother would be coming home soon. It had been wonderful news. They were all joyously counting every minute until their return. Their homecoming would be sweet.

Eden cuddled Michael close, cherishing the warmth of him in her arms.

"It seems I'm always destined to find you in the Garden of Eden."

Logan's voice came to her and she went completely still. She was shocked by the power of the heart-rending response that tore through her.

"Logan?" Eden said his name in a whisper as he appeared before her.

"Hello, Eden," he said quietly, seeing her holding the infant.

"You came back—"

"I told you I would." He paused, then added, "I missed you, Eden."

Logan assumed the baby was an orphan she'd taken in at the Haven. He drew closer and saw that it was a beautiful baby. Then the infant turned to look up at him and smiled. A jolt of visceral recognition jarred Logan. He lifted his gaze to Eden's.

"We have a child?" Logan asked hoarsely, a wide range of emotions tearing at him. Eden had borne his baby, and he'd never known. He hadn't been there to help her.

Eden had feared incrimination and anger from him. Instead, she saw only awe in his eyes. "Yes. I named him Michael—Michael Logan Matthews."

She stood up with the baby so he could see his son more clearly.

"He's beautiful—just like you," Logan said, his heart aching with tenderness at the breathtaking picture his wife and son made.

"Why did you come back, Logan?"

"Because I wanted to tell you one last time that I love you, Eden." He looked down at her hand then. "You're still wearing your wedding ring."

"I never took it off. I couldn't."

"Why?" he pressed. "Because of the children?"

"No. Because I love my husband," she finally confessed in a broken voice. She had fought against it, tried to deny what had been in her heart all this time, but her feelings for Logan had never changed.

"Can you ever forgive me for hurting you?" Logan asked. He wanted to take her in his arms, but he wasn't sure yet if he dare try. "I want to spend the rest of my life proving how much I love you. With the war, everyone has lost so much. I don't want to lose our love."

The months apart had helped Eden to know the depth of her feelings for him. She looked up at Logan and saw the man she'd fallen in love with. He might not be Reverend Logan, but she loved him nonetheless.

"Do you have any plans to return to your calling as a minister?" she asked.

Her question lightened Logan's mood.

"No," he answered with a grin. "But I had thought of heading west away from the ugliness of these last years. We wouldn't be Yankee and Rebel there. We could truly be a family. I wasn't sure if you would be willing to leave the Haven, though." He knew how much the orphanage meant to her.

"I think I know who could take over for me. Camille and her husband, Darrell, have been working here regularly. They'd be wonderful with the children."

"You're sure?"

She nodded and handed him Michael for the first time.

Logan took his son from her and held him

close. The baby nestled against him, trustingly.

"We can start all over again, Eden."

"I'd like that." Eden rose up to kiss him sweetly. "I love you, Logan."

"I love you, too."

And in that moment, they knew their love was strong enough to overcome all the pain of the past. Together, they would find a way to build a future of love and happiness.

Bobbi Smith · SECRET FIRES · The Half-Breed

In the midst of the vast, windswept Texas plains stands a ranch wrested from the wilderness with blood, sweat and tears. It is the shining legacy of Thomas McBride to his five living heirs. But along with the fertile acres and herds of cattle, each will inherit a history of scandal, lies and hidden lust that threatens to burn out of control.

Chase knows he has no legitimate claim to the Circle M. After all, his father made it painfully clear he wants nothing to do with his bastard son or the Comanche girl he once took to his bed. But Chase has his own reasons for answering Tom McBride's deathbed summons. He has a job to do as a Texas Ranger, and a woman to protect—a woman whose sweet innocence gives him new faith that love born in the darkest night can face the dawn of all his tomorrows.

___4853-1 $5.99 US/$6.99 CAN

Dorchester Publishing Co., Inc.
P.O. Box 6640
Wayne, PA 19087-8640

Please add $2.50 for shipping and handling for the first book and $.75 for each book thereafter. NY, NYC, and PA residents, please add appropriate sales tax. No cash, stamps, or C.O.D.s. All orders shipped within 6 weeks via postal service book rate. Canadian orders require $2.50 extra postage and must be paid in U.S. dollars through a U.S. banking facility.

Name_____

Address_____

City_____ State_____ Zip_____

I have enclosed $ _____ in payment for the checked book(s).

Payment <u>must</u> accompany all orders. ❑ Please send a free catalog.

CHECK OUT OUR WEBSITE! www.dorchesterpub.com

BRIDES OF DURANGO: ELISE
BOBBI SMITH

Elise Martin will do anything for a story—even stage a fake marriage to catch a thief. Dressed in a white lace gown, she looks every bit the bride, but when her "fiancé" fails to show, she offers ten dollars to the handsome gentleman who just stepped off the stage to pose as the groom. As a fake fiancé, he is all right, but when he turns out to be Gabriel West, the new owner of her paper, the *Durango Star*, Elise wants to turn tail and run. But she can't forget the passion his unexpected kiss at their "wedding" aroused, and she starts to wonder if there is more to Gabriel West than meets the eye. For the more time they spend together, the more Elise wonders if the next time she says, "I do" she just might mean it.

___4575-3 $5.99 US/$6.99 CAN

Dorchester Publishing Co., Inc.
P.O. Box 6640
Wayne, PA 19087-8640

BRIDES OF DURANGO: TESSA

BOBBI SMITH

Tessa Sinclair owns the local boarding house where she not only takes care of her guests, but every unfortunate she comes across. Brimming with compassion, Tessa is so busy rescuing other people she doesn't notice the dangers she continually faces but marshal Jared Trent does. In fact, he notes every move the willful beauty makes. The most daring of all being the position she takes up in his heart. Tessa prides herself on seeing the best in everyone, but Jared Trent's determination to curtail her activities sorely tests her patience. As handsome as he is infuriating, Jared unearths feelings Tessa has never experienced before. And as he helps extract her from one perilous situation after another, she realizes she wouldn't mind getting caught in some close encounters with the dashing lawman himself—little dreaming he will unveil the love of a lifetime.

___4678-4 $5.99 US/$6.99 CAN

Dorchester Publishing Co., Inc.
P.O. Box 6640
Wayne, PA 19087-8640

Please add $1.75 for shipping and handling for the first book and $.50 for each book thereafter. NY, NYC, and PA residents, please add appropriate sales tax. No cash, stamps, or C.O.D.s. All orders shipped within 6 weeks via postal service book rate.
Canadian orders require $2.00 extra postage and must be paid in U.S. dollars through a U.S. banking facility.

Name_____
Address_____
City_____State_____Zip_____
I have enclosed $_____ in payment for the checked book(s).
Payment <u>must</u> accompany all orders. ❑ Please send a free catalog.

WESTON'S BOBBI
Lady SMITH

There are Cowboys and Indians, trick riding, thrills and excitement for everyone. And if Liberty Jones has anything to say about it, she will be a part of the Wild West show, too. She has demonstrated her expertise with a gun by shooting a card out of Reed Weston's hand at thirty paces, but the arrogant owner of the Stampede won't even give her a chance. Disguising herself as a boy, Libby wangles herself a job with the show, and before she knows it Reed is firing at her—in front of an audience. It seems an emotional showdown is inevitable whenever they come together, but Libby has set her sights on Reed's heart and she vows she will prove her love is every bit as true as her aim.

____4512-5 $5.99 US/$6.99 CAN

HALF-BREED'S
Lady
BOBBI SMITH

To artist Glynna Williams, Texas is a land of wild beauty, carved by God's hand, untouched as yet by man's. And the most exciting part of it is the fierce, bare-chested half-breed who saves her from a rampaging bull. As she spends the days sketching his magnificent body, she dreams of spending the nights in his arms.

___4436-6 $5.99 US/$6.99 CAN

Dorchester Publishing Co., Inc.
P.O. Box 6640
Wayne, PA 19087-8640

Please add $1.75 for shipping and handling for the first book and $.50 for each book thereafter. NY, NYC, and PA residents, please add appropriate sales tax. No cash, stamps, or C.O.D.s. All orders shipped within 6 weeks via postal service book rate. Canadian orders require $2.00 extra postage and must be paid in U.S. dollars through a U.S. banking facility.

Name_____
Address_____
City_____State_____Zip_____
I have enclosed $_____ in payment for the checked book(s).
Payment <u>must</u> accompany all orders. ❏ Please send a free catalog.
CHECK OUT OUR WEBSITE! www.dorchesterpub.com

BOBBI SMITH

The LADY & the TEXAN

"A fine storyteller!"—*Romantic Times*

A firebrand since the day she was born, Amanda Taylor always stands up for what she believes in. She won't let any man control her—especially a man like gunslinger Jack Logan. Even though Jack knows Amanda is trouble, her defiant spirit only spurs his hunger for her. He discovers that keeping the dark-haired tigress at bay is a lot harder than outsmarting the outlaws after his hide—and surrendering to her sweet fury is a heck of a lot riskier.

___4319-X $5.99 US/$6.99 CAN

SOMETHING SOMETHING BORROWED, BLUE

ELAINE BARBIERI, CONSTANCE O'BANYON, EVELYN ROGERS, BOBBI SMITH

Here to capture that shimmering excitement, to bring to life the matrimonial mantra of "Something old, something new," are four spellbinding novellas by four historical-romance stars. In "Something Old," Elaine Barbieri crafts a suspenseful tale of an old grudge—and an old flame—that flare passionately—and dangerously—anew. In "Something New," can Constance O'Banyon arrange an arrogant bachelor father, a mysterious baby nurse, and a motherless newborn into the portrait of a proper South Carolina clan? In Evelyn Rogers's "Something Borrowed," a pretty widow and a gambler on the lam borrow identities—and each other—to board a wagon train West to freedom—and bliss. In "Something Blue," Bobbi Smith deftly engages a debonair cavalry officer and a feisty saloon girl in a moving tale of sexy steel and heartmelting magnolias.